Two unsuspecting lovers stumble upon the blueprint for love . . .

Calliope Allbrook takes a job in lovely, sunny Adelaide, Australia, hoping to lose herself in her work as a balm for her broken heart. And if it weren't for the handsome hunk renovating the house next door, Calli would never even have looked up from the garden she is designing for her latest client. But rugged Kellen Dee is just the cure the beautiful heiress needs. After all, he has no idea who she is, so he certainly won't see her as a meal ticket. Then there's the fact that Kell's deliciously sexy—and incredibly good with his hands . . .

From the moment Kell takes her in his arms, he knows Calli is more than just a fling. Then the blue collar bachelor learns he's not sharing his bed with just any woman, but the wealthy daughter of the man who could make Kell's construction business a success—and Kell the kind of well-heeled man worthy of Calli's love. But he'll have to be careful his ambitions don't trip up his heart . . .

Books by Virginia Taylor

South Landers
Starling
Ella
Charlotte
Wenna

Romance By Design
Sets Appeal
Perfect Scents

Published by Kensington Publishing Corporation

Perfect Scents

A Romance By Design Novel

Virginia Taylor

LYRICAL PRESS
Kensington Publishing Corp.
www.kensingtonbooks.com

Lyrical Press books are published by
Kensington Publishing Corp. 119 West 40th Street New York, NY 10018

All Kensington titles, imprints, and distributed lines are available at special quantity discounts for bulk purchases for sales promotion, premiums, fund-raising, and educational or institutional use.

To the extent that the image or images on the cover of this book depict a person or persons, such person or persons are merely models, and are not intended to portray any character or characters featured in the book.

Special book excerpts or customized printings can also be created to fit specific needs. For details, write or phone the office of the Kensington Special Sales Manager:
Kensington Publishing Corp.
119 West 40th Street
New York, NY 10018
Attn. Special Sales Department. Phone: 1-800-221-2647.

First Electronic Edition: September 2017
eISBN-13: 978-1-5161-0008-8
eISBN-10: 1-5161-0008-5

First Print Edition: September 2017
ISBN-13: 978-1-5161-0012-5
ISBN-10: 1-5161-0012-3

Printed in the United States of America

Author's Foreword

I have been helping to develop a National Trust garden for three years, realizing that thinking someone ought to do so wasn't as much help as me being someone and offering. Renovating part of the three acre plot has taught me quite a bit about plants and the natural healing powers of gardens.

Chapter 1

Calli Allbrook stood, key in hand, her suitcase beside her, contemplating the old stone cottage she intended to house-sit for the next three months. Birds flittered through the nearby trees while clouds scurried across the pallid spring sky.

THUNK! Startled, she dropped the key. The fence next door shook and rattled. A male voice swore loudly. Glass shattered and tinkled onto stone. Footsteps clumped, a hinge squeaked, and a door slammed. She glanced nervously at the tumbledown, overgrown wreck of a house behind the fence. A tad conscious of her overreaction to the neighbor's noise, she scrambled up her key.

The main house on the allotment had been built at the front of the double block. Her separate accommodation was sited on the back corner. The attached carport sat farther along the back fence, sheltering Judge Adrian Ferguson's black Jaguar, a luxury model white Mercedes, and her own twenty-year-old green Ford, not an edifying sight alongside the judge's more expensive choices.

She pushed open the aqua door of the tidy little cottage, hoping that while the judge relaxed in the Mediterranean, she hadn't taken on a larger commitment than she could manage. But, of course, she had to if she expected to reclaim her professional reputation. She had already seen the outside of her prospective lodgings last week when she had walked the judge through her plan for the design of his garden. Surmising that he had done as good a renovation here as he had on the interior of his spacious bluestone house, she glanced around. The area had been replanned as four spaces.

Three opened into each other; two at the front, one the sitting area, and another the eating area, separated from the white kitchen by an island. A coffee machine stood on top. She craved real coffee. For the past month, she had lived on the cheapest foodstuffs she could buy.

With a happy hitch of her shoulders, she made her way past a soft caramel leather couch facing a television set and two floral armchairs. Opening the door into the fourth space, the bedroom, she spotted a luxurious king-size bed. Before she unpacked, she checked the en suite bathroom. The gleaming white tiles served as a welcome relief from the pink, shared bathroom in the bedsit she had occupied since she had sold her own house a month ago.

Living in this hidden far corner while she worked on the garden of the main house, alone and undisturbed, would give her time to reexamine and finally put her life back together. By the time she had folded her underwear into a drawer; hung up a row of shirts, a skirt, and a jacket; and had pushed a few old gardening clothes onto a shelf; dusk shaded the room gray. She switched on the lights and closed the plantation shutters, glancing pensively at the bed. This morning she had performed one last cleaning round of her bedsit. She could sleep for a week, offered the chance.

Except, she hadn't given a thought to breakfast in the morning. With only a fond hope, she wandered out to the small refrigerator. Her new employer had been gone a week, yet he had stocked a few staples for her, including butter and long-life milk. She found the coffee pods needed for the machine, a canister of teabags, jam, and peanut butter in an overhead cupboard, and cornflakes and dry crackers in a storage cupboard. Without trying to locate a shop, she could make a nice unhealthy snack before having an early night.

Tomorrow morning, she hoped to mark out various areas in the garden. In the not-too-distant future, the judge would be the proud owner of a new garden more suited to the style of his stately home. His present garden had been planted twenty years ago with rows of standard iceberg roses and English box hedges. Her plan was for a softer, more casual layout. The judge had approved her budget and had signed the various contracts needed for her to go ahead. That way, she didn't need credit with trades or suppliers, fortunately. She had none.

After plastering peanut butter thickly on the crackers, she sat back in the comfortable armchair to watch the news on television.

Her startled lurch caused the cracker to hit her nose when a yelling voice fronting a heavy rock band screeched that he would rock her. Even the thick stone walls of the cottage vibrated with the noise. The iron roof rattled in protest.

"Turn the music down," yelled a male voice in the distance.

Wiping the brown gloop off the tip of her nose, she stood, and peered out through the shutters at the grass tennis court at the front of the cottage and the crushed granite driveway, presuming—hoping—that the noise came from the glass-breaking neighbor rather than from invaders armed with stereo equipment. No one appeared to be partying on the court, but barbeque smoke trailed in from next door. Apparently the glass-breaker had outdoor culinary plans for the evening.

With a groan of resignation, she shut the window firmly and went back to the television news. The aroma of cooking meat meandered into her living space through the air vents, apparently knowing she had nothing interesting to eat. The background rock music continued to thump, competing with outbreaks of noisy laughter and shouted conversations. Although predominately male noise, the higher pitched laughing of women pierced the chilly night air. Despite her barbeque envy, she dozed off in front of the television.

She awoke suddenly to the sound of a car engine revving.

"Goodnight. See you soon," called a female voice.

Lower tones and more revving of engines, perhaps motorbikes, and loud conversations continued for some time. Then, after a squeaky gate finally slammed shut with a metallic rattle, she wandered into the bedroom. Now would be her chance for a peaceful night of unbroken sleep.

She had told her family she would take a short break, implying that she would be travelling. No one other than her family had the number of her new phone. Given brain space, she could work out how she had ended with such a discombobulated life.

"Poor choices," her mother had said, but Calli had always made considered choices. She always dated suitable men who had come from her background, had approximately the same education, welcoming parents, and suitable jobs. As soon as she thought she might have found *the one*, he decided to find someone else. So, after two unsuccessful relationships, clearly not marriage material, she had decided to work on her career instead.

"Great idea, Calli," her sister had said, eyeing her sideways. "Like you don't already have a good career."

Calli had, of course, but not an independent one. She had worked in the family business, but she thought that might have been part of her problem—always being an Allbrook and never being Calli. Taking up with Grayson in a purely business relationship seemed to be a sensible idea, killing two birds with one stone. She could be Calli, she could present the gardens she would like to do instead of the gardens her father thought suitable, and not worry about her personal life ever again. That was then. Months ago. Her life had morphed into *now*.

Sighing, she changed into her pajamas and slid between fresh clean sheets. Her mind drifted. Tomorrow, she would start the most beautiful garden she had ever designed—one that would cause new customers to line up begging for her services. Then, she would be hired for bigger and better projects, and she would be so famous that—

CRASH.

She leaped out of bed in her panic, and stood, trying to find her bearings. *Crash.* The high-pitched squeals of bottles tumbling into a plastic bin, *crash, crash*, with each, about a hundred. *Crash.* Perhaps the neighbor was throwing away his wine glasses, too. *Crash, crash, crash.* She rubbed her forehead.

After breaking all his bottles and glasses, he started on his outdoor furniture.

Bang. Smack. Thud. Whack. Crash.

His back door slammed after an amplified squeak of the hinges. Now that noisy neighbor had cleaned up, he would surely have to sleep. She lay awake, waiting for the next noise, but she must have been exhausted because she awoke clear-headed in the morning. And ravenous, despite a sore throat.

She ate a bowl of cornflakes, drank a cup of tea, showered, and dressed in an oversized sleeveless sweatshirt and knee-length gym pants. After tucking her hair behind her ears, she pulled on a baseball cap and donned her sunglasses as she usually did for her morning jog. She opened her door and a cat brushed her ankles as it wobbled into the house.

The dirtiest creature she had ever seen dragged itself up onto the pristine couch.

"The judge's new furniture is not the place for you, I'm afraid." She hawked, hoping to clear her voice, but she had a clog there that she couldn't shift. "I must ask you to leave," she whispered, trying to sound cross, which didn't work without any sort of volume. She pulled the door wide open, hoping the cat would recognize that her expression looked outraged.

The scruffy dun-colored cat blinked a pair of bleary eyes at her, and subsided into a circle of matted fur.

Not wanting to touch the filthy thing, Calli stood undecided. "So, you don't take orders, hmm?" After some thought, she filled a saucer with milk. "Have that while I'm gone, but as soon as I get home, you will have to leave."

The cat barely acknowledged her almost inaudible mutter. Calli tucked a ten-dollar bill and the house keys into her pocket. If she spotted a supermarket while she investigated this upmarket area, she would buy cheese, fruit, and bread for herself, and a can of food to tempt the cat outside again. She had never been a cat lover, though she did feel a modicum of sympathy for the creature's unkempt condition. When she got back, she would call the animal rescue people.

She jogged up the crushed granite driveway to the street and decided to go left to take a better look at the noisy neighbor's property. Although she couldn't see much more than yesterday, she had a chance to note the details of the dilapidated sight behind the low redbrick fence.

Trees hid the façade of the house with only the tallest point of the Tudor roof visible. The date of the build could have been the early 1900s, and likely was. This one in a less affluent area would divide up nicely for six new family homes. Here, not a chance. Two at the most.

A shiny new SUV sat in the street outside. A man with forearms covered in tattoos sat on the wall. He wore black from head to toe—black T-shirt, black jeans, and black shoes. His hair had been cut with a hipster wave in front and short-short sides.

His companion stopped Calli's breath. Tall, dark-haired, and impossibly handsome, he stood feet apart, arms crossed, his startling blue eyes momentarily raised to glance at her as he finished his sentence. "...might be happier in another area." He offered Calli the sort of wry half smile that would floor a woman who was not immune to men. "Morning."

She smiled instead of trying to speak, glad that a neighbor had decided to complain about the noise last night. At least she knew the glass and bottle breaker looked like a gangster, not the sort of man to cross. She just might not complain about the noise if it happened again.

As for his current accommodation, she wouldn't recommend saving too many of the trees growing in the jungle at the front, among them Tecoma, feral olives, and Rhamnus, the blowfly bush. A recent hacking showed a weed-covered path. Steps led up to a once gracious veranda, tessellated like the step and most likely missing tiles, too. Overgrown branches and leaves hid the rest of the house.

A few more puffing breaths past the same unsightly overgrowth took her to rusting iron gates guarding an opening wide enough to drive a carriage through. The building behind looked like a two-car garage with an addition, possibly on old laundry house. The roof had caved in. In front, sat a couple of work trucks—one with a tray, and both possibly dumped for the duration of the resident's stay. She hoped this would be short if he planned to host more loud parties with his carnivorous pals.

Though, not even a gangster would have a party every night. She could be a good uncomplaining, cowardly neighbor once a week if need be. To go out herself wasn't an option. She didn't intend to socialize for quite a while, not until she had lived down her humiliating fall from grace.

Her downhill trek led her to a group of shops, comprising a doctor's surgery, a chemist, a physiotherapist, a dentist, and a small supermarket. On the other side of the road she spotted a pizza shop and a coffee bar, which unfortunately advertised an array of small cakes. Farther down the road sat a petrol station and a hotel. She wouldn't need to go too far for anything she needed.

She jogged back up the hill with the makings of her lunch. The cat made a faint mewing sound as she entered the cottage.

"No, I didn't forget you," she said, using a throaty whisper and a faked smile. She tried clearing her throat again. "Who could? Now, look what I bought for you. Why don't you move yourself off that nice clean carpet and come into the kitchen to eat?"

The cat blinked, slowly stood, and slithered over to her, making that strange noise the whole time.

"Food." Calli winced in revulsion as filthy fur touched her leg. "Follow me." She went into the kitchen area and opened the can. The stench of fish wafted out. "Ah, the aroma of the sea. Nice fish. Yum, yum. C'mon, c'mon. That's me calling you without a voice."

The cat wearily subsided on the floor near the couch.

She planted her fists on her hips. "Don't you dare die now that I've spent half my money on your food. Don't you dare."

Apparently the cat didn't heed whispered threats. The thing closed its eyes. Her skin crawling, Calli marched over and picked up the cat, which appeared to be mainly matted fur covering fine delicate bones. For no reason that she could name, because she didn't like cats, her eyes filled with tears. "You're starving. You couldn't even make it to the food. Don't worry. I'll put it right under your nose." Suppressing her distaste, and blinking back tears, she moved the cat to the dish and the saucer. The cat wobbled onto its feet and nosed at the milk, then began to lap, slowly and delicately. When the tiny puddle of milk half disappeared, the cat looked at the food and then at Calli.

"You don't have to eat it all right now. When you have energy, you can start." The cat licked the fur on its chest. Tears squirted from Calli's eyes. Starving and filthy, the cat still had some pride in its appearance. Although Calli didn't care much about hers these days, she knew a lesson when she saw one.

"Okay. You've won me for the time being. I won't call the rescue. I'll take you to the vet instead. We'll give you a chance. Everyone deserves a chance." She wiped at her nose with the back of her hand.

She was an *everyone*, too.

* * * *

Kellen Dee, known as Kell by his brothers and friends, and Killer by guys who wanted to deride his luck with the female sex, swept the discarded nails into a pile. The shapely young jogger this morning had been a welcome sight. The job he would begin this week was starting to look more interesting.

The well-heeled residents in this area were reputed to be doctors, but only specialists; lawyers, but mainly high court judges; politicians from either party; businessmen, the most successful; and anyone else with up to three million to spend on a house.

The jogger could be a wife of any of the aforementioned, and he would probably never know, but her beautiful long legs had been an enervating sight. If he could watch her every morning, he would be happy to stay for the three months he had estimated he would need here to run a chainsaw through the garden and effectively swing a sledgehammer inside the house.

He glanced idly around the room at the top of the main area where he would begin his destruction this morning, having taken a couple of days off work to make sure of a good start on his new renovation project. All the old cupboards needed to be removed from the bedrooms, as well as a water-stained part of the ceiling in the upstairs hallway. Fortunately, unlike his current housemate, he didn't have a hangover. Abstemious, and not about to end up like his alcoholic father, he had kept his intake last night to a single glass of beer.

The staircase creaked and Trent appeared. Tall and gangly, with light hair and eyes, he had a peaceful nature. He also thought he had an artistic bent, which left him open to constant ragging.

"I saw Steve outside. What did he want?" Trent massaged his forehead, wincing when the light from the window hit his eyes.

"He thought he'd left his sunglasses here last night."

Trent creaked out a laugh. "Is he having separation anxiety already?" Steve, briefly the employer of Kell and Trent in his theater set construction business, last year had married Lonny, ex-hairdresser and stylist to the stars, and now had a one-year-old pesky son.

Kell shrugged. "Maybe."

"He tried to get me to leave with him again last night. I told him I wanted to finish this house with you first."

"He's a hometown boy. For him, moving to Sydney is a big deal."

"Yeah, but he'll do better with his business there. How about Lonny, though? A contract for a TV makeover show. You and me, we're getting left behind."

Kell squared his shoulders. No one would leave him behind. He had plans and nothing or no one would distract him from his course. "Don't fret. You'll be back working with him in a couple of months."

Trent nodded and heaved a sigh. "You starting in here?"

Kell nodded. "I think I can reuse some of the wood."

"From the cupboards? Yeah. Good quality stuff, man. What are you going to do with it?"

"Haven't decided. I'll put it into storage. See these floorboards? Jarrah." Kell licked three fingers, squatted, and moistened the boards. The wood turned a clear mahogany red. "Beautiful. I'm thinking about taking them up, too. Can't see much reason to leave them here. I can do this floor with composite instead, because I'll carpet the place."

"What job do you want me on first?"

"Start gutting the garage and laundry. Then we can knock down the outbuildings. I'll want to put up a fence for the subdivision, too. Or you can do that. Remember, I want to keep anything salvageable. And be more careful of the leadlighting. I can make money out of that. I don't want any more breakages."

"I didn't know it was there. Vandals must have taken the window out and then decided to leave it," Trent said with stiff dignity. "I wouldn't mind having a go at restoring the broken one, though."

"No point. I'm not reusing it. I'll sell it. How did you get on with the nurses last night?" Kell gave Trent a sideways glance.

Trent had somehow never learned how to pick up a woman, though he was a nice guy and reasonably intelligent. A year or so ago, Kell had let the well-meaning idiot go on a double date with him. Since Saturday, two days ago, when they had moved in to flip this house, Trent had been angling for another invitation.

A long running joke said one woman wasn't enough for Kell and he "dated" his two at a time. He never commented. The women involved also never commented since spicing up Kell's reputation also made their own look more interesting. His brothers maintained that the women ignored him and enjoyed themselves with a good gossip while he slept. The truth lay somewhere in between.

Kell was a cynic who worked long hours. Since he didn't drink, nights out with the lads invariably ended up with him driving everyone home and pouring them into bed. Like any other sexually active male, he'd done his fair share of sexual experimentation, but when he wanted female company, one woman at a time was enough for him. However, if he happened to be attending an event where one of the guys, namely Trent, would be sure not to have a date, most of the women he knew had a bestie he could take along as a spare.

In all, he'd never met a woman he wanted to keep around permanently. Could be he was simply waiting for the right woman to come along. He hoped he would recognize her when she did, or if she did. In the meantime, he kept his relationships on a strictly casual basis. A man with a mission, he would go nowhere if he tied himself down.

"Well enough," Trent said, turning and heading toward the stairs. "How about if you organize a double date with them? Then I might be in with a chance."

Kell ran his fingers over his stubble. The spare women last night had been invited by Trent in a roundabout way. "When you're interested, you need to do more than sit back and watch."

"I'm trying to learn from the Killer."

"Ask them about themselves. They're people like you and me," Kell said impatiently. At twenty-eight, he was two years younger than Trent who by rights should have settled down a while ago. "The next time I meet a couple..." Reaching the bottom of the stairs, he walked off, leaving Trent to assume whatever he liked about the conclusion of the sentence.

He glanced around the downstairs area as he boiled the water in the electric kettle. The place might still have a kitchen but the last update must have been a good fifty years ago. The cupboards, although made out of good English oak were...well, made out of good English oak, which meant each had been lined with paper that didn't stand a chance of protecting the wood. The insides had rotted, but the doors were still good and would scrub up well after he removed them. He planned to put them back again refitted onto a laminate carcass.

His real-life, everyday self was a cabinetmaker. He earned a good wage, but his elder brother, now an architect, had made quite a few dollars out of renovating the worst house in the best street in their old neighborhood. Jay had then married, found himself a better job, and had scrambled out of debt with the sale of his house. Jay's wife had advised Kell to go into flipping houses, deciding he had the skills. She had proved right. A few months ago, he had sold his first flip, making enough money on the deal to fund a mortgage on this tumbledown house-and-land deal.

The local council, fat and greedy with the profits from suburban infill, had already approved his subdivision plan. Within the next few months, he would do up the old house on this side of the block to exhibit his cabinetry work. For the other side, he also had plans. A while back, the major property development company in the state had hired his small team, consisting of him, a carpenter, and an apprentice, to help catch up on a shopping mall job. Seeing the scope, Kell wanted more jobs with the company, but like every other business in the state, he had to prove himself first. AA & Company only took on the best.

Knowing he had to earn his way in, he spoke to the company's property manager and put forward his proposition. He would renovate the house on his double block, and if AA approved of the job he did, they would take on the build of the new house on the other side, and share the profits.

The property manager had nodded. "Three months. You'll want to show your management skills, too." A handshake sealed the deal.

Kell had no time to waste. This morning, the remaining roof tiles would be lifted off the old outhouses and stacked onto pallets, ready to take to the salvage yard. He could also sell the cleaned bricks from the demolition, the best of the reclaimed wood if he didn't find another use for the quality lengths, and the old leadlight windows.

This time next year, if AA took him on, he would end up with a good steady income, and the means to expand his business. In the meantime, he had moved out of the caravan he had parked inside his workshop to camp in this house he was renovating. Eventually, he would have the money to buy himself a pretty good home in a classy area. Then, *no one* would dismiss him as a lowly tradesman.

Chapter 2

Calli checked where to find the nearest vet and wrapped the cat in a towel. One look at her bundle by the receptionist, and she was ushered into a tiny cubicle.

"She's a pretty girl," the leathery vet said, his careful eyes and gentle hands checking out the cat, not Calli, who was rarely called pretty, even by men her own age. "She came a long way to find you. Look at the pads of her paws. She has done some travelling."

Calli cleared her throat, trying to force her voice. "Why would she want to find me? I don't even like cats."

"She's not yours?" His brown-eyed gaze connected with hers.

"She walked into my house. Sorry for whispering. I think I have a touch of hay fever."

"So, you want me to euthanize her?" He stood back, staring at her, his expression impartial.

"I promised her I would help her if I could." She lifted her shoulders, blinking at him.

He examined Calli's expression for some seconds, and then he wiped the cat's eyes with a wet cotton ball and squeezed ointment into them. "A cream Burmese I would think. De-sexed and starving. Put this ointment in twice a day and clean her eyes as often as need be."

"Will she be okay?"

He shrugged. "She was looking for someone. It might have been you. No charge if you are planning to give her a home."

Calli moistened her lips. She could offer the little cat a home until the creature was strong enough to be passed onto someone who liked cats. "Would I be allowed to give her a bath?"

"Good luck," the vet said, already on his way to the next patient in the next cubicle.

Calli made a nest out of her oldest T-shirt when she arrived home, and put that and the cat close to the milk and fish. "What shall I call you?"

The cat gave her a bleary-eyed blink.

Calli shrugged. "Hobo?"

The cat staggered out of the towel and nosed at the fish.

"Hobo it is. Now, will you be okay while I earn my living? I'll come back at lunch time and check on you."

The cat ignored her and daintily sniffed at the food.

Calli changed into her gardening gear: jeans, a stiff new khaki work shirt, and her old work boots. She jammed on a khaki military hat and sunglasses. With her diagram in her hand, she grabbed up a spray can of marking paint and strode over the rolling green lawn to the area of the garden in front of the main house. The cat would either be better or worse when Calli saw her next. She hoped for the former. The sooner Hobo fattened up, the sooner she would find a good home.

The cream paving from the cast iron front gate led straight to the door. Calli planned to change the paving to gray slate, laid French style. The iceberg roses standing sentinel on either side had to go, and not because of the new wider path. For this lovely bluestone house, she wanted a base of blue and silver, forming a softer and gentler, more cottage-like entrance to the old and gracious property.

Without stakes and string, she didn't attempt to spray the straight edge where the lawn would end at the planned garden bed. Instead, she sprayed a small dot at one end and the other, and filled in the line with a few dashes. As she moved to do the same on the other side of the path, she heard, "You! Out!"

She raised her head. Standing by the front gate, the impossibly handsome stranger from this morning glared right at her. His lowered eyebrows showed his disapproval of her, but she stood, staring straight back at more than six feet of annoyed male, his fists planted on his lean hips, taking his morning neighborhood-watch duties one step too far.

Although conscious that she looked far from her imperfect best, she instantly reacted to his imperious manner. She'd had enough of men telling her what she could do. He could get rid of her neighbor with her blessing, but other than that, he could mind his own business. He appeared to be able to speak civilly to the gangster next door, but not to a harmless woman. As she rose to answer, her throat completely closed over. "Me?" she asked in a husky whisper.

"Put down that can."

She rose to her full height of five-eight, ready to set him back into his place. Trying again, she forced through, "Now, j—"

"Don't make me come in and take it," he said in a dangerous tone.

Backing a little, she held up a placating palm and began a far from ladylike hawking of her throat, and finally managed to say, "I'm the gardener," in a voice that sounded like a scaredy-cat with laryngitis rather than a fully-grown woman.

His dark eyebrows arched with disbelief. "Well, buddy, in that case you would know the name of the owner of the place." He folded his arms across his manly chest and stared down his nose at her. The morning sunlight emphasized his wonderful cheekbones and made chiseled angles of his clean-cut jaw.

She smiled at her challenge. At this time of day, still before ten and wearing jeans and a sweatshirt, he could be a doctor, a lawyer, or possibly an architect, but he was most likely a professional sportsman. His clear skin said healthy living and his perfect haircut said *money*. He looked about the right age to be a footballer. She knew a few lived in this area. If so, he would be married. She didn't know why she tried to see a ring, but angling her gaze to his left fist took her eyes to the front of his well-packed jeans. She hastily glanced back at his face. His relationship status had no relevance at all to his infuriatingly melting effect on her.

"Buddy," she repeated, belatedly realizing he thought she was male which capped her indignation. Tallish she might be, and square-shouldered, but she had all the girly bits in all the right places, too. Not that any showed under her stiff shirt. However, no matter how she looked, he had apparently decided that the spray can she still held and had somehow pointed at him, was a weapon. She lifted the can higher, narrowed her eyes, and aimed more directly at him. Her thumb toyed with the nozzle, her lips firm.

"Don't even think about it," he said in a deadly tone.

She paused. Of course she shouldn't. Aside from that, if he wrestled with her for the can, he might knock off her hat, and then he might recognize her. Not too long ago, her picture had not only been splashed across the daily paper, but also flashed on the news screens. At this stage, she couldn't deal with any more opinions of her character. She drew a resolute breath.

"I'll have the name of your employer right now."

She lowered the can. For all she knew, he might be a very good friend of her employer, who trusted her not only with his garden but the keys to his house. She had no business offending a stranger. But to keep her self-respect she couldn't give in without a show of resistance. "Horace Rumpole." She raised her chin.

"Try again," he said through his teeth.

"John Deed."

"One last try, smart-arse."

She thought he had relaxed slightly. "Adrian Ferguson," she said, taking her thumb off the nozzle of the spray can.

His eyebrows lowered as his gaze pierced through her. Finally, he unclamped his lips. "Keep in mind that around here, neighbors look out for each other." After a terse nod of his head, he went on his way.

She didn't watch, although she wanted to. That was one hunk of a yummy man, not a dimpled charming man like Grayson, but his polar opposite. Pushing out a huff of self-impatience, she turned back to the garden and sprayed more blue spots onto the lawn, marking out where she expected the string lines to go.

She wished she had checked to see where the neighbor lived. When the judge came back, she could tell him and make the story funny. Then she laughed. The story was already funny. Mr. Neighborhood Watch thought she was a boy.

Then again, for a woman who had been shown only too often that she had no appeal, that wasn't so funny.

At about one, she stopped work for lunch. The cat had again curled on the couch, leaving the food dish half-full.

"Progress," Calli muttered, scraping the stale food into the bin. She swallowed a long glass of water, and hacked out a cough, clearing her throat, momentarily.

Hobo glanced in Calli's direction, but her eyes seemed to be leaking again. Calli made an ick-face. The idea of cleaning gunk from the cat's eyes made her stomach churn. The idea of being so heartless as to leave the cat in misery caused her to find a couple of cotton balls and wet them.

She gingerly sat beside the cat. "Help me here. I don't know how to do this. I'm going to wipe your eyes, right? Here goes."

With a tentative hand under the cat's chin, she tilted up the little furry face. Quickly she wiped the first eye. The cat sneezed.

"Well, that was easy, don't you think?" She did the second and, not with any confidence, she squeezed a row of ointment across each of Hobo's eyes. The cat sneezed again and curled up into a dainty, weary ball. For a bundle of filth, she had elegant pretensions.

Calli washed her hands and picked up her phone, thumbing numbers while she ate her cheese sandwich. First, she confirmed the order for the pavers and the sand. Next, she checked with the paving company she had always used. The job would be a large one, and she had already booked the work team.

"Monday next week," she said, repeating the date, noting that the more she spoke, the better her voice. After concentrating for a moment, she realized she had hardly spoken to anyone in the past few weeks. Now with all her cat conversations, she almost sounded normal. *Use it or lose it* seemed to be the cure here, though when she forgot to drink she also did her voice no favors. To make sure of her hydration, she drank another two long cool glasses of water.

"You don't have any water either," she said to the cat, and she filled a large breakfast bowl with water for her scruffy companion.

"I'm off now. Keep yourself clean, or wash yourself, because if you aren't shiny bright when I get back, some time tonight you are having a bath. No one ever got well lying around in their own dirt." And she gave a reluctant laugh because she sounded like her mother.

After rinsing out her cup, she closed the door behind her and stepped back into a clouded spring day. For a moment she paused, glancing briefly at the dividing fence. The Tudor house remained silent, but a distant clank and the murmur of male voices could possibly be the gang discussing their next hit while rattling their numchucks. Or not. Whatever the business of the people next door, she could mind her own.

However, she was pleased to see that the gangster had left for the day. She knew this because his SUV hadn't returned. Probably even thugs had regular employment. Nevertheless, her idle speculation about her tattooed, bottle-breaking neighbor could certainly hold elements of truth. He looked like a biker. Tattoos might be trendy, but his didn't look arty, and the rev of the motorbikes last night had been threatening. Likely he had gathered together the other members of his gang to break bottles on a Sunday night, expressing an antisocial protest against recycling. She actually laughed aloud at her clever cycling pun as she pulled her gardening gloves back on.

Despite the gray sky today, this coming summer was predicted to be as dry as the last. During winter, the judge's garden had dried out considerably. Calli couldn't remember the last time she saw rain, and she needed to install a new water-saving irrigation system before the heat set in.

Since the whole garden would be changed, she would also need to change the hose grid. Although the old drippers had kept the garden alive, the new plan using less water would make the garden lush. In the meantime, she ignored the blockages and the leaks, managing to hand water the plants that showed the most wilt. Normally, she supervised the gardens she designed, leaving others to perform the hard slog. These days, she couldn't afford laborers, but apparently venturing out of her comfort zone was doing her good.

As she had supposed, performing the work herself kept her mind on the job rather than on her woes, the worst of which was caused by her decision to bankroll her partnership with Grayson. The people who cared for her, friends and family, had queried his background, but after the failure of two personal relationships with men from the "right" backgrounds, she had seen this as snobbery. She thought she had made a sensible choice, but she hadn't.

For the first time since the man she had trusted with her start-up business had left with her money and reputation, she realized that she had begun to relax. She appreciated being offered a chance, and she would certainly give the judge her best effort. He trusted her to do a good job despite her having such a pitiful record. All she wanted now was to reclaim her credibility with her family, friends, and anyone she had ever worked with or whom she knew.

Sighing, she marked out the spot for the fountain in the back garden.

Chapter 3

Kell inspected the ceiling in the old laundry room. Normally, on Mondays his appointment book was filled with visits to prospective customers who wanted kitchen estimates. He'd done two last Friday, freeing up part of this week so that he could help with the demolition while he plotted the changes.

"Good work," he said to Trent who stood on the top of a ladder in the center of the old laundry building attached to the garage. Trent had been hired for a nominal wage and free board. "We should get a couple of hundred for this."

Trent grunted and shoved his crowbar under the hole he had made to remove the ceiling rose, cracking off half a sheet of plastered horsehair, which dropped to the floor amid the cloud of dirt and dust that had accumulated over a hundred years. Like Kell, he wore a white disposable coverall.

Kell moved out of the way, his eyes covered with one hand while he adjusted his facemask. "Do you like the garden next door?" he asked, still annoyed the little dickhead had threatened him with a spray can.

"It's okay if you like classy gardens."

"That's what I thought. He's got a gardener, a young lad."

"How young?"

Kell shrugged. "Eighteen, maybe. The kid is working there alone, if you believe that." He glanced up at Trent. "He threatened to tag me, but he's not such a smart-arse as he thinks. I got him to tell me the name of the neighbor. He's a judge."

"You don't see him around much."

"His cars haven't moved from the carport since we've been here. The house looks deserted." Kell took a leap to the side. The next plaster length thudded to the floor, scattering the accompanying detritus to the far corners of the room.

"And an eighteen-year-old is digging in the garden?" Trent waggled his eyebrows, almost concealed behind the layers of filth dropped on him from the roof cavity. "If you see him burying something, you might want to make sure it's not a body." He laughed.

"He doesn't look tough enough to dig a hole, let alone drag a body into it," Kell said sourly. "He's a skinny little thing."

"It'd be interesting, though, if we discovered a serial killer."

Kell started stacking the shattered lengths of ceiling. "It wouldn't be interesting to kill a judge. It'd be downright bloody stupid. I'd start out with someone less noticeable, like a handyman."

"But if you were killing so that you could steal money, judges earn a bit."

"There you are!" said a satisfied female voice. The doorway darkened as Vix Dee, Kell's sister-in-law entered.

Kell straightened, removing his mask to smile at the pretty blonde wife of his older brother, Jay, the architect who had found this property and advised Kell to take out a mortgage to buy the best deal Jay had seen in years, or so he said. "I hope you didn't hear Trent plotting a murder."

"No. I heard *you*. Which particular handyman do you plan to kill?"

"Other than Trent? None of us earn enough to make the effort worthwhile." He brushed the dust off the shoulders of his coverall.

"I brought lunch for you both." She smiled at him. "It's not often you take days off work and since you're taking those days off to do more work, I thought I could help by supplying food."

Trent backed down the ladder. "Great." He removed his mask and wiped his sleeve across his dirty face. "I can't tell you how much I didn't want to buy a pie."

"Why would you buy a pie when you must have a houseful of leftovers from the barbeque last night?" Vix shook her head. She had contributed most of the leftovers, if not most of the main meal. She thought she had to feed the world, and her wealthy family certainly supplied more than their fair share of good healthy sustenance to the less fortunate.

"I ate the cold sausages for breakfast." Trent, as skinny as three-ply, decided he needed more protein than Kell, who had to content himself with pretzels and a tomato salad, which he hadn't particularly minded although he wouldn't admit that to Trent who thought he had scored.

"I have a rather large basket of food I need to get rid of before everything spoils. You'll have to come out to the car and get it. I wouldn't be surprised if I had a few pork pies in amongst everything else, but I think it's mainly the usual for this time of year—oranges, honey, pâtés, cheeses, a ham, rye bread, nuts, too, I think. I took out the fresh vegetables because I knew neither of you would, um, have time to cook healthy meals."

Kell nodded, faking detachment, but he honestly thought Vix was the most adorable women he had ever met. He had never known anyone quite as generous as her, or quite so embarrassed by her wealth. He tried not to be embarrassed by her wealth, too. Accepting gifts he could never pay back was hard, but Vix knew this and suffered with every thoughtful gesture she performed. He and the others could do no less than appreciate her consideration.

"Since you brought bread, we could set up a table and stop for a while."

"Fortunately, I brought a tablecloth, too." She laughed.

Kell shook his head with rueful amusement and wiped his hands down the sides of his filthy coverall, catching Trent's glance. They both knew she had come to fuss over them like a mother hen. When they were building the theater set she painted, she had done the same. Jay was the luckiest man in the world. But Jay had made his own luck. Kell intended to make his own, too.

Kell envied his brother nothing other than his wife, who he richly deserved. Jay was the older brother who had cared for his siblings the way a parent should, working to support them while their father drank. Kell didn't like to remember the bad times, but since his toughness had been formed by the bad times, he had little choice. "Where did you park?"

"Out the front. You parked across the drive and so I couldn't get in." Her voice held a tone of accusation.

Kell nodded, indicating the plaster sheets on the floor. "I was about to pack this rubbish into the truck bed."

Vix lifted her shoulders. "So, I sincerely hope I don't embarrass you."

Wary, Kell scratched his ear. He couldn't guess why the way she had parked her car would embarrass him, but as he reached the driveway gates, he spotted a bright racing red in the street. "A Ferrari," he said in awe.

She looked guilty. "Jay hasn't seen it yet. He won't be pleased, but I'll only have it for a couple of days. My father sent over the basket in it. He thought it was time I had the Beamer serviced."

"You shouldn't let him boss you around like that," Kell said, trying to sound severe. "Hell, if my father did that to me…." He glanced at Trent.

"And if my father did that to me…" Trent shook his head, his eyes bright with suppressed laughter.

She pursed her lips. "I know you both think I'm ungrateful, but I live in a conservative area of town. This car does not suit my lifestyle."

"It suits mine." Kell ran his hand over the polished hood. He wanted to lie there, arms outstretched, hugging the expensive car, but instead he shrugged and tried to look detached. At that moment, the gardener from next door poked his head out of the driveway of the judge's house. His skinny face disappeared quickly.

Kell frowned. He hoped the kid wasn't scouting before doing something nefarious, but what could the kid do? Steal a car? He seemed to have left an old heap of his own in the carport. The judge probably told him not to park on the street. A car like that would give the classy neighborhood a bad look.

"You know when we were talking about murder?" he said to Vix. "The neighbor next door is missing and a kid is hanging around the place."

She looked surprised. "That's Adrian Ferguson's house."

"How do you know?" Kell said, and he wished the words back. Vix and her family knew everyone rich or connected.

"It's a heritage house. It's listed. Everyone knows Adrian owns it. Aside from that…" She looked uncomfortable. "He's a friend of my father."

"Have you seen him recently? The judge, not your father."

She shrugged. "I think he is touring the Mediterranean."

"Why would you think that?" He narrowed his eyes as he gazed at her.

"Because he and his wife went with my stepmother's sister and her husband."

Kell sighed. "Let's get this basket indoors." He grabbed one handle and Trent took the other.

"If he was dead, I would have heard, because my stepaunt certainly would have said something to my stepmother." Vix walked down the side of the house.

Once this area would have been sheltered by an open veranda with a view onto a tennis court, but the roof had long since been dismantled, which saved Kell the trouble of knocking off the tiles. And the old tennis court had been lost in the weeds. "Well, the kid is up to something."

"I'm sure Adrian will be very glad to know you are keeping an eye on his place." She opened the back door of the house and stepped aside so that Kell and Trent could enter ahead of her. "If someone is planting a bomb to surprise him when he gets back, he would like to know before he opens the front door."

"You may think this is funny, but the kid was wearing a disguise and snooping around." Kell walked through the back lobby to the kitchen.

Vix followed behind Trent. "I'll go and talk to him."

"Then he'll know we're onto him," Trent said, puffing a little. He grunted as he helped lift the wicker hamper onto the table. "It's best if we keep cool."

"Do you believe he is doing something wrong, or don't you?" Vix gave them both a schoolteacher frown.

Kell inclined his head to the side. "I think it's unlikely that anyone would employ a gardener to spray blue spots on the lawn, especially when they're away."

"So, I'll talk to him. You two would only scare him off. At the moment you look like a couple medical examiner's assistants. And with your masks, you would be downright scary. Lunch will be ready as soon as you are." She raised her eyebrows at their garb.

"If she wasn't my sister-in-law, I would suspect her of wanting to check out my body," Kell said to Trent.

"She's seen better." Trent was already struggling out of his filthy white coverall as he headed toward the bathroom.

"Let's hope he leaves the bathroom clear for me," Kell muttered, having been annoyed by Trent's habit of leaving his towels on the floor of the bathroom for the past three days.

Vix seemed to be on another track entirely. "You know, this is a beautiful house." She glanced around the kitchen.

"I don't see it, myself." Kell couldn't imagine who would want a kitchen double the size of the average living room, with a tiny laundry and bathroom opening into the same space. He would need to reconfigure. "I could make this room look pretty special, but it's not worth too much bother."

"Isn't it listed?"

"That's why I got it at a bargain price. Every other buyer wanted to knock it down." His mouth hitched with dissatisfaction. "I only have permission to get rid of the later-built outhouses. I want to do a quick reno and then get on with my life."

"The brickwork is something special," she said, completely ignoring his words again and getting right back onto her own track. "My gran's house was like this. When she sold it and went to live with my father, the man who bought the place added on a modern extension."

Exasperated, he raked one hand though his hair. "I suppose that's what will happen here. I'm not a builder. I'm a chippy, and I do interiors. I can't afford to waste money on extensions. I need to get in quick, make a profit, and get out."

She sighed. "My mind sees this place all spruced up and beautiful again."

Lifting one palm, he rubbed a thumb over the ends of his fingers. "Money. When I can afford altruism will be the time for me to think that way."

Her cheeks turned red and she nodded. He didn't like bringing up her situation, but he had only stepped onto the first rung of success, unlike her father who had built a taller ladder and hauled his family to the pinnacle. One day Kell might do that.

"Your turn," Trent said, returning a little sprucer than when he had left. "It's a shame we don't have any clean plates."

"They're in that cupboard above the sink." Vix shot him a frown. "Don't try your helpless act with me. I'm married to Jay who can set a table as well as I do."

"That's because he's been domesticated. I'm still training Trent," Kell said on his way to the bathroom where he yet again picked up Trent's towel and washed.

By the time he returned, the card table in the center of the kitchen had been spread with a red tablecloth and dotted with white plates. Bread, ham, cheese, pickles, and a salad to eat, and he was a new man. Vix left the food in the fridge and took the basket back, likely for her father to refill.

Kell liked knowing that one of the richest men in the state was putty in his gentle daughter's hands.

* * * *

The afternoon flew by while Calli concentrated, referring again and again to her diagrams. She wanted sudden views in the garden and hidden nooks. She wanted beds of color, patches of sunlight, and swathes of green. On paper, her plan seemed feasible. While she ducked through the old haphazardly planted undergrowth, the job looked bigger than she could manage. However, she had to manage. She had made a mess of her personal life and her business life, and she was tired of being used.

She whacked at the stake marking one of the curved edges for the front garden, using her righteous energy productively. For too long she had been no more than her parents' daughter, and she had to find another self. If she wanted to change herself and her life, she had to do so now. Before she finished this job, she would be a whole new Calli. She gave an extra whack to the next stake.

During the afternoon, she finished shaping the new front garden. Re-plotting the complicated back garden would take her more than a week, in her estimation. She stripped off her gloves as she returned to the cottage and the cat, who greeted her with a raised head and a blink.

Calli put fresh food out for the animal, a bare mouthful, which seemed to be the amount Hobo could manage. She watched the cat eat for a moment and then she changed into slim black pants with a loose top patterned in black and white. With her short toffee-colored hair brushed back, she doubted anyone would look at her long enough to recognize her. She had omitted the lashes she had always worn and only added gloss to her lips.

Her slight nod to vanity was her black-and-white striped heels, which made her as tall as the average man. Satisfied she looked neat and clean, she took herself and her phone to the local pub for a bar special. The place employed a cook and not a chef, and the cook couldn't cook. In between web searching for plants on her phone, she picked at the watery vegetables from the serve-yourself bain-marie. After cutting off the fat, she ate the greasy roast lamb, wishing she wasn't hungry enough to do so, and she left after taking the last mouthful. She could drink good coffee at home, since the cottage was now her home.

Dark had descended when she arrived back. Lights glimmered through the forest surrounding the house next door. She now knew more than one person lived there, since the white SUV had left during the day. Later, she had seen two white-wrapped men, one blonde woman, and a Ferrari.

Perhaps because walking into a dark house alone at night spooked her, her mind began to hover over her speculations about the neighbors again. As the SUV hadn't been there during the day, the tattooed gangster wasn't either of the white-clad men. The only car to arrive had been the Ferrari. Women rarely drove Ferraris, therefore one of the men would have brought the blonde, or she lived in the house next door, too.

Why would the Ferrari macho stereotype, usually a youngish male who wanted admiration from other men or, of course, beautiful blondes, live in a dilapidated property hidden by trees? Why would he wear white coveralls? For cleaning? Unlikely. Or not? Momentarily letting her mind wander over cleaning, aka, body disposal, she hesitated in the doorway—but she couldn't let her imagination loose when she only had herself to spook.

Deliberately relaxing her shoulders, she switched on the main light. A body disposer wouldn't be interested in her. She hardly had a body at all, and she certainly didn't have any mob connections. Aside from that, she had nothing to snitch to the police about, other than Grayson, of course. Her worst problem was the smelly cat.

"Hi, puss," she said to Hobo, who stretched, and then soft-footed off the couch, aiming a reproachful glare at Calli. "What have I done? I've been out. Whatever has happened, you can't blame me."

Hobo did a figure eight around Calli's ankles and then paraded to the fridge where her food dish sat empty.

"Very impressive. I suppose you expect me to fill the bowl again. Well… okay. But don't take a single bite unless you agree to have a bath." Calli spooned food into the bowl and set the dish in front of the cat, who ate like a taster in a cooking competition, taking tiny bites and pausing. "I hope you realize you have compromised yourself by accepting a bribe."

She decided the cat had nodded in agreement. Grabbing her bottle of shampoo and one of the towels from the bathroom, she left the kitchen sink to fill with warm water while she made a pad that covered the drainer. "How to bathe a cat," she said in a companionable voice. "In one easy lesson. Finished dinner?"

Hobo lifted a paw and began cleaning between her toes with her teeth.

"Don't worry about that." Calli picked up the cat, tested the water's temperature with her elbow, which anyone knew to do, and with trembling hands put the cat in the water, which reached just past her knees. "Could you sit? No. Is it okay if I scoop water over you?"

The cat gave her an unreadable glance, but other than a slight shudder, she accepted having water scooped over her. Calli soaped her up, rinsed her off, cleaned her eyes, and then as gently as she could, she patted the bundle of bones dry. Without her matted fur covering, the cat was frighteningly delicate. On the plus side, washing a cat was rather like washing a teddy bear, but actually nicer, because the cat purred while she was being dried. Calli had no idea why the vet had said *good luck.*

Finally, Hobo decided she was dry enough and she sprang onto the tiles and ambled across the carpet to the front door. She glanced back at Calli as if to say, "C'mon."

"If your need to go outdoors is in any way embarrassing, don't tell me. And if you run away, remember I don't care. I won't have to clean your eyes again." Calli opened the door.

The cat disappeared into the night. "I didn't mean it," Calli said, her fingers pressed to her cheeks. "I do care. Please don't make me search for you."

Within a few minutes, Hobo returned, glanced at the open door, glanced at the garden bed beside the open door, adopted an expression of complete innocence, and rolled herself in the dirt. Then she shook herself, bounded back inside the house, and curled up on the couch.

"So, that's your true opinion of my bathing skills?" Sighing, Calli perched beside her and reached for the television remote controller. A crime show flickered onto the screen, lights flashing, actors clumping around in blue latex boots and *white coveralls.* She changed channels to a cooking show, even worse, because the food looked edible. Switching off the set, she listened for noises in the night. Not even an air conditioner hummed.

She couldn't go to bed before eight at night despite being physically exhausted. Instead, she folded her arms and stared at the ceiling, noting a tiny cobweb in the corner. She breathed out and stared at the cat, who slept soundly. Tomorrow she would buy a book to read. Tonight she would think about what she would do first in the morning. Breakfast. Jog. Move a few plants from the front garden to the edge of the veranda facing the tennis court. The sun didn't reach that area until the late afternoon. Then she had miles of brown plastic piping to cut and fit for the new dripper system. She dropped her chin onto her chest, thinking. Then, with her jaw forward, she stood, kicked off her shoes, pushed up the sleeves of her sweater, and grabbed a white chair from the dining area. In the darkness of the night, she could peer over the neighbor's fence—just to make sure they didn't nurture a marijuana plantation or run a meth lab.

After switching off the light, she carried the chair to the side fence. Listened. Nothing. She took a step up onto the seat. The street lamps gave her a clear but gray view into the neighbor's property. Immediately under her nose stood the overflowing smelly bin and a brick path leading to the back door. She hadn't made herself into a snoop to watch her neighbors but to put her mind to rest about their illegal activities. Or so her mind insisted.

The property had the same back boundary as the judge's. The house ended where the judge's main house started. The backyard resembled the front garden, weedy and speckled with feral trees. Calli had no view through to the garage, but she knew a large area of land lurked between the house and the outbuilding. This meant the marijuana plantation would be out of sight, if the gangster grew marijuana. The meth lab would be in the crumbling garage, which would be a good disguise for a meth lab.

The yellow light from the windows of the main house lent menace to the shadows. Without any sort of warning, while she was peering through the weeds, the back door of the house creaked open. She had time to see a rangy man in dirty jeans open his eyes wide with surprise when he saw her. "Killer," he shouted wildly.

Terrified, she immediately ducked down, huddling on the chair while clutching at the fence post. Was he yelling for someone to kill her? Surely they wouldn't. Neighbors spied on each other all the time. In some areas, neighbor watching was considered to be an essential sport.

Her heart thudded in her chest, and she thought about calling out that she hadn't seen a thing. She cleared her throat, and his back door slammed. The thump of footsteps. A bump against the fence, which rocked. Moving, she whacked her knee, and the chair tilted. She grabbed hold of the fence post, but too late. The chair tipped over, and she fell onto the upturned seat, the heels of her palms and her knees planting into the dirt. She quickly arose, only to be thrown onto her belly.

A heavy shape landed on top of her. "Got you, you little varmint."

The neckline of her top jerked up under her chin, almost choking her. She froze. Her heartbeat went into overdrive, and her pulse pounded in her ears. She tried to turn but the man put his elbow around her neck. The weight of him held her down.

"Isn't it time you went home?" he asked in a silky voice.

Her body tightened into defense mode, stiff and ready to fight back. "Not your business," she managed to say in husky, breathless voice. "Get off me!"

His weight lifted off her, but he had a grip on her top. As he stood, he dragged her up with him. "Explain why you are still lurking around," he said in a terse voice.

Almost crippled by the tackle, she turned to face him, tangled in her skewed top.

He examined her, his hand tightly gripping her shoulder. Then, he blinked and stiffened into a visible double take. While she stood frozen to the spot, her blouse settling back into place, he morphed into the dangerously handsome Mr. Neighborhood Watch. The palm that had flattened on her shoulder shifted to his hip, his whole stance expressing surprise. "You."

Her heart dropped. She hadn't expected him to recognize her face when he had only seen her in sunglasses and a hat. "Instead of worrying about what I'm doing, you should be concentrating on the gangsters next door," she said through clenched teeth, bravely taking a step back.

"The gangsters next door?" His expression relaxed into the sort of amusement that would cause the elastic in women's undies to melt.

Her shoulders eased. "And their meth lab."

"Meth lab?"

She folded her arms. "Or marijuana plantation."

"Marijuana plantation?" His eyebrows lifted slightly.

"I already know you have mentioned to one of these people that they might be happier living elsewhere. I heard you this morning. I can certainly report suspicious activity. The gangsters in there are probably making a fortune while you're running around at night scaring poor innocent residents."

He re-angled his stance. "You're a resident?"

She flicked her head toward the darkened cottage. "That's how I can hear what's going on next door."

"Noisy, are they?"

"No. Suspiciously quiet. Well, except for last night. They played loud music and laughed and broke bottles. I expect they were having an orgy after counting the millions they extorted from people during the day." She straightened the neckline of her top.

He pressed a loosely curled fist to his mouth while he examined her face. "I think this neighborhood deserves further discussion. Tomorrow night over a meal, perhaps?"

"I think you should back off the property before I call the police." She took a step back to the door, clenching her bare toes onto the lawn.

"What's going on over there?" said a voice from behind the fence.

"I've had complaints about you," Mr. Neighborhood Watch called back.

"Me?" the voice said in indignant squeak.

"And I would suggest you dismantle your meth lab before the police arrive." Mr. Neighborhood Watch pushed his hands into his back pockets, and nodded at Calli, as if to imply he had the situation covered and was in collusion with her.

"Okay," the voice said. "It sounds like you're talking to a woman."

"As it happens, I am. The eighteen-year-old boy turned into the jogging girl."

"Story of your life, isn't it, buddy? I expect you don't need my help." The voice sounded bitter. The back door squeaked and banged.

Calli stood for a moment staring at a face that even in the shadows set her heart thudding.

"The police won't arrive in time, and they won't find any evidence," he said, holding her gaze.

She moistened her lips, her intake of air icy cold. "You're one of the next-door neighbors, too, I presume?"

He shrugged, as if it didn't matter. "About the bottles—we thought the cottage was empty."

All of a sudden, she remembered his comment to the man over the fence. "You've seen me jogging?" She wet her lips. "Is that what you meant when you said *you*."

He nodded. "We're working on the house until the marijuana crop is ripe enough to harvest. The meth lab is Trent's. I don't have anything to do with it."

"And you're staying there while you work." She hesitated and, in case he had seen her picture in the paper as her father's spoiled dishonest daughter, she tested him with, "I'm Calli."

He gripped her palm. "Kellen. Now, about that dinner...."

"There's nowhere around here you would want to eat. Look, it's been interesting talking to a gangster, but I have a pile of work to catch up with."

"Right." Kellen reached behind her and grabbed the chair. "Where do you want this?"

"I'll take it inside."

"I'll take it inside. It's the least I can do after throwing you to the ground and landing on top of you."

"If I can carry it outside, I can carry it inside." She lifted her chin.

His expression deliberately patient, he took the chair to the door and waited for her. "I understand that you don't want a strange man wandering into your house. How about if you wander through mine tomorrow instead and check the whereabouts of the meth lab? It would save you climbing the fence at night."

She firmed her chin. "I expect you wouldn't want me to arrive until you've had time to hide everything."

"Come for lunch," he said, passing the chair to her. "We have a houseful of food."

"I might," New Calli said, surprising herself. Apparently she wasn't quite as staid as she had thought. Or Kellen's reluctant amusement had relaxed her. "At about one. By the way, how did you get into this garden?"

"I jumped the fence." He backed away, a crooked smile on his face. "I'll show you." In two steps, he had hold of the top of the fence, lifted to the extent of his arms, and vaulted. "See you at one tomorrow."

Chapter 4

"You might be sitting here thinking I fell for that smooth line," Calli said to the cat as she tucked up her bare feet beneath her on the couch. "But I sure as heck didn't. Yes, I did say I would go to lunch, but first he asked me out to dinner. Ha! He must have a whole lot to hide. You need to watch out for men who pretend they want a date when you don't have your hair or makeup on. I don't mean bald—don't get me wrong. I mean without, you know, a bit of camouflage."

The bundle of bones opened her golden eyes with surprise. She seemed to have natural eyeliner herself and probably couldn't see a reason to worry about makeup.

"You're right, of course. He was trying to change the subject. They do that." She pressed her lips together, knowing that she had never been man-bait. She had to tell herself the truth. The men she knew saw her as either contemplative marriage material or the useful daughter of her influential father.

Despite the smoldering amusement in his eyes, Kellen hadn't been trying out his charm. He didn't even know her. He wanted to appease her. The thought that she might report him for coming onto the judge's private property and accosting her must have had him worried. By asking her over to lunch, he meant to calm the situation. Little did he know that offering food to her was about the smartest thing he could do, even if he did have a marijuana plantation or a meth lab, which she no longer really believed or likely never had.

And judging by the shows she saw on television, drug dealers didn't have offbeat senses of humor like Kellen's, which in the normal way of things she enjoyed. The obvious had never appealed to her. The sexiest thing about a man was a brain and a sense of humor. Although the two should go together, quite often clever men didn't "get" her and they made her explain, which dried up her conversations and jolted her confidence. And then, of course, she decided she wasn't smart enough, and she let them dump her or swindle her. Her relationships that began with admiration and high hopes, ended with her losing part of herself.

Tonight, however, she had stood her ground, despite the fact that Kellen had knocked her flying, and he had scared her. If nothing else, she could be proud of herself for that. Although everything she had thought for the past two days had been turned upside down, she had come out ahead. Instead of living on her own near gangsters, she lived near a couple of tradesmen trying to earn a wage, just like her. She no longer felt alone. If she could manage to be friendlier toward them, she might be comfortable by herself. She might not be spooked by noises in the night.

She might not tell saintly lies to herself, either.

Sliding down in the seat, she crossed her arms over her chest, grumping. A month ago she would have sworn she would never look at another man, and here she sat, trying not to imagine Kellen without his clothes. Her body hadn't connected with a man's for a very long time, certainly from pre-Grayson days, and almighty Kellen had lifted her to her feet with a tug of her shirt. Primitive, of course, but very manly.

Judging by the width of his shoulders and the way he had tossed her around, he had Muscles, with a capital M. She happened to be very keen on toned men, or looking at them. Well, she was a healthy young woman. Naturally she would look twice at a man as easy on the eyes as Kellen.

"And you didn't hear me say that," she said to the cat, who gave a huge, utterly bored yawn.

* * * *

Kell strode into the kitchen. "Jogger Girl's coming to lunch tomorrow."

"What happened to the dinner date?" Trent asked sourly, scrubbing at the plates they had used for the evening meal.

"That was a no-goer."

"Does she look as good up close as she does when she jogs past?"

"It's hard to tell without a light, but she feels good."

Trent shot him a glance. "You copped a feel?"

"Let's keep this above the belt." Kell folded his arms across his chest. "I tackled her to the ground. I might have enjoyed that a little longer if I'd known she was a female. She can't pass for a boy when you're up close. She smells like a woman."

"You tackled her to the ground. And then you asked her for a date."
Trent nodded resignedly and shrugged. "I suppose that's automatic for you."
"Only when I tackle women to the ground. You're going to leave those dishes to drain, I hope. I don't want this house-sharing deal to deteriorate into a couples' thing where you wash and I dry." Kell frowned.

"It was better when we didn't have any dishes."

Kell absentmindedly picked up the tea towel Vix had left. "It was also better when we had no food in the house. Then I wouldn't have fallen into the trap of asking Jogger Girl to lunch. She said she would come at one tomorrow." Surprising himself, he laughed. "She's crazy. She says we're drug dealers, and she is coming at one to inspect the place."

"*And* she was standing on a chair peering over the fence." Trent grinned. "I think we have a live one this time. You don't want to get too friendly, though, Killer, because if she lives next door, she'll be hard to shake off."

"That won't be a problem." Kell wiped and stacked the plates back into the cupboard. When he lost interest in a woman, he simply told her he needed to move on. Not keeping a woman on the hook seemed to him like the most efficient thing to do. He had let his first girlfriend at the age of sixteen hang around far too long because he didn't want to hurt her. Then he hurt her anyway when she realized he had lost interest. Making a quick break had to be less painful than the subsequent crying scenes she put him through.

Trent pulled up a chair to the countertop and started fiddling around with the diamond paned leadlight window he had retrieved from the bin, likely trying to work out how to remove the glass he had broken without damaging too much lead. Kell wandered outside to his hastily erected shed where he had stored the cream-painted wardrobe doors salvaged from the bedrooms upstairs. He wanted to strip the paint off one and see if the natural wood might be worth repurposing.

Recently he'd been experimenting with vintage styles, and he liked using wood with different textures and colors in his kitchens. When asked to do a bedroom or a study, sometimes a customer required more than shelves or cupboards, and he was always on the lookout for good solid slabs of wood that could be turned or carved, or made into a desk or a special set of shelves. Invariably, he ended up supplying laminates or two-pack sprays, but given the choice, he would work on the high end of quality rather than the disposable. Only the well-heeled considered wood that would require maintenance, but only a wealthy person would be able to afford this house.

As he raced his scraper over the painted surface, he speculated about Jogger Girl, whose reaction when he had tackled her to the ground was remarkable, considering she was female. She hadn't yelped or screamed. She'd been quite determined not to let on that she was a woman. Interesting. Then she had faced him, ready to fight back, which had given him a scare when he realized he could have hurt her. He admired her pluck.

Eventually, he revealed an inlaid pattern of various woods beneath six or more layers of paint and decided that instead of sending these doors off to the salvage yard, he would keep the lot. He could certainly make use of the designs one way or another, though not in the new bedrooms. The old house needed to be brightened up and he planned white cabinetry upstairs. He had a look in mind for the kitchen: the old reclaimed oak cupboard fronts with cream floor tiles, and light quartz countertops, a combination that generally appealed.

When he finally wandered back indoors, Trent was already snoring in one of the two camping beds Kell had deposited in the old sitting room at the front of the house. He sighed. A male roommate didn't have the same appeal as a female, but wasting two rooms in an about-to-be-renovated house seemed ludicrous. He switched off the overhead light and dropped his clothes onto the floor, slipping naked into his sleeping bag.

The next thing he knew, Trent was standing over him, shaking his short wet hair in a spray of droplets over Kell's face. "The hot water's off. You'll get a cold shower."

"You don't need to sound so cheery about it," Kell said, squinting at the daylight. "I'll get Luke around to see what the problem is." Yawning, he stretched his aching body, and glanced at his watch. "Has Jogger Girl been by yet?"

"Half an hour ago. Like clockwork." Trent pulled on his work shirt. "I found a place online where I can buy lead strips for the window. I might drive over sometime today."

"Good idea, but let's not get into the habit of a chat before coffee, huh?"

Trent grinned and disappeared, leaving Kell to grab his clothes and head off for a cold shower, not that he needed one. Jogger Girl was interesting, but he hadn't yet seen her in the daylight. She could be as rough as sandpaper for all he knew.

He and Trent cleaned and stacked bricks all morning and he almost forgot about the lunch date until Trent reminded him. "Get out the tablecloth, too," Trent said, waggling his pale eyebrows. "Women like that."

Kell had barely walked into the kitchen when he heard, "Yoo-hoo," from the open front door. One step out the doorway, and he glanced along the passage. The black silhouette against the daylight was shapely with long hair.

"Hi, Kell. I knew you two would be working hard. I brought you some lunch." A pretty blonde wearing tight jeans and a brownish top walked through the hall toward him, her long scarf floating along behind. She wore a big multi-colored bag slung over one shoulder.

He searched into the distracted fog of his mind for her name. "Emily," he said, finally.

She reached for his shoulders and gave him a lingering kiss on the lips. "Hi, Kell." She had attended his barbeque on Sunday with the other nurse. He must have said he was taking part of the week off.

He had met both the women while he had been standing with Trent in a queue outside a nightclub last week. One started up a flirtatious conversation and had asked for his phone number. He obliged, she entered her number in his phone, but being female, they were invited inside the venue by the bouncer first.

"Before you go," Trent had said, "Kell will give you his address. We're having a barbeque next week, if you're interested."

Kell duly handed over a business card, to which someone with a pen had added his address. The queue looked never-ending and he normally worked seven days a week and so he decided to leave. Trent left with him, but he was sure the women would turn up at the barbeque. They had.

She smiled up at Kell. "The food is a belated host gift for you. I didn't bring a thing on Sunday."

Apparently, she had decided to make a move, either on Trent or him. He hoped she was interested in Trent because he had shown interest in her at the barbeque. Aside from that, Kell had invited Calli to lunch when he never made a play for a woman. At this stage of his life, a woman was only a momentary distraction. Glancing away for a second or two, he remembered why he had acted out of character. Calli intrigued him. "Where's your friend?" He ought to remember the name of the other woman.

"Working." Emily made a face. "We do shifts. I have the day off."

"So, you often work on weekends?"

She nodded. "Where should I put lunch?"

Even had Trent not been interested, Kell knew he couldn't tell her to leave the food and skedaddle. "As it happens, we were about to sit down for a meal. The gardener from next door is coming over. You're welcome to join us."

She looked taken aback. Naturally, she expected to stay with her lunch. "So, shall I help in the kitchen?"

"Sure thing." He led the way. "I've done the tablecloth. I'll set out a few plates."

She put her bag on the countertop and pulled out two long baguettes filled with meat, cheese, and salad. He passed her a knife and she cut the bread into sections and placed them on a large plate. "Four," she said. "Right?"

"Four." He sliced a plate of ham and glanced ruefully at the salad ingredients.

She took the hint and put a mixed salad together, placing the bowl in the center of the table with a fork and a spoon he handed her.

He glanced at his watch. "I'll call Trent." He moved toward the back door, which opened.

Trent walked in. He glanced at Emily and his eyes widened. Then he gave his goofy grin. "Emily. Did you bring Amber?"

She smiled back. "She's working. I thought I would bring lunch instead for you workers, but you seem to have plenty."

"But we don't have plenty of women to look at, so it's good you came. Should we start without next door?" Trent asked Kell.

"You think I do lunches often enough to know the etiquette?" Kell asked with an amount of attitude. He didn't mind Trent being so pleased to see Emily, but he didn't want this lunch to be a date with two women, eating healthy baguettes like the poncy types who lived around here. He had asked a gardener to eat with him and his tradesman mate. This wasn't happening as he thought, a casual sit-down with fellow workers.

"Knock, knock," he heard from outside.

"Come straight through," he called, and in walked Tag Artist wearing a thick work-shirt, jeans, and work boots, like on Monday. He placed his fists on his hips, frowning. He had asked Jogger Girl for lunch, and her alter ego had arrived.

Her mid brown hair, cut short at the back and longer at the front, framed her well-defined cheekbones and jaw line. With a clear-skinned face, a slim elegant nose, gleaming silver-gray eyes, and thick dark eyelashes, she shortened his breath. Pure class. He could look at her for half an hour and still enjoy the view.

She glanced at Trent, Emily, the table, the food, and back at him. The expression on her face didn't change from mildly interested. "Hi," she said to all. Like last night, her voice sounded husky. Sexy.

He made a blank of his expression. Long ago he had learned to do that; a lifetime ago. Indicating the other two, he said, "Emily dropped by for lunch, too, and I keep Trent around to take care of the marijuana crop."

She faced him. "You told me he is in charge of the meth lab," she said with a mock-innocent widening of her eyes.

"Me? Oh, no," Trent said, pulling out a chair for Emily. Impressive. Impressive, also, that he had remembered the name of her friend. "I'm an artisan, not a druggie. My normal job is to build theater sets, but I'm helping here for a couple of months before I whip off to Sydney to build another." He said this to the back of Emily's neck.

Kell used his head to indicate a place at the table for Calli. He pondered pulling out her seat but was saved the trouble when she moved around him and sat. Then she smiled at Emily. "I'm Calli from next door. I don't know if Kellen remembered my name so this is a tactful reminder."

"Thank you." Kell sat. "She's a member of the drug squad," he also said to Emily. "She heard the party on Sunday night and deduced we were all on drugs—a logical assumption."

Emily glanced at Trent. He shrugged. She looked back at Calli and smiled. "Hi, Calli. I'm a nurse. I don't want to know drug dealers, either. I deal in drugs all day. That's enough for me."

Tag Artist smiled at Emily and then turned her gaze to Trent. "Theater sets. That sounds interesting," she said, and that started Trent off.

During Trent's spiel, Kell resisted adding that he also built sets when needed. Instead, he acted the waiter, kept passing food and pouring glasses of water. He also discovered that Calli had a scratch along the back of her hand and a callus on her middle finger. She ate like a starving poodle, which in a lot of ways she resembled, being elegantly shorn, long limbed, and graceful. Also, largely silent. She absorbed other people and kept conversations going with interested questions.

"You look familiar," Emily said to her while she passed the salad.

Calli smiled politely. "I hear that a lot. I must have that sort of face. I've been told I look like Hilary Swank, for example."

Emily laughed. "It must be the short hair."

"Ellen DeGeneres, also a woman with short hair," Trent said, with a look of concentration. "You don't look like her."

"Interesting to know." She picked at the scratch on her hand nervously, which intrigued him.

"I also make decorative screens," Trent said to Emily, trying to get her attention back again.

"How interesting," she said, still staring at Calli.

"I've got one outside I could show you. You might want to see some of the leadlight I'm thinking of repairing."

"Leadlight? Like in churches?"

"Like in old houses. We're going to put in plain glass here. Nobody likes the old stuff anymore." Trent rose to his feet and Emily slowly rose to hers.

"Lead on," she said, with a puzzled shrug at Kell.

He smiled at her, pleased that for once Trent had used his initiative. If he exerted himself, he might get a date.

"Nice lunch. Thanks. I must get back to work." Calli rose to her feet. "And I'm not nobody."

He rose, too, strangely put out that she didn't to want to stay longer. "I didn't think you were. Or do you mean you like leadlight?"

"I can't imagine why anyone would tell you to remove the original windows from this house."

He rubbed the side of his neck. "People these days like clear views."

"Some people like a few interesting elements kept in the older houses. Not everything, of course. The whole update doesn't need to be vintage but in this kitchen, if it was renovated properly instead of rebuilding, you could have a real butler's pantry and larder. Everybody wants those."

"There's not enough room."

"That," she said, pointing at the side-by-side laundry and bathroom, "is the old larder and the old pantry. They only need to be re-incorporated."

"Those two rooms are going to be the new modern kitchen and the rest of this room will be a casual living space," he said annoyed that, yet again, his plan was being questioned.

She started toying with the top button of her shirt as if stalling. "Maybe you ought to get the owner of this place to talk to a few land agents before he makes that decision."

"Maybe I ought to look over the judge's plants and give you my advice on gardens."

"That would be a waste of time." She laughed. "I can already see you don't know a thing about horticulture."

"We haven't started on the garden here, yet. But I can tell you, those shady trees out the front are staying." He crossed his arms, knowing he sounded riled.

"That's what I thought." A dimple appeared just below the curve of her cheek. "I also thought I was invited here to look over the place."

"You should have gone with Trent," he said, his voice a growl.

"I don't want to be the third wheel. Anyway, I have to get back to work. But I can see now that you are both renovators and not drug dealers. The tattooed man was a red herring." The dimple came and went again.

"Steve?" He frowned. "He doesn't even live here. He's a respectable married man with a child."

She lifted her shoulders. "Well, he shouldn't wander around looking like a gangster."

"You'll be pleased to hear that his wife doesn't like his tattoos, either."
He gave her a superior smile. "If she had noticed him earlier, he might
not have them."

"So, it's her fault?"

"It's always the woman's fault."

Instead of laughing, clocking him one, or giving him a smart-arse
comment, she pressed her lips together as if censoring herself. He couldn't
imagine why. Although he didn't necessarily want to argue with her, he
enjoyed a bit of give and take.

"What did you mean when you said 'that's what I thought' about the
garden?" He ushered her toward the front door.

"You people don't know a weed from a plant," she said over her shoulder.
"You don't have a real tree in the garden, though I suppose those feral
olives almost count as trees. But the councils around here want them gone."

"What about the tree with the shiny leaves?"

"That's also feral—the blowfly bush. It used to be planted as a hedge
and it's a good strong plant, but it produces berries that birds eat and
now the seeds have been scattered far and wide. When it grows into the
bushland, it's a real menace, like the olives, and like that lantana you are
also growing. The seeds from that are dire."

He considered the earnest expression on her face. "Perhaps you could
give us advice about the garden."

She stared at him, worrying at her bottom lip with her teeth while she
considered. "I'll help you if you help me," she finally said.

"What do you need help with?"

"Lifting, mainly. A bit of digging." She inclined her head to the side,
watching his face.

"So, you give me an hour, and I give you an hour?"

"My time is more valuable than yours."

"Says who?"

"I have a degree. Therefore I'm paid at professional rates." She tilted
up her elegant nose.

"I have muscles." He smiled, crossed his arms and pumped up two
biceps with his thumbs.

She blushed a bright pink, turned on her heel, and said as she walked
through the door, "Deal."

* * * *

Calli went straight back to work in the garden again, trying not to let
Kellen's unexpected smile shift her focus.

Having overeaten, she experienced a certain amount of sluggishness—but a great amount of satisfaction because of the best meal she had eaten in a week. Tasty baguettes, fresh and crisp. Wonderful salad and lush plump ham. Nothing but the best for Kellen, and that included pretty Emily.

Two months ago, Calli had been an Emily. She had looked like Emily, with long stylishly colored hair. She had worn the same makeup as Emily, with the same thick black eyelashes, the same careful eyebrows, and probably the same brand of lipstick. She could make a checklist of Emily's clothes: caramel high heels, check; Zara jeans, check; loose knit cashmere top, check; designer scarf, check-check-check.

Emily had adopted the classic look shared by women who expected a comfortable marriage to a comfortable income. Callis and Emilys didn't stand out from the crowd. They hoped. They kept themselves neat and clean while waiting for the right man to come along. Since Kellen was clearly not the right man for Emily, the smartest thing she had done was to disappear with Trent.

Trent, an artisan with enthusiasm for his work, had a far more comfortable marriage potential than Kellen. Though what would Calli know about that? Her only two real relationships had been with men who could at best be described as *marking time*. She hadn't been enough for either of them.

Neither Calli nor Emily should waste a second of her time slavering over an alpha male like Kellen, the macho type who expected a woman to prepare lunch for his buddy and the gardener next door. Had his attitude not been so outrageous, Calli might have experienced a short moment of yearning.

Though, what sort of savvy businessman would let his tradesmen remove leadlight windows from an old house in this exclusive area? Even without a renovation, the place would be worth a mint. The land alone was worth a million, give or take a dollar or two.

She clicked her tongue as she stepped back to check the forty-five-degree curve she had used to take her staked-out path around the house from the back patio to the side veranda. This area overlooked the tennis court on the shady side of the house in front of her cottage. From here, she could see nothing of the house next door other than the overgrowth and the roof. The house next door certainly had potential.

She almost laughed. Her former imaginings about Kellen being a gangster now seemed ludicrous. When she had entered his current residence, she had seen a place as neat as any occupied by two single men. They slept in camping beds in the front room, but she hadn't noted clothes scattered all over the floor. Similarly, the kitchen, while old fashioned, had no dirty dishes lingering in the sink, no filthy tea towels slung over chairs. Drug dealers would have plastic bags filled with dried leaves lined up along the countertops, or brown paper packages tied up in string.

She smiled wryly when she realized she was humming "these are a few of my favorite things" from *The Sound of Music*. Drugs weren't her favorite things. She had been called straight by Grayson's crowd, and straight she was, if not downright disapproving. She should have rethought her business plan the first time she saw Grayson with a white line, but he had shrugged and smiled. Her mind-story had told her he was too smart to continue. Her new cynicism told her most of her money would never be retrieved.

The paths she planned took her all the way around the house. Between the judge's house and the sandstone two-story on the other side, she would plant a formal row of white crepe myrtles softened with a border of the sea lavender, a pretty block-out of the fence. Along the back, fruit trees with raised beds of vegetables in front would keep the judge's young grandchildren amused. A child could have such fun in the garden, picking fruit, planting, and harvesting food.

Memories of her own childhood came and went, and she disciplined her mind to the job at hand. Tomorrow her load of stones would arrive. In the back garden, the paths would be wood chip with a rock border edging, hard and soft together to make a textured contrast. If Kellen or Trent barrowed the rocks to various points for her, her job would be made so much easier. Her working life, that was.

The other part of her life where she worried about money, hoped to redeem herself, wished she had been stronger, smarter, and less willing to believe extravagant stories, seemed to be receding into the background. Passing scrutiny when she had been so closely examined by Emily, pleased her. She had wriggled out of the *I know you from somewhere* questioning— Where did you go to school? Do you know so-and-so?—quite neatly. Her new life might go as planned, with her getting on with her work, earning her wages, and proving herself businesslike.

Finally her parched throat took her back to the cottage for a glass of water. The cat greeted her at the door and edged past, tail cocky as she left to find a spot to do her business. Time had flown. Now past five, Calli could end work for the day. She changed the cat's water, and put her food bowl in the sink. In two days, Hobo had changed from wretched bundle of bones into a confident bundle of bones. Her eyes still wept, but with healing tears and not pus.

After Calli had washed and changed, she examined her face in the mirror, thinking that somehow she looked less tired, although she was physically exhausted. And hungry. Tomorrow she would need to go to the bank to see if her starting wage had been deposited. The cat still had half a can of fish to consume, but tonight Calli would be eating crackers again. The lunch should have tided her over, but she still had an empty space to fill.

She peanut-buttered her crackers, joined them two by two, and took them on a plate with a white chair outside to eat in the waning daylight. Her door smacked behind her.

"Is that you?" she heard a male voice say on the other side of the fence. Since she didn't know if she was being addressed, she kept quiet.

"Calli?"

"Yes. Did the sound of the door bother you?" she said with an amount of exasperation. She had complained about the noise. Now she was the noisy neighbor.

"Not at all. It's me—Trent. Come to the fence, and we can talk." The top of his head appeared, and then his eyes, crinkled as if he was smiling.

She stood and moved over to him. "What do you want to talk about?"

"I heard you needed help with lifting. While I'm cleaning bricks, or stacking tiles, I need a change of position from time to time. I can help you almost any time you like. A break would do me the world of good."

"Trent, that's wonderful. Can you come over here to talk to me? I'm just about to make coffee."

"Real coffee?"

"Pod coffee."

"I'll have to walk around. I don't take fences in a single bound like Super-Kell."

"Kell? You call him Kell?"

"When I'm not calling him 'Killer.'"

"I'll start up the machine."

She put two cups on the warmer, connecting the two names, and actually blushed, mortified that her overactive imagination had led her so far astray. For no reason at all, she had scared herself. She went outside again to watch Trent chugging down the long driveway. "Sorry I don't have cookies, too," she said, holding the door for him to enter. "The larder is quite bare."

"We have a couple of packets to spare. Kell's sister-in-law brought us a basketful of stuff from the country. Even fruitcake. Do you like fruitcake? We won't eat it. I'll call Kell and ask him to toss some stuff over the fence."

Chapter 5

Calli stood in her doorway hot with embarrassment as Trent yelled for Kell. Kell answered back, and packs of cellophane-wrapped *stuff* sailed over the fence before Kell, whose hands then gripped the top of the fence. First, his face appeared. Then, somehow, he lifted to the full extent of his arms, placed one foot on the top of the fence, and swung his body over, landing upright on Calli's side.

"Real coffee," he said, still looking totally cool, because that's what he was—a deadly package of calm and inscrutability. If she hadn't known he was a tradesman, she would have guessed he was a businessman, a corporate lawyer; a man who was used to keeping his secrets close. He rubbed his hands together as he walked into the cottage, which appeared to shrink around him. "I hope I can control my tremors. That's if I'm invited with my cake and cookies?" He frowned at her half-eaten peanut butter crackers.

"Cake is the entry fee today. Please, take a seat."

Since Trent had said he and Kell wouldn't eat the fruitcake, she emptied a pack of his pistachio and white chocolate cookies onto a plate, and passed each man his coffee as soon as the cup filled. "Milk?" She took the carton from the fridge and put a small amount in each cup before sitting.

Then she salivated. Her hand trembled as she reached for a cookie. She didn't want to speak. She wanted to savor the first taste of empty calories she'd had in a month. She crammed her mouth full while the men savored the aroma of the coffee.

"Coffee," Trent said in a reverent voice. "Now the only thing missing is hot water for my shower in the morning. Did you get hold of Luke, Kell?"

"Luke is my younger brother," Kell said to Calli. "He does my plumbing. If you like cheese, we have too much in our fridge. And ham." He glanced at Trent.

Trent nodded. "Hell, yes. You can get really sick of all that healthy stuff." "Do you have a phone?" Kell drummed his fingers on the table while his heart-bumping gaze assessed her.

She nodded, thinking about glorious fatty cheese and how to look casual about him getting rid of some ham in her direction.

He pulled his phone from his back pocket. "Put your number in here, and I'll put mine in yours. Then if you need anything, you can call me."

"I used to wonder how he picked up women," Trent said in a voice of resignation. "Living with him is like taking on another apprenticeship."

"Calli is a woman alone tucked away at the back of the block. I, for one," Kell said in a dark voice, "would like to know she has someone to call if she has a problem." He gave Trent a reprimanding glance. "And, I don't want to scare the hell out of her if I drop in to see her."

"You could knock on the fence."

"And you think that won't scare her?"

"Would it?" Trent stared at her.

"Not now, because I've met you. But if someone snuck up behind me in the garden, I might not be too brave."

Kell's mouth relaxed. "I'll get the ham and cheese."

Calli picked up his phone and added her number, trying not to see how many first-name women he had there already.

Kell came back with a small wheel of brie, a triangle of blue-vein cheese, a box of expensive-looking crackers, a shrink-wrapped hunk of ham, a pack of dried figs, and a bag of walnuts. "The cheese is a bit fancy for us," he said as he dropped the food onto Calli's kitchen countertop. "So are figs and walnuts."

Trent nodded in agreement. "You have to feel sorry for Jay, Kell's brother. He has to eat this sort of stuff a lot these days." Bringing the coffee mug to his nose, he inhaled the aroma and made a sound of pleasure. "I'm a pie and sauce man myself."

Calli glanced at him and didn't believe a word either man had said. Both had healthy bodies and good skin. They were being inordinately generous, and she had no way of paying them back. She sighed, staring at the wonderful offerings. "You realize that I'm not going to be able to charge you for my horticultural advice now. This more than compensates for anything I can do for you."

Kell looked down at her, his dark eyebrows lowering. "Accept this as an apology for tackling you last night. And since I'm giving away food I was given myself, I'm hardly being noble." He folded his arms and squared his determined jaw.

"He doesn't have a noble bone in his body," Trent said, his eyes sparkling with humor. "Believe me. On his best day, he's a selfish bastard, and I should know because I've been working with him."

Kell lowered himself into a chair again and picked up his mug. "He's complaining because he had to wash the dishes last night. I'll call *him* names when it's my turn." He took a long gulp of his coffee and sighed with appreciation.

"It's never your turn. One thing you are *not* is domesticated," Trent said, his voice resigned.

Calli tried to concentrate on her cup. Sitting as close as she did to Kell, she knew he had showered recently. He smelled clean and soapy, which was the best sort of odor on a man, an aroma a woman wanted to breathe in and then lick off. Her insides flared with unwelcome lust while she stared at the coffee in front of her. "I know insults between guys are terms of endearment." She tried an off-hand tone, which sounded slightly husky. "I have a brother, though you guys would be tougher than he is. For example, I don't think he would consider taking a cold shower." She drummed her fingers on her thigh, hoping she had made a leading statement.

"I wouldn't be considering it either unless I was forced," Trent said dourly. "Kell doesn't care. He wasn't brought up soft like me." He eyed Kell.

"How long do you think it will take to get your hot water back again?" she asked Kell, still hoping, and trying to bat her naked, probably invisible eyelashes.

He glanced at the table. "Two weeks to a month. Luke didn't see any point in repairing the pipes in the old bathroom since we need to put in an en suite and a main bathroom upstairs. One thing we've got upstairs is plenty of space for bedrooms and bathrooms."

"A month?" Trent said in a tone of outrage. "I'm giving you my notice now."

"Don't be a wimp."

"Geez, Kell. It's early spring. The cold weather hasn't ended yet. This sunny break won't last. Though, maybe I could shower at the gym." His face twisted with thought.

"Or," Calli said, her voice hopeful. "You could shower here. In exchange for work in the garden."

Trent moistened his lips. "Done. I'll give you double the time I take in the shower."

"So, that would be a minimum of ten minutes?"

"Say quarter of an hour."

"So, I'll get an hour every four days, unless Kell wants a hot shower, too?" She risked a quick glance at him.

"I'll be okay with cold."

She didn't let her disappointment show. "So, Trent, are you any good at throwing rocks into a wheelbarrow?"

"I worked for a bricklayer when I left school. I've done my apprenticeship in rock-throwing and I can throw bricks, too. When do you want me to start?"

"The delivery is expected tomorrow. Any time from the end of this week."

"Not any time. You're still working with me," Kell said with a sideways glance at his friend.

"I've never been so popular." Trent nodded at Kell. "Well, boss, let me know when you can spare me."

"When we've got those outbuildings down and all the bricks cleaned." Kell gave Trent a hard stare.

"Are you going to reuse them?" Calli asked, knowing that waiting a week or two for free labor wouldn't be a problem.

"Sell them. People buy the old bricks for paving." He lengthened his legs under the small table and his knee touched hers.

Her leg reacted by lurching out of the way, embarrassing her. "I know. I use them sometimes in my gardens when I'm doing an old house." She willed her expression to remain impartial.

"Do you do many gardens?" Kell narrowed his gaze at her.

"I used to. This is my first for six months." She fingered the handle of her cup, seeing the tip of a cat's tail twitch near the other side of Kell. "I moved onto design work instead." And Grayson had done the bookwork that would never balance, not since he had taken her money and disappeared. She had sold almost everything she owned to stave off bankruptcy after he left, and even now she still owed money to her father who she should be able to pay back after this job, as long as she could keep her living costs minimal.

"What sort of design work?"

"Horticultural. That turned out to be my main interest." The rest of the cat appeared with a sneaky intrusion onto Kell's lap.

He didn't even look at Hobo. His big hand covered her back and his fingers massaged behind her ears. The little cat's eyes slitted with pleasure as she settled on his knees, purring. "What made you take up gardening?"

Calli tried to look casual, because strictly speaking, she hadn't taken up gardening. Gardening had taken her up for the time being. Her initial degree had been in horticulture, to which she had added garden design as an adjunct to her family's business. Then Grayson had convinced her to put all her money into a horticultural start-up she would run with him, designing new gardens for old homes. "I thought it would be an interesting way to earn a living."

"Isn't it a bit too physical for a woman?" His thumb found a spot on Hobo's back that caused her to writhe with ecstasy.

"Not really. I don't do much heavy work—mainly the designing. Normally I design and then supervise my workers. This job is different. I needed time out for a while and when I was offered this garden and the cottage for three months, I decided I could do the whole thing myself because I had three months instead of a few weeks."

"So, this is virtually a working holiday for you?"

"Yes," she said, eagerly grabbing onto the idea. "Time out away from the rat race. I can, actually, lay bricks and set stonework. If I had to, I could also barrow all the rocks around the garden, but I would rather pay someone else to do that. The judge left me enough money to pay a laborer."

"He paid you before he left?" Kell's raised eyebrows expressed his astonishment.

"I'd be a fool to try to diddle a judge, wouldn't I?"

"There's that." Kell gathered up the cat, placed her on Calli's knee, and plonked his empty mug on the table. As he stood, he indicated to Trent that he should, too. "Thanks for the coffee. Much appreciated. Sorry I threw you to the ground."

The disgruntled cat leaped off Calli's lap and stalked back to the couch.

"Me, too," Calli said, placing a palm over her lumbar region with a faked pained expression. But she wasn't sorry. She could still recall his hard body against hers. At the time she had been scared. However, the memory of his raw masculine aggression remained with her, shortening her breath. Although she knew manly men existed, they didn't usually didn't take much interest in her. The men who did were usually university graduates whose main interests were hauling socially acceptable women from one exclusive function to the next. "Look before you leap, next time."

His eyebrows lifted, as if in amusement. "Do you want a next time?"

"That wasn't an invitation. It was simply friendly advice."

"Yeah, we better get going." Trent rose to his feet. "I want to finish cutting the wood for my new screen before the light fades."

"You'd better not let our neighbor know you'll be using a power tool at this time of night. She expects visits from the neighborhood watch when you empty bottles into your bin at night." Kell's sideways glance stayed firm. "I don't know what she would do about real noise."

She frowned at him. "She would probably ignore it. How do you cut out your screens, Trent?"

"Mainly with a band saw these days. It's kinda noisy." He glanced at his feet.

"What materials do you use?"

His eyes refocused on her and brightened with enthusiasm. "Lately I've been using recycled wood because that's trending now."

"*Trending,*" Kell repeated in a deliberate voice. "He used to do leaf patterns, but all the hardware shops are selling those in cut metal. So, now he does arty wood screens."

"I like the look of the weathered wood in gardens," Trent said, his tone lofty. "I'm no good at drawing anyway. But I could charge more if I could add a few new floral designs."

Kell slowly shook his head, his expression resigned. "I never thought any of my guys would mention floral designs."

Trent ignored him and glanced at Calli. "You know about gardens. Can you draw flowers?"

She moistened her lips. "Botanically or artistically?"

"I wouldn't know the difference. If you could give me some ideas, I could shift your rocks for free."

"The way you guys bargain, you'll be broke in a month," she said, exasperated.

Kell sighed and tried to usher Trent out the door.

"Come and see my screens tomorrow, Calli," Trent called as he was dragged away. "You might be able to advise me, who knows?"

She laughed. She liked Trent, who reminded her of a bouncing puppy. He had energy and enthusiasm, and a sort of innocence. Although he was nice looking, he didn't have the cut and polish of mind and body that so attracted her to Kell. She could be friendly with him without being in any danger of falling for him. And that was what she needed at this stage of her life—a friend who wanted nothing from her but the drawing of a flower.

Kell? Well, she didn't know what he wanted from her, but she suspected that he was used to full-on admiration, the like of which Emily had displayed. He would treat the other woman as badly as he had yesterday when he had sent her off without a second glance to see Trent's screens. He would treat most women that way—easy come, easy go, and if they chased him long enough and hard enough, he would give them a tumble.

She breathed out slowly. She wouldn't mind a quick and uncomplicated tumble herself. But, no. Not with a tradesman who lived next door. Any distraction in her life right now should be with someone more her type. Aside from that, Kell was probably a man whose supersonic looks let him think that any woman was easy prey. Although handsome men attracted her, male preening annoyed the heck out of her. The new Calli wasn't about to be impressed by anyone because of the way he looked. One lingering heartfelt sigh about how Kell's behind neatly packed his jeans, and she squared her shoulders. Time to get to work.

In her special accounts' book, she had ruled up columns, heading the top of the page with the amount of money she had been paid for the job. She had already entered the prices of her paving, sand, and stone. She added the quote for the delivery and the work. The plants she ordered would not be sent for some weeks, but she bargained for a good price, which she had also recorded.

The judge had banked the total she quoted him for the full job, materials, and labor. Who did the labor was immaterial. She estimated the work would be finished in one month but she had the cottage for three months on a house-sitting basis, which would save her a small amount of money on rent during that time. In the deal, she was expected to drive each of the judge's cars once a week. No punishment, that, and she planned to take the Jaguar out the next time she needed a trip to the shops.

So, after she had finished the judge's garden, she would still have free accommodation for two months. With luck, she would find other work in the meantime, and she would earn more money. If she could manage to live on fifty dollars a week during her stay, she would be able to pay her father back for the amount he had paid in her name to the garden supplies' wholesaler, to the tradesmen who had laid her concrete, to the bricklayers who had worked on her garden edgings, and to the suppliers of sand and bricks, bills that had never been paid by Grayson from her funds. In time, she would grant herself permission to use her accounts again. At this stage, she bought at retail prices, where her money had the same value as any other customer, but as soon as she deserved credit again, she could quote for new design jobs. Because of her debts, she would be a laborer for another three months.

Already she had gained enough positive thoughts to see her life turning around. Whereas before she could only focus on her hurt and humiliation, she could now see her way ahead. Her parents had been disappointed in her, not for losing her money, but for losing her mind. Neither could believe that a daughter of theirs would be so unbusinesslike as to put all her money into a partnership with a man who had not contributed a single dollar.

"You thought he had some special knowledge that you lacked?" her mother had asked, showing the frown lines on her forehead.

Yes, Calli had. She thought Grayson had the charm she lacked to run a business, and the ability to sell her ideas. Of course, she could design whatever a client wanted, but sometimes she thought she could do better, given the right persuasive words. She had lately realized that the right words stemmed from enthusiasm, but he faked that as well. He had charmed her right out of her money and she had let her parents down the same way she had let down her tradesmen, suppliers, and contacts. She hadn't seen Grayson for the person he was, a user. She had only seen his dimpled smile and heard his weasel words. Never again would she accept anyone at face value. A person would have to prove him or herself before she offered her trust.

Reminded of her mother, she clicked on her phone and sent a text. *Love you. You might be proud of me yet. Love to Far. XX*

Her mother had accepted that she would return as soon as she had her head on straight. Far had growled and said he would send out a search party if he didn't regularly hear from her. Since she had sent her first text before the carrier had arrived for her excess baggage, her father would be placated by this next message only three days later, which she thought was very regular and also smart. If he decided to find her, she would be found, without a doubt.

Her phone tinkled and a message from her mother lit up the screen. *Love you, too. Far wants your address.* She turned off the phone; she had to fix her problems without the help of her parents, which they had offered and would continue to offer until she had proved self-sufficient, moneywise. A daughter of two such wonderful people would naturally want to be independent and correct her own mistakes. She decided they knew this as she cupped her chin in her hand, staring at her accounting, which to her looked balanced.

Her figures would remain healthy if she did something she had never done before, not previously having to worry about money. For a change, she had listened to the hype and decided to shop at the Central Market in the city once a week to buy the ingredients for her meals at little more than wholesale prices. She had wasted fifteen dollars this week already on food, including the meal at the hotel, therefore she would need to list exactly the items she needed for the week and no more. She sighed. From now on, she would be cooking the basics.

She cheered a little when she remembered the blue-vein cheese. The judge had spinach in his garden. Blue-vein and spinach would be a treat with gnocchi. One meal down and only thousands more to plan. Although she had never been quite so organized before, she plotted her meals for the week.

In the morning, she would drive into the city at around seven, be back home by eight, and working in the garden by nine. An early night would be in order. The day had been full, and certainly enlightening. Kell, who had apparently been employed to renovate a house on one of the most exclusive streets in one of the most exclusive suburbs in the state, planned to get rid of bricks he ought to be using for the renovations, if only for a few interesting paved paths outside.

His employer didn't appear to be at all cluey. Whoever he was, he had no styling sense whatsoever. If she had a scrap of generosity, she would share some of hers with Kell. Then again, a man with his confidence wouldn't listen to a woman anyway.

* * * *

Using the last of the daylight, Kell hefted and squared two pallets of reclaimed bricks in the main driveway. He stood back, his eyes narrowed, staring at fruits of his and Trent's labors. They had knocked down the old garage and the old laundry. The old-fashioned bricks were smallish, pale, and battered, but had a more attractive low-key appearance than the larger, knife-edged, more aggressively red modern clay bricks.

Perhaps, as Calli had hinted, he ought to reuse more of the originals than he had planned, maybe as fire surrounds or even a feature wall, both suitable for that vintage look he wanted. He slowly rubbed his chin for inspiration. Yes, he would keep them, but he couldn't use them all. He would end up with enough to build a small house, far more than he wanted.

Jamming his hands into his pockets, he strolled past the shed where the band saw still intermittently whined. Trent would work all night if not reminded to stop. The man had a need to create. In a way, Kell shared the passion, though he was a craftsman rather than an artisan and he suspected Trent was the same. After working on theater sets, the other man preferred the word *artisan*, though.

Kell moved into the doorway, watching his companion pile his lengths of cut wood against the wall. "Finished?"

"I guess I could do with a meal. So, you want me on demolitions again tomorrow?" Trent raised his gaze to Kell's.

Kell read Trent's ultra-sneaky expression. "I don't think Calli is your type."

"Ah. You want to keep me away from her for my own protection?"

"You need to make a decision. Do you want to run after a gardener or are you interested in a nurse?"

"The nurse being Emily?"

"Or Amber."

"Do you think they would be interested in a threesome?"

Kell leaned against the doorway, trying to give the impression of man seriously considering this idea. "Nope," he said eventually. "Emily seems to have a bit of class."

"Do you think *she's* my type?"

"Did you impress her with your attempt to fix the leadlight window?"

Trent laughed wryly. "I think I puzzled her with my screens. She had made a decision about me, and I wasn't fitting into the right box."

"You like to play the dumb tradesman."

"I always thought I was one." Trent narrowed his eyes at Kell. "Are you planning on further contact with her?"

"Well, there's Amber to consider, too," Kell said, keeping his tone casual.

Trent clamped his jaw. "Which one do you want?"

"I haven't decided, but Amber hasn't turned up since the barbeque."

"You know, most men contact women they're interested in." Trent still looked tense.

Kell shrugged. "Did you get Emily's phone number?"

"I'd look like a real jerk if I did, wouldn't I? She came to see you, not me. Don't you have her number?"

Kell gave Trent a look of incomprehension. "Why would I keep her number? Do you know which hospital she works at?"

"So, you don't share, huh? Yeah, right. I could call and ask to speak to Emily, a nurse," Trent said in a sarcastic voice. "I'm sure the reception desk would be happy to page her."

Kell relaxed in the doorway, leaning against the frame. "Good luck."

"I can't tell you how much you piss me off. You can pick and choose women, except of course Calli. You've thrown all your best lines at her, and she has thrown them all back."

Kell decided not to answer. He didn't have lines. He barely had a coherent thought stream when he spoke to her. Straightening, he prepared to return to the house.

"What would *you* want with a woman who looks like man and gets her hands dirty?" Trent said as a parting shot. "You like them in heels so high they totter instead of walking."

Kell frowned. "She doesn't look like a man. Did you see her eyelashes?"

"You can't have every woman, you know. She would naturally prefer me. I'm arty. She's arty."

"You're about as arty as a plank of wood."

"That's where you don't understand art. A plank of wood is arty."

Realizing he had almost shown his feelings, Kell forced himself to relax. "You're right. You two have plenty in common. I'll stick with Emily and Amber, who can totter along with the best of them." He stalked off. Calli. Who said he wanted Calli? The woman was nothing but skin and bones. When she had opened her fridge, he had been shocked. She had nothing there but long-life milk. Perhaps she had anorexia? No. Every time he had seen her lately, she had been stuffing her face. He couldn't imagine her in heels, though last night she had looked smart in casuals. Of course he didn't want Calli. She had short dark hair. He preferred blondes with long swinging hair a man could wrap around his wrist while he pulled her toward him for a steamy kiss.

Emily, or Amber, was more his type. Maybe he should call Emily. She had taken the trouble to put her number on his phone, and she had brought lunch. Nice girl. Pretty, too. And he would make Trent happy if he could double date with Amber. No, Trent wanted Emily. Kell had noted his expression. The man had a crush. Kell would have Amber. That was if he called Emily, which would be complicated if he was planning on asking to arrange a date with her and Amber and Trent.

He skimmed through his phone numbers. He found Emily's, selected her name, and she answered almost instantly.

"Hi. Kell Dee. The man you treated to lunch yesterday. What do you say to a trip to the wineries with Amber and Trent sometime on the weekend?"

"Sounds lovely. I could do Saturday afternoon. I don't know Amber's roster. Can I call you back tomorrow?"

"Sure thing." He switched off his phone. Yup. Complicated. If Amber couldn't make it, he could hardly take back the invitation. Damn. Next time, Trent could get his own date. Disgruntled, he found the design he had mocked up for the kitchen.

With nowhere else to work, he sat at the card table and examined his plan. Calli had insisted that everyone wanted butler's pantries. He already knew the pantries were growing more popular because he had two orders in progress at the workshop, but he intended to construct a regular kitchen here, needing the extra space for the entertaining area. After he had taken off the old cabinet doors and drawer fronts, he would get his carpenter to build the carcasses to fit.

He had planned nothing flashy for this house, all simple and expensive-looking. A butler's pantry, aside from taking up much needed space, would need extra cash and possibly be a fad that would soon pass. He had borrowed as little as possible for this house, but maybe... He rubbed the back of his neck while he thought.

What would a gardener know about kitchens, anyway? Why would he listen to her when he had ignored Vix's advice?

And why did he want to bed that damned pest? She made his skin itch. He must be working too hard. His brain had dropped into his pants, and he could only think about shiny short dark hair, a slim square-shouldered body, and a soft sassy mouth. And she smelled like peanut butter, which was a rare turn-on. He laughed.

Nothing would cause more of a problem than dabbling in sex with the woman who lived next door.

Chapter 6

When she awoke, Calli realized she hadn't made a formal plan about the use of the shower in the morning. She had no idea what time Trent would drop by. She would have hers right then, which would give him an hour before she left for the market at seven.

She hurried through her shower, ate her staple of cornflakes, dressed, and by the time she had fed the cat and let her out for an ablution's break, Calli remembered she had packed her shopping bags in one of the boxes she had sent to her parents. Although frustrated with her lack of forethought, she beat the peak-hour traffic to the city. However, without a nice big bag or nana trolley, she first had to spend a few precious dollars on a plastic carry-all from the nearby supermarket.

Her total haul took her two trips to the car. She had noted the price of a trolley and decided to buy one the next week, having calculated that she would be feeding herself very nicely for less than thirty dollars, saving twenty of the thirty she would need for the trolley. In the meantime, she had bought packaged gnocchi at fifty cents a serving, fruit for under two dollars a kilo, and seasonal vegetables—leeks, cauliflower, green beans, and fresh mushrooms—almost all with her loose change.

When she arrived home, the cat awaited her on the doorstep, and took a keen interest in the unpacking of the food. By leaping onto the countertop and trying to open the brown paper bag, Hobo indicated she would be interested in a mushroom or two, but when Calli presented her with one, Hobo blinked in astonishment that anyone would have imagined she would eat a raw vegetable.

As Calli cleared up, someone knocked on the door.

"Am I too early for a shower?" Trent asked as she opened the door. The cat sprang up onto the couch and studied him, her expression aloof. "Your timing is perfect. Good, you brought a towel."

"I thought you might charge me ten minutes extra if I didn't." He wriggled his eyebrows. "I brought my own soap, too."

"I would have charged you five minutes for both, don't doubt it. And I'm putting my timer on now." She gave him an entertained grin, indicating the bedroom with the bathroom beyond.

"You'll join the millionaires' club within the year at this rate," he said as he opened the bathroom door. "Very nice. Thanks for this, Calli."

She smiled, despite knowing that men and bathrooms were incompatible. Nothing could be more certain than she would have to clean up after him. However, he opened the door well within the ten-minute time span with his towel slung around his neck and dressed in the same clothes but with wet slicked-back hair.

"Ten minutes," she said as he walked to the outside door.

He nodded and hesitated. "Is it too early in the morning to ask a favor of you?"

"That depends what it is."

"It's a personal thing." He shuffled his feet. "Would you come to the Barossa Valley with Kell and me on Saturday? Emily will be coming, too. We'll be doing lunch and a bit of wine tasting."

"You're asking me out on a date?" Her mind said no-no-no; she didn't want to watch Kell romance Emily. She didn't want to see Emily making doe eyes at him and accept being his servant.

He shook his head. "Just a regular foursome. Kell asked Emily and her friend Amber, but Amber can't come. I told him I would ask you, and he said okay."

"So you *are* asking me out on a date?"

"No. I'm asking you for Killer."

Her heartbeat went into overdrive. "Why can't he ask me for himself?"

"Because he thinks you'll be my date."

She swallowed her disappointment. "If he wants to be with Emily, why are we going to all this trouble? Can't he just go with her?"

"I don't want him to. I don't think he is the man for her. I think I am."

"That's very romantic, Trent." She had been ridiculous to hope that Kell might give her more than the time of day or even that he might be shy about asking a woman for a date. He didn't have a shy cell in that whole big gorgeous body of his. "So, why don't you ask her and skip all these complications?"

"Like every other woman, she wants Kell. He would play with her for a couple of weeks and then get bored. I don't want him sleeping with her. If I end up marrying her, I don't want to know she was with him first."

"You're serious about Emily?"

"Couldn't be more serious. I spent most of last Sunday night at the barbeque talking to her. She's a nurse. She's smart and kind, not Kell's type at all. He likes frivolous women who just want to have fun, no strings. She's the type a man would want to settle down with. I made some headway two days ago, but she is still thinking she is interested in Kell."

"And I'm somehow supposed to sidetrack him? I'm hardly the frivolous type myself."

"You're cool and calm. You're not interested in him. He takes that as a challenge. I think you could sidetrack him for a while by doing that thing women do."

"Do I want to know what that is?"

"Hot and cold." He scratched his neck. "Friendly, but not too friendly. Interested, but not too interested. If you do, I'll make it worth your while. Whatever time you spend distracting Kell on Saturday, I'll pay back in rock-shifting."

She narrowed her eyes and concentrated on his face. "What sort of lunch is in this deal?"

He laughed. "It won't be wrapped in paper. This will be a regular date, but he will think you're mine. I'm sure I can peel Emily away from him with your help."

"You've got more faith in my charms than I have. Mind you, I would do almost anything for a restaurant lunch. And what could possibly go wrong with a plan that will have me playing myself?"

"Well… " He looked slightly dubious. "He likes you, I think, and I won't be worse off if he spends the night with her, because that was always in the cards. But I have to at least try, don't I? What is it about him, other than his looks, anyway? Why do women drop by all the time, wanting to feed him or wanting the other thing?"

She kept her face expressionless, but apparently she had at least one trait in common with Kell's women—looking at him and instantly thinking about the *other thing*. "I don't see it myself." She tried to use a cool and calm voice instead of a lying voice. "He hasn't exactly impressed me. First, he thought I was a boy, then he thought he could order me around, and then he tackled me. I wouldn't say we have made a good impression on each other."

"He said you have long eyelashes."

"What?"

"I've never heard him say anything about a woman's eyelashes before. That's when I thought I might get away with using you to distract him." Long eyelashes? When did a man ever notice something like real eyelashes? "I've never been used to distract a man from another woman. I hope I'm not going to embarrass you and myself, but yes, because I'm irresistibly drawn into any old nefarious scheme by blatant flattery. I'm your date for Saturday, and I'll try to get between Emily and Kell. And what do you think of that?" she asked her best advisor, the cat. "Me trying to distract Mr. Bossy?"

Hobo considered the weighty matter for a moment before deciding to sleep on her answer. She curled herself in a neat little ball and closed her eyes.

"I think she's quite relaxed about it."

Trent laughed. "Mr. Bossy? Kell?"

"Well, he did accost me a time or two."

"He called you Tag Artist first and then Jogger Girl. Funny how you both make up names for people. Oh, and I won't need a hot shower again. I can manage with cold water if Mr. Bossy can. Now you'll earn a couple of hours help from me whenever you want, which is a better deal for you." With a pleased smile on his face, he left.

She rubbed the back of her neck, puzzled. A better deal for her? He was trying to help her? She ought to fall for him instantly, and why not? She liked him. He was clearly a good guy. If she had a brain, she would fall for good guys.

Then again, she doubted that she had ever really fallen in love with a man. She had seen *suitable* and *unsuitable* in her mind, and she had chosen to date the suitable until that really hadn't worked for her. The suitable guys saw other women as more suitable than she, except for Grayson, whom she suited right down the ground, being too gullible to see past his charm. She couldn't say all men were rats, but she could say she was no judge of character. She seemed to be attracted only to men who would let her down.

"Hobo. Excuse me interrupting your sleep, but why did you insist on snuggling up to Kell? Does he lure everything female or can you sense empathy?"

Hobo's ears twitched.

"Right, I'll ask you when you're in a better mood."

Calli strode outside to a humid spring day with an overcast sky and began to dig up the small plants she didn't plan to keep. Being canny, however, she potted most. She just might be able to pay back her generous neighbors with plants as well as advice.

* * * *

Kell eyed Trent sideways. "You smell like a rose," he said as Trent strode into the kitchen with a satisfied expression on his face.

"There's something to be said for a hot shower," Trent said, his voice smug. "Lucky that Emily contacted you so early, though, because I had a chance to ask Calli, and she said yes." He tossed his towel into the old bathroom, which would soon be demolished.

According to Calli, the room had once been a generous larder. Kell hadn't revised his initial plan. He would use the space for the greater part of the new kitchen, and the room Calli had decided was the old butler's pantry would remain the laundry room. Another bathroom would be built upstairs. The master bedroom would have an en suite.

"Yes to a date with you? Well, good luck," Kell said, keeping his expression set and disinterested. "But remember, it's not a good idea to sleep with a neighbor. However it goes, it will always be awkward."

Trent stared at him for a few seconds, and then he nodded. "I like her. She's funny. Unlike you, my first thought when I see a woman isn't connected to sex."

"I would hope not at your age." Kell caught the banana thrown at his head, snapped open the top, peeled off the skin, and took a bite. "I have to go to the workshop today to make the cabinet doors for the Richmond house. I'll be there tomorrow, too. We're behind at work, and I need to catch us up again." He dropped the banana skin into the bin.

"I'll carry on with clearing up, then. I'd make a start on the ceiling upstairs, but the plasterboard hasn't arrived yet. If you think you might want to reuse any of the leadlight, I'll see how I go with repairs."

"If you get tired of cleaning bricks, come to the workshop. I can always use another pair of hands."

"Thanks, Kell. I appreciate the work. You're a good man. Don't let anyone tell you otherwise."

Kell blinked. "No one has." No one had but his father, of course, who in drunken rages had called all his sons worthless. A kid who hears that loud enough and often enough certainly has doubts about himself. Although his first thought when he met a woman probably *was* connected to his other brain, his second thought was to work out how quickly he could get away without being drawn in. Morning-after were not for him. He didn't want to chance having his father's words proved. As long as he could keep sex casual and relationships distant, his worth or lack of would never be discussed with him.

While he worked on his customer's glossy, laminated kitchen, he stayed on track, concentrating on the job at hand. He liked his work. He enjoyed installing new cabinetwork and seeing his customers satisfied. Unlike the consultants at the bigger firms, he didn't give advice on color schemes or try to palm off cheap and nasty work as something special. He simply provided whatever the customer asked for. Here and there he suggested changes, but mainly his customers had their tastes catered to.

Being his own customer in his own house, the red brick Tudor, he needed to decide exactly what he would install. No rocking of boats. Simply a couple of white bathrooms upstairs with Shaker-style cabinetry like in the kitchen he planned. Maybe pale granite countertops with the polished wood. The formal rooms, the sitting room and the dining room, needed nothing other than good carpets and well-painted walls. The place had to showcase Kell's cabinetry and little more.

The kitchen would be his showpiece. Women cared more than men about kitchens. If their ideas wouldn't work for one reason or another, often related to plumbing, he would tell them why, but most wanted exactly what they wanted. If he'd had more room, he would have considered Calli's opinions about redoing the butler's pantry and the larder, but he needed a laundry room downstairs, and he had no other space; nor any other space for informal living—unless he could incorporate the dining room, somehow. Hardly anyone wanted formal dining these days. He rubbed his forehead.

On Friday, he installed the new kitchen he had completed for his customer—an elderly woman with a tiny house and a need to give tradesmen cups of tea and little cakes. Meeting her made him wish he had a more immediate family. All he had was his two brothers and two sisters-in-law, though the tribe was growing because of Luke's three sons. Perhaps Kell was growing soft, thinking that way. He shook the thoughts from his head. Looking at happy marriages of others wouldn't change his mind about settling down.

During the late afternoon, he accepted an order for another new kitchen, this one larger than usual and with a butler's pantry squeezed into one corner. Two sinks in one small space. He shook his head over the idiocy.

On Saturday morning, he arose early. Today he wanted to make sure he looked like the kind of guy who would go wine tasting, a know-it-all about the better things in life. When it came to wine, he knew red from white and there his knowledge ended. But despite her work-roughened hands, Calli was all class. He could tell by the way she talked, her porcelain white teeth, her fine expensive skin, and her neat and perfect haircut. She was a tall and healthy smart-talking woman. When she gave him sass, he wanted to lift her off her feet and swing her in the air, and when he brought her down again, he wanted to kiss her until she lost her cautious expression. Somehow, she brought out the big kid in him, though he had possibly never even been a little kid. He had always been careful and watchful. Her candid observations made him want her in a way he had wanted no other woman before. And she had barely even glanced his way. She would be interested in men with her sort of class, a private school education, a degree or two, and parents with a swimming pool and a tennis court. He had none of those, but he would eventually have some of those. He would never have more than he could earn himself. To attract a woman like her, first he would need to tone down his naturally terse manner and relax, be more casual like Trent. Likely, he could do that.

He made sure of a good workout in the gym, and he took a long hot shower while he had the opportunity. The morning passed quickly while he completed the weekly chores, stocking up his fridge with the staples, sitting in the Laundromat reading his phone messages while waiting for his clothes to be washed. Most of the messages were related to work and none were urgent.

Finally, with more than one clean shirt to his name, he drove home, plotting how to shift Emily onto Trent. He wanted Calli to himself this afternoon.

* * * *

With only a vague idea of how to be man-bait, Calli took the time to pamper her skin. After her shower, she blow-dried her hair, which took about a minute. She even applied a light coating of makeup and a heavier coat of mascara. Long eyelashes, huh?

Not expecting to socialize while she was living in the guest cottage, she didn't have an extensive wardrobe to choose from. Finally, she decided her black slacks would do for a day in the country, and she had a loose amber top that contrasted with the light gray of her eyes. She knew what Emily would wear. Exactly what Calli would have worn if she had all of her clothes with her. Nevertheless, she didn't want to be stuck in heels if she had to clatter from one winery to the next. Boat shoes would do.

She squirted perfume around the bathroom and walked through the haze. Subtle, she hoped, and she grabbed her big black casual bag. She had agreed to drop in next door when she was ready. Apparently the expectation was that the guys would be waiting and she would take longer.

She trudged through the jungle next door and took the stairs to the veranda. The front door cracked open as she reached the top.

"I heard you coming," Kell said, moving aside so she could squeeze past him into the hallway. She smelled soap on his skin, saw his dark stubble, and felt the male heat emanating from his big body.

Her eyes met his, and she knew the rest of the day wouldn't be fun at all. For the whole time, she would not be able to have a real expression on her face or use real words when she spoke to him. Fake Calli had been hired to distract him. "It must have been the swishing of the scythe ripping through the overgrowth that gave me away."

His mouth lifted on one corner in acknowledgement of the hit. "Hold still."

She took a step back into the wall despite his order, her breath shorter than a healthy woman would normally expect after climbing four steps. She raised two eyebrows and stayed expressionless, despite the wild beating of her heart.

"You collected a leaf on your hair."

Her gaze focused on the skin of his corded neck and a bolt of lust hit her in the lower region of her body so hard that she almost gasped. The pulse in her throat went into panic mode. She could think of nothing but the movement of his chest while he breathed, and his arm brushing her shoulder when his fingers reached into her hair.

He removed a tiny scrap of leaf litter, which fluttered onto the worn carpet runner. "We can't have Trent's date looking like she has gone through a bush backward, can we?" His breath warmed her cheek.

She managed a silent swallow. "That's a very flattering description of my hairdo," she said in a ridiculously shaky voice. "Do you throw those sorts of compliments at your own dates, too?"

His eyes focused on her mouth and stayed. "You look very nice today. Clean, for a change."

She laughed, almost glad she couldn't phase him. Today he would simply be her newest challenge. He was used to women chasing him, and he wouldn't turn a hair even if she propositioned him, which she didn't plan to do. Only one thing was certain. She couldn't fascinate him. "You look very nice today, too," she said, more to take back control of the conversation than to compliment him.

If she told him that he looked so sexy in his tan cotton pants and cream cotton-knit sweater that she wanted to tear out Emily's eyes, she might be speaking the truth but not helping her own case at all. Today she needed to keep him interested by letting him think she wasn't, a tactic that worked best with his type, not that she knew firsthand. She had to accept Trent's opinion and remain just a tad out of Kell's reach. "Say that to Emily when you pick her up."

His dark eyebrows lowered. "Do you imagine I've never been out on a date before?"

"Not at all," she said politely. "I'm simply helping you get a second date. For instance, if you pushed up your sleeves this far, you would improve your chances by about fifty percent." She took his wrist carefully and pushed the cotton knit about two inches higher. "Women love nice forearms."

His eyes turned smoky. He didn't move. "Don't you think that might be a little contrived?"

"You're right, of course. You're the dark and dangerous, mysterious type. You need your date to be intrigued. Nice knit, by the way."

Without acknowledging either of her comments, he turned her toward the back of the house with one hand on her hip, indicating she should walk ahead. "I'll lock up. We'll leave by the back. Trent is outside opening the driveway gates."

Throbbing with anticipation, she moved smartly through the house and opened the squeaky back door. "I hope it doesn't rain today. I didn't bring a coat."

"We'll never be too far from the car." After locking the back door, he guided her toward a gray SUV with *KD Cabinetry* stenciled on the door in white.

So, now she knew he would be his own driver. "Do you mind if I sit in the front? I get carsick unless I do."

Without taking a scrap of notice of the pitiful expression on her face, he opened the passenger door at the front and she stepped in, over the first hurdle, as it were. Now Trent could sit with Emily, and Calli could begin to earn a few hours free laboring in the garden. Kell backed the car out of the drive and Trent closed the gates. He grinned at Calli when he leaped into the back seat of the car.

During a desultory conversation about the Saturday morning traffic and the crowds of home renovators in the hardware stores, Kell's GPS guided them to Emily's house. Emily didn't look too excited to be put into the back with Trent, but within minutes the two were chatting companionably, including Kell and Calli in the conversation about the best place to go for lunch.

"Do you have a preference?" Kell asked her in a quiet aside.

"If we don't have a booking, it would be best to try somewhere not too popular." She didn't want to see anyone she knew, but Emily had the opposite agenda. The busiest most annoyingly trendy place was chosen during a conversation that whiled away the time along Main North Road.

After Kell drove through Gawler, the scenery suddenly changed. Flat green plains turned hilly and rows and rows of grape vines travelled up and down and took sculptural curves. The roads narrowed and the verge trees grew taller and greener. Calli had always loved the Barossa Valley. By the time Kell pulled up the car at the end of a winding track, she was ready to stretch her legs.

The shabby chic restaurant had been constructed of old corrugated iron and a recycled shed. The view at the top of the small hill took in the neat grape vines and the surrounding roses planted to keep the bees toiling productively. Unfortunately, the parking area was only half-full. Calli had hoped to see an overflow so Kell would be forced to go elsewhere. She sighed and waited for Trent. He managed to put himself between Emily and Kell, who led the way into the place. A waiter showed them to a table for four. In a swift and smooth move, Trent pulled out a chair for Emily.

Calli hesitated. Kell motioned for her to sit diagonally opposite the other woman, which put her onto a cushioned bench seat along the back wall of the restaurant. He sat beside her and opposite Emily. Trent sat opposite Calli and beside Emily. Now Kell could watch Emily without having to turn his head. He could just as easily ignore Calli. Unfortunately, she couldn't ignore him, or his man-spread.

His knee sat against hers. Should she mind? She decided she did and so she gave his knee a slight shove. He glanced at her. The menus arrived promptly along with the wine list. While she decided on duck terrine, his knee edged toward hers again. She knew without looking. She had never been more conscious of a man in her life.

"Do you have a wine preference?" he asked, his breath warm on her neck.

Her insides thudded with lust. She breathed out. "Something light, white, and dry."

"A Semillon for me," Emily said to the waiter who stood by her shoulder.

"The same for me," came from Trent.

The waiter queried Calli with his eyes. "A Riesling. House," she said with a smile.

"And, sir?" He stared at Kell.

"Water will do for me."

The waiter left.

"It's good to see that you're taking your duty as the designated driver seriously." Calli took a quick glance at Kell and a longer glance away.

"I take everything seriously. For instance, this menu. What do you think I might like here?"

"The kangaroo or the rabbit with broad beans."

"You said that without any hesitation. Should I be suspicious? What are you ordering?"

"The duck."

"Why wouldn't I like the duck?"

"Because it's served with preserved figs. I see you as a rare steak eater rather than a gourmand."

A line formed between his eyebrows. "There's no steak on the menu."

"Which is why I suggested kangaroo."

"So, are you four steps ahead of me?"

"Only three." She gave him her blockbuster smile without meaning to, and he stared at her mouth.

Her insides went into a complete meltdown. She glanced toward Trent, but he was focused on Emily who was concentrating on Kell. Calli would have liked to connect with Emily, but today Emily was having no part of her. The whole eye contact thing was missing, which was good, really, when Calli was planning on distracting Emily's man, who almost seemed to want to be distracted. Unfortunately, he was also distracting Calli.

Perhaps she shouldn't have sipped her wine before her food arrived because her wine had disappeared.

"Do you want another?" Kell asked as her duck was placed in front of her.

"Not if we're tasting wines after this. One should be plenty." Although she was nowhere near being intoxicated, she had lost one of her inhibitions. She patted his knee that now warmed the outside of her thigh.

His fingers covered hers. For a moment, her arm went into lock mode and then she remembered she was meant to distract him. When he moved her hand to his inner thigh, she let him, and when he slid his fingers between hers, she said, "Oops. Sorry, Kell. I was distracted for a moment." She put both her hands on the table and since everyone had been served, she quickly picked up her knife and fork.

His gaze burned a hole in the side of neck. She now had his attention, and she had no objection to that whatsoever. Being Fake Calli lifted a weight from her shoulders and probably a few creases from her forehead. For a while she could forget about her money problems, forget what a fool she had been. She didn't have to worry about Emily's feelings, because Fake Calli wouldn't.

She loaded her mouth with duck terrine, noting the line of new customers being escorted to the large table near the window. A bustling, some jostling, and the edge of a handbag swiped Emily's hair. "So sorry," said the owner of the bag, beautiful Melody, the girlfriend of a buddy of Grayson's. She didn't glance at Calli because she wouldn't. She'd been born bored, and she was too interested in pushing ahead to her table. Nevertheless, Calli had an anxious moment. As she watched, a tableful of people she knew arranged themselves to look important.

Sooner or later, someone would recognize her and come over. Though, maybe not. She looked different with her hair dark and short. Nevertheless, she ate quickly. "Are you enjoying the kangaroo?" she asked Kell.

"Yes. Are you enjoying the duck?"

"Do you want a taste?"

"Absolutely." He turned in his seat and gave her the sort of look-over that would curl another woman's hair.

Not Fake Calli's, of course. She took his fork and pushed on a slice of duck. As she handed the morsel over, she realized she should have fed the food to him. That sort of thing was supposed to be sexy.

"Nice," he said. "The kangaroo's better."

"I notice you're not offering any to me."

"Take what you like." Again his words seemed full of innuendo.

"I'm considering that." Her eyes met his and again she lost her breath. He was better at innuendo than she, but not half as good at hiding his nefarious thoughts.

His mouth curved and his eyes darkened with appreciation. "Can't wait," he said under his breath.

After that, she could barely swallow, let alone concentrate. Finally, lost in her thoughts of his hard body entwined with hers, she finished her meal. She glanced at the large table. Already Grayson's crowd had begun to circulate around the room, a normal occurrence for people who wanted everyone possible to recognize who the in-crowd was. She didn't see Melody and the place was crowded and noisy. "If we're about to leave, I'll take a lipstick break." She aimed her words at Kell, not expecting Emily to want to gossip with her, and she proceeded quickly to the ladies' room.

She had left the stall, washed her hands, and was reapplying her lipstick when Melody stepped out of another stall. She stopped still and stared at Calli. "You!"

Chapter 7

"Lovely to see you again, Melody," Calli said, hoping to escape with an easy brush off.

Melody pasted a deliberately wide-eyed expression on her classically beautiful face. "I can't say the same about you." Every feature, from her fine arched eyebrows to her delicate sculptured mouth was perfect.

Six months ago, the sight of Melody had filled Calli with envy. The other woman epitomized Grayson's crowd, among who numbered minor celebrities, and beautiful people with dazzling smiles and bad memories for names. Calli, as an independent career woman, had been welcomed with open arms into the group. Her ego recently torn and tattered by the second of her two failed relationships, she had needed nothing more to convince herself that she could be a success in her own business, despite her father's blatant disapproval.

Today, Calli glanced at the other woman and recognized that the beige she wore in varying shades matched her personality which, rather than her bone structure, helped her blend with Grayson's crowd. Bores, the lot of them, on hindsight, with their collective opinions and ability to concentrate on the trivialities of life. Endless speculation about others passed as normal conversation within the group. This should have been a warning to Calli, but she let Grayson's smooth words paper over the deficiencies of the in-crowd.

"I didn't think you would have the nerve to show your face for years," Melody drawled.

Calli turned on the tap to wash her hands. "There's nothing much wrong with my face that can't be fixed with makeup, like yours." And she breathed out. From mouse to lion in one sharp sentence.

"You know what I mean." Melody's mouth turned sulky. "Stop trying to make Grayson into your scapegoat. He had to leave the state, you know. And without a cent."

Two of the doors in the set of four stalls were locked, which meant two other stalls were also occupied, but Melody apparently didn't mind involving at least two innocent bystanders in a scene.

Then the main door swung open. Her gaze fixed on Calli, Emily took a step inside, her expression militant. She pulled up with a frown when she noticed Melody. Totally ignoring the other woman, Melody continued, her voice full of righteous indignation. "It's all right for you. Mummy and Daddy will get you out of trouble. But poor Grayson! You used him as your free laborer, you spent all his money, you ruined his business, and you made sure he couldn't get credit anywhere."

"I don't suppose my version of the story would interest you a whole lot."

"You disgust me." Melody flipped back her shining auburn hair, swung around, and with the tails of her beige silk scarf flying, she left the room.

Calli's cheeks warmed. Her gaze met Emily's. "An old friend," she said, swallowing her embarrassment.

Emily stepped closer, her mouth a thin flat line. "I thought I recognized you the other day. Then I remembered the story in the newspaper. Nice photo, by the way, though you've changed a bit."

"Thanks." Calli activated the blower to dry her hands. Anyone could look her up at any time, see the facts, and draw whatever conclusion they chose. "The reporter had a field day."

Emily waited for the noise of the dryer to stop, her handbag held close to her chest as if for protection. "A woman who did what you did…and you seem to be working your magic on Trent, too. One thing I'll make sure to do is to warn him not to give you a cent."

Calli tried for a blank expression although the other woman's harsh words hurt. "We're bartering. I don't want his money." She was glad to hear her voice contained no emotional content whatsoever. If anything she sounded as if she could not care less.

"I have no idea what he sees in you. But if you hurt him…"

"Trent?" Calli blinked, puzzled. Suddenly Emily cared about Trent?

"Trent." Emily planted her fists on her hips.

"Have you told him who I am?"

"Not yet. I don't want to spoil the day. But I can't keep what you did to myself."

"Why not?"

Emily blinked "Because you clearly have a pattern. You're already using him as a free laborer."

"I don't suppose you read what I had to say in the article?" Calli collected her bag, ready to leave the ladies' room.

"What else would you say? You're connected. That poor man wasn't. He didn't stand a chance against your family's influence."

Calli left the rest room. The court of public opinion seemed to be unanimous. And she couldn't do a thing about it other than to keep trying to prove herself.

* * * *

Kell settled the bill while Calli and Emily occupied the restroom. "If you've decided Emily is your date now, you can pay half the bill later," he said to Trent as he arrived back at the table.

Trent frowned. "I was always going to pay half the bill. And it's not a matter of me deciding Emily is my date. I think she decided that when you put her in the back of the car with me."

"As a matter of fact, Calli put herself in the front with me." Kell didn't mention the carsickness. Better Trent thought Calli was interested in Kell. A physical relationship with the woman next door would be tricky for Trent. Not so much for Kell. He always made his intentions clear. Sex was sex, and he wasn't planning any more than that. Once a woman knew he wasn't interested in a commitment, she wouldn't want to be stuck with him for any longer than the time she tried to change his mind. "I don't object to taking her off your hands." He remained standing, a crooked smile on his face. "We may as well wait in the front lobby for them. Where do you want to go next?"

"We can taste the wines here, then move along the road. I don't care. I'm not planning on buying more than one or two bottles. Nice lunch, hey?" Trent followed Kell back into the lobby.

"Uh-huh." The best part being Calli's interesting reactions.

Kell hadn't expected her to play along with him, but she had played like an expert, leaving him more than hot and bothered. Normally he wasn't so impressionable, but the way she had leaped at him from a standing start had more than surprised him. He had the idea she was stringing him along, though he didn't know why. If he got her alone somewhere, he could check that out. Unfortunately, he didn't know his way around the wine country, and he couldn't imagine where he might find an opportunity. She seemed more knowledgeable about the food in the area, which said she had been here a few times before. If he could hold her attention a little longer, the day might not turn out to be a dud after all.

Finally, Calli strode back and, making no eye contact, she took a position between Kell and Trent, talking idly while waiting for Emily who arrived soon after. The women ignored each other, which suited Kell because Calli grabbed his arm and practically dragged him out of the place.

"Where to next?" she asked, so close to him that her soft breasts pressed against his upper arm. He needed to breathe deeply for a moment.

"Do you have a preference?" He covered her hand with his, keeping her snuggled against him.

She smiled with more appreciation in her eyes than he would have expected for such a simple gesture. "We have the choice of more than one hundred and fifty wineries and eighty cellar doors. Why not drive and stop where you can't see too many people? I'm here to taste. What about you, Emily?" she said over her shoulder.

"No preference. Anywhere will do." Emily sounded terse.

Kell led the way to the tasting room across a well-kept lawn, and the four lined up along the redwood bar. The barman kept up a stream of sales talk while others tasted the wines. Despite not drinking, Kell stayed close to Calli's side. She seemed to want him there, almost as protection, which puzzled him. Also, the fact that the women didn't speak puzzled him. He seemed to be in the middle of a silent war, and he could only assume the women had had words in the restroom. About what, he couldn't imagine. Not Trent, surely?

During the next hour, they wandered into and out of another four wineries. Although Kell didn't see how, the group had divided into two couples. Either Trent would buy a bottle, or Emily would. Neither Kell nor Calli bought wine, but Calli sure threw down the tastings. Her eyes grew glossier and her cheeks pinker, and she laughed loudly. She clung to him tighter. She had him so sensitized to her touch that he tolerated an aching half erection most of the day.

If the car parks hadn't been so full with other tourists, he might have tried to hustle her out to the car. One quick episode would have taken off the edge, but no such luck. Trent and Emily trailed them the whole time. He could barely get in an innuendo let alone anything else.

He dropped off Emily first and Trent escorted her to the front door of her unit. Although the couple had quite a long conversation, when he came back into the car, Trent had a grin from ear to ear. "Yes!" he said in an exultant voice. "I've got a real date with her. She has asked me to go to a party with her tonight."

"Good work, Trent," Calli said, glancing at him. She sounded tentative.

Trent's glance back looked wary, if not downright confused.

Kell didn't know what that was about, either, but he didn't care. As soon as he got Calli home, his real day would begin. He glided the car into his driveway, pulled up, and saw that Calli had opened her door. He would have to speed around the car to get to her before she escaped. "Not so fast. I'll do a Trent and escort you to your front door."

"Don't worry. Thanks for today. It was…." Right then, a loud splat of rain hit the bonnet of the car, followed by a cloud-load that drowned out anything she might have said. She pulled the car door shut and sat watching the deluge, the expression on her face wry.

"Stay right there," Kell said, turning the engine back on and activating the screen wipers. "I'll back up and drive you to your door."

"No need. This is too heavy to last. It'll be gone in a trice."

By that, he assumed…what? That he hadn't read her body language correctly. That she hadn't succumbed to his fatal charm? That she had simply wanted to be polite today, and that she was disappointed that Trent had hooked up with Emily?

"I'll make a run for it inside," Trent said with a *want to talk* expression on his face. "I'm going to change and drive back to Emily's place. Likely, I'll see you later tonight."

Kell didn't want to talk. He wanted to grab Calli into his arms and kiss the heck out of her before he took her to bed—hers, he hoped. The need he had for her made him edgy. Trent opened the car door, pulled up the collar of his shirt, and dashed toward the back of the house, chased by a second deluge, which stopped as suddenly as it had started.

Calli opened the car door. Fresh wet air blew in. "As I tried to say, thanks for today. And thank Trent for me, too, though I must say I don't think he is much of a date. He mainly left me to you. I'm thinking now, he might have used me as a decoy." She didn't sound annoyed.

"You're not racing off like this. We kind of had a date, and I will return you home safe and sound."

"I live next door, for pity's sake."

He leaned across her and pulled her door shut. "I'm driving you," he said, determined, and he swiveled to stare through the rain-bleary back window as he did a Formula 1 speedy reverse of his car down the drive. The wheels swooshed in the mud.

A quick flip of his forward gear, and he was out into the street and turning down the judge's drive. He pulled up in the carport between the Jaguar and Calli's 1990s green Ford. Certain she would open her door before he could, he leaped out of the car to grab her before she raced off, but she waited, and he got to do the first gentlemanly act in his life—help a woman down out of his car and escort her to her front door.

His shoulders squared to prepare him for his ultimate disappointment. He walked beside her while she scrabbled for her keys in her big bag with almost frantic haste.

He pushed his hands into his pockets and drew a deep breath. "I don't normally have this effect on women. Some don't even mind talking to me."

"I need to be on my own."

"I need to be with you," he said in the mildest voice he could manage.

She lifted her gaze, and when his eyes met hers, he saw a kind of hopelessness that made him reach out and pull her against him, his hands resting lightly on her back. She buried her face into his shoulder. Her heart pounded against him. She didn't push him away. Her fingers curled into the sides of his sweater, tightening the fabric. He put his hand on the back of her head, stroking. "I would like to think this is passion for me, but maybe you just want to be held. Did you think you were Trent's date? If so…"

"Of course I didn't." Her voice was muffled into his collar. "I know he wanted Emily. I was meant to distract you, that's all."

"You did a fair job." He slid his hands down onto her hips, his lower body indicative of her success.

"I can feel how distracted you are, you know. And that particular distraction is distracting me."

"This one?" He moved his hips slightly, not easing his erection in the slightest.

Her head moved in assent.

"Look at me."

She lifted her face. His gaze held hers for a long moment, trying to read her thoughts. He saw no rejection, and he lowered his lips to hers. She tasted like wine and salted nuts, and she smelled like fresh rain. Her hips moved, tantalizing him, and then she hooked her arms around his neck and lifted so that she edged his penis between her legs. He groaned, his hands clutching her buttocks to hold her there, to move her against him. His skin heated, and his intake of air grew forced. He dragged his mouth from hers. "Your key. Let's get this door open."

She pulled in a breath and nodded, her eyes large and bright, her lips soft and red, and again began scrabbling through her bag. He couldn't wait. He wanted to break down the door and get her onto her back. Finally, she pulled out the key and pushed it into the lock. She swung the door open and shoved inside, him right behind. He snatched her bag and threw it at the couch. Then he grabbed her up again, running his mouth across the soft skin of her neck, while with desperate haste, he sped open her zipper. He jerked her undies down while she fought to open his pants.

"Back pocket. Condom," he said in a gruff and urgent voice, taking her mouth with his, his need frantic.

She snatched his wallet before he did, so he opened his own pants. She toed off her shoes and presented him with the unwrapped condom. He slammed shut the door with his foot. He had to have her right then. While he stretched on the condom, he moved her back against the door. With one of her buttocks in each hand, he lifted her onto his hips. She wriggled, and his penis found her hot moistness. She slid her arms to his shoulders and clung, and attached her mouth to his with avid greed. He sucked her tongue into his mouth, at the same time moving his fingers along the hot wet temptation of her vulva, sliding, sliding, until the catch of her vagina.

"I'm ready. I've been ready since lunch." And with that she urged the tip of his penis into place.

If he had shoved in, he would have come instantly. He stayed as still as he could, hot with need, but cold with purpose. This wasn't a woman he would use. This was the woman he would love, again and again. He took her mouth, experiencing the taste of her, the smell of her skin, her hair, and the begging of her body. He stayed, leaving her to inch him inside her. He groaned with pleasure.

Even when she had accommodated his full length, he remained breathing heavily, retaining iron control even though her bare heels pushed into his buttocks, urging him on. Unintelligible sounds of throaty need whispered against his neck. She finally made slow sideways rocking movements of her hips, leaning the back of her head against the door, gasping for breath. "Please, please."

He had wanted her to beg him. He needed her to want him as much as he wanted her, but he was so close to climax himself that almost any movement would end him without giving her the ultimate pleasure. Trying to keep his mind elsewhere, he pulled back and plunged, desperate not to let his desires control him. Whispering soft words of love, he slid his hand down between them and found her hard little clitoris, which he treated to a gentle nudge and a circling tease. And she bucked, making those woman-noises into his neck. Never had a woman come for him so quickly.

Her inner tightening almost took him out, too, but he stayed in place until her clenching stopped, until her soft noises of pleasure turned into relaxed breathing. He began to move then, and his climax arrived faster than he hoped. Nevertheless, he didn't berate himself when he knew his woman had been pleasured first—*his woman*. He stayed heavy inside her, expecting to subside while her body relaxed.

She stared at him, her smile a mixture of embarrassment and pleasure. With a tender expression on her face, she lifted her hands to cup the sides of his face, showing every sign of being about to unhook her legs from his waist. Before she could, he grabbed the end of the condom and slid out of her.

"There's no gracious way to do this," he said, his voice regretful as he peeled off the limp latex. "Unfortunately."

She laughed, pushing her hair back from the warm sheen on her face. "Put me down, and you'll be able to pull your pants up and walk to the kitchen trash."

He did both and washed his hands while he was there. His body still thudded, though, with sated lust and a slight apprehension. She seemed too dismissive, too casual about an act that had a strange significance to him.

"I like food after sex," he said gruffly, hoping to stay a while longer.

"I like food all the time," she said, stepping back into her undies and pants. She did this in a particularly elegant way. Everything she did was elegant, and fascinated him—from the way she kissed, to the way she touched his face, to the way she orgasmed. "The least I can do after that lovely lunch is make you a bacon-and-egg sandwich for dinner." Her querying expression completely disarmed him.

Normally, this would be an awkward moment. The woman would let him know she wanted the same again, or she would be slightly embarrassed she had wanted him in the first place, or she would automatically assume... anything at all. Calli simply accepted that what happened had happened, and life would go on as before. "Or I could go out and buy fish and chips for us. Do you want fish and chips?"

She stretched languorously. "If you need to get back to the house, I'll understand. I'm sure you don't want Trent to know about your sex life any more than I want him to know about mine."

He rubbed his fingers over his stubble. "He's my work buddy, not my guardian." Perhaps he should have said he wouldn't be making love to her again, but that would be a lie because he would, and as soon as he could. "And why would I care when you know bloody well we haven't finished with each other yet?"

Her eyes rounded. "We haven't?"

"So, if you think you can easily get rid of me, I'll have a bacon-and-egg sandwich. I'm not letting you out of my sight for a while yet."

"I need to freshen up, first. I've had a big day, and I plan to watch TV after I have eaten." Flicking her fingers through her crisp hair, she headed for her bedroom.

And if that's what she wanted to do, he wanted to do that with her, though he could put together a more satisfying plan in an instant. She disappeared into her bathroom. He glanced at the couch, prepared to wait, and the cat unfurled herself. She blinked at Kell, made a graceful leap to the floor and did a Beyoncé walk to the front door, all swaying tail. There she sat, waiting for a minion.

"Is the cat allowed out?" he called.

A voice from the depths echoed back. "Leave the door open so she can come back in."

Instead, he stood in the doorway staring at the dusk and the wet black rooftops over the road. The rain had left a sheen on the landscape, the freshness of new beginnings. He didn't know what he had expected to do after making love to Calli, but somehow he felt compelled to find out. After a few minutes, the cat came back, and he shut the door behind her. When he settled onto the couch, the cat insinuated herself onto his lap and began purring like a buzz saw. He automatically scratched behind her ears and under her chin. Within minutes, Calli wandered back, too, her hair perfect and her lips glossy, Jogger Girl again—a fit specimen of expensive womanhood.

She put her hands on her hips, looking outraged. For a moment he wondered what he had done. "Why does that cat ooze around you? I feed her, and she barely notices me. I bet she doesn't even know my name."

He grinned, bent over the cat, and put her mouth near his ear. "Whisper the name of your woman." The car purred. "Calli, she said, but she doesn't know your surname."

"We've never been formally introduced. She wandered in here the other day and that was that."

"I'll introduce you if you tell me."

She swallowed. "Calli Opey."

"That's a mouthful. I don't know if she will be able to pronounce the whole lot. Did you hear that, Cat?" The cat nodded with a little help from Kell's hand. "She says it's okay if you keep feeding her, too."

"Humph." Calli stalked over to the kitchen with mock affront. "Do you like rhubarb sponge? I picked some stalks from the judge's garden this morning so I could make a dessert, too."

"I don't know. I've never tasted rhubarb, but if it comes with a sponge, I'm bound to like it."

"Never had rhubarb? Where on earth were you brought up? Every good Aussie kid has had rhubarb."

"My dad didn't ever cook. He bought takeaways. My mother died soon after my younger brother Luke was born, and I have no memories of her."

"Not a one?"

He shook his head. "Not a one. Fish and chips was my staple diet unless a neighbor turned up with a casserole or something. No one turned up with rhubarb."

"I'll get the rhubarb cooking, in that case, and heat the oven. This is one of the few things I can make without a recipe. It was a standard dessert at our house."

He wanted to go over and be with her, but not prepared to look gormless, instead he turned on the TV and watched the news. Nothing of note had happened, being Saturday, and the cat decided to sit on his shoulder instead. "Hey, there," he said to the fur close to his face.

Calli laughed from the kitchen. "She just can't get close enough. What are you doing tomorrow?"

"Tomorrow I'll be back at work on the house."

"What's your real job?" Her gaze connected with his.

Although he would have liked her to think he had a high enough income to flip houses as a recreational sport, he couldn't manage a lie. "I run a small cabinet-making business, and I have another kitchen to finish this week. Doing the house is my extracurricular activity."

"Who owns the house?"

"The bank owns the house. I have a small interest in it."

"You? You own the house? So, *you* can make the decisions as to the renovations?" She sounded interested.

"And I can't fit in a butler's pantry," he said, staring at her back.

"Have you taken some advice on this?"

He lifted his eyebrows. "My own."

She began whipping up something in a bowl. "This is an exclusive area. The people who buy here have enough money to send their kids to private schools. You have a four-bedroom house there. You certainly need room for at least four bathrooms."

"*Two* bathrooms."

"With two bathrooms and no informal entertaining space, you'll be selling to the lower end of the market."

"The house is meant to demonstrate my fit-out skills. After that, anything I get for the place will be profit."

"Any buyer would build on. You will be providing a bargain for someone else."

He shook his head. "Why would anyone keep a house that's probably a hundred years old and ugly as well?"

She grabbed a steaming pot off the stove and poured cooked strings of pink rhubarb into a casserole dish. "For that very reason. People with plenty of money want to mix with other people with money. The older the money, the higher the status. An old house with a history is very appealing to people with new money. You need to know your market."

First, he frowned at her. He didn't need a lecture. Then, he moistened his lips. "So, what are you saying?"

"Don't leave someone else to make the profit you ought to be making with the house." Turning away from him, she scraped the batter she had whipped into a creamy blob onto the top of the casserole.

"So, add another two bathrooms?"

"One. Build an extension, and you'll have room for a downstairs powder room, a half bathroom." She placed the dish into the hot oven. "You'll want to extend a large entertaining area out from the kitchen to overlook your beautiful garden."

"You're angling for the garden job." He drew down his eyebrows.

She looked across at him and the ends of her mouth turned up. "I wouldn't mind the job, but that's not my prime concern. I think you need to squeeze out every cent you can from the house. The old lady who lived there—"

"How do you know an old lady lived there?" He switched off the TV.

"Guess work. Whoever lived there didn't do renovations or any sort of rebuilding, therefore he or she didn't have a good income. I'm guessing he or she inherited the family home and remained there until old age while living on a pension."

"I bought it as a deceased estate, and you're right. The old lady was in her late nineties when she died. She had no close relatives."

"People these days like large kitchens and separate laundry rooms. You have a large kitchen and you'll need to build a new laundry room."

He put the cat on the couch and wandered over to the island that separated the kitchen from the dining space. "I'm going to leave the laundry room where it is," he said, folding his arms across his chest. "I'm not extending back."

"If you build a new laundry room and reconstitute the butler's pantry, that would be a magnificent selling point." She glanced at him. "And the downstairs bathroom could easily convert to a nice powder room. That's a great way to impress guests. You have it all in that house, and you have the old reclaimed bricks to build it."

"That would add weeks to the renovation time."

She found a frying pan, one of those thick expensive ones, and she placed it on top of the stove before pulling a plastic pack of bacon out of the fridge. "The rashers are frozen together. See what you can do about separating out a few slices." She put the pack on the island in front of him and went back to the fridge to take out a carton of eggs. "An extension would possibly add another quarter to your selling price. I'd say your quick clean up of the house would get you close to a million. In this area, you would get over a million, perhaps 1.5 for a four-bedroom house with a modern extension."

"You sound as if you know that." A lump of four bacon slices came apart from the block and she took them, replacing the plastic pack in the freezer. Interesting way to keep bacon.

"I do. I used to work for a property development company. I designed the gardens for all the new builds and all the renovations. You learn a lot when you're around the big business end of town. Now, where did he put that toaster?" She found the thing in a cupboard under the island, and she plugged it onto a socket she found there, too. "These islands are handy."

"Everyone wants them these days."

"You certainly know your market for kitchens."

"Are you going to put frozen bacon into that pan?"

"The ice will steam off before they cook. Fresh bacon is a lot nicer, but when you're a single person, you can't eat too much before it goes off. I suppose you've found that, too."

"I don't do a lot of cooking." He settled on the stool near the island while she cracked a few eggs into the pan and put bread on to toast.

"Hands, or knife and fork?"

"Hands."

She took two plates from an overhead cupboard and filled the toaster with another two slices of bread. "See those two tablemats? Pop them on the table, would you?"

He did as asked while she served up two neat bacon-and-egg sandwiches, his twice the size of hers. He waited for her to sit first, having learned that nicety from his brother who had learned a bit of class from his wife. Handy trick.

He had probably made himself hundreds of bacon-and-egg sandwiches in his lifetime, but the one he ate with her was the best. Even the rhubarb sponge was tasty. The way she treated him and spoke to him, made him feel like an interesting person, not a prospective partner or simply a sex machine. "So, what do you want to watch on TV?"

"Are you staying?"

"We don't have TV." He settled down again, and she sat beside him. The cat sat on his lap. This was about as domestic as he had ever been, and he laughed.

Calli glanced at him in query.

He put his arm around her, and she snuggled into his chest. For a while he stayed like that, holding her, but she began to undo his shirt buttons, and one thing led to another.

Chapter 8

Calli wished Kell could stay the night, but of course that was impossible when she didn't want Trent to know that she had been so frantic to have sex with Kell that she had practically jumped him, not once but twice. The second time she had managed to drag him into her bedroom first, but she hadn't quite managed to draw back the cover on the bed. Fortunately, he had seemed more than eager to cooperate.

Neither time had she been completely naked. Nor had he. She would like the full deal, naked and in a bed, and she had absolutely no doubt he would comply with both, had she made the request. The man had complete confidence in his body, unlike her, though she was certainly building a little. He had a way of making a woman feel uniquely interesting and very much desired.

In the lamplight, she glanced over at him, lying on his side facing her, his lips curved and his eyes a mystery. Her insides a shaky mixture of desire and uncertainty, she moved her hand to his shoulder—and her phone rang.

During the past few weeks, she hadn't answered any calls. Her family sent text messages, and her needy body was inclined to ignore the sound. However Kell, clearly not as focused on her as she was on him, reached over and behind her to the bedside table.

"Yours," he said, his voice sex-husky as he passed her the phone.

In the belief that she would look normal rather than persecuted, she glanced at the screen and saw the number. "It's my sister. Don't worry. I'll send her a text later."

"So, if you don't want to talk, how about if we take a shower?" His eyes smoldering, he placed her phone back on the bedside table and rolled onto his back.

"Okay." She watched while he sat up in one fluid motion and pulled the white T-shirt he still wore over his head—and she was a goner again. His chest was everything she had imagined, hard, broad, with short dark hair in T across his nipples and arrowing to a trail that led under his chinos that he had only very recently pulled back over his narrow hips. "How many condoms do you have?"

"That's an interesting question." He rolled slightly, jammed his hand into his back pocket, and dragged out his wallet. After a quick inspection, he gave a grin as lascivious as any man's could be. "I'm provisioned for a couple of days as long as I don't get too ahead of myself."

Dressed in an unclasped bra and her amber top, she sashayed into the bathroom, him right behind her, undressing as he walked. He almost teased her to death in the shower, apparently not about to try anything too slippery, but she had decided to take whatever she could get while she still could. Soon enough he would hear the gossip about Calli, the tempter of men—the woman who knew how to part them from their money.

She had to prove herself to herself, but not to Kell, nor to the whole wide world. Without a doubt, Emily would tell Trent the story she had heard in the women's room—not true, of course, but deniers always looked guilty. He would repeat the story to Kell as soon as the two spoke again. On the plus side, Trent might not return tonight—which made no difference in the long run. Kell would eventually hear, no matter what. Therefore, she may as well keep him for the night if she could. "If you hide your car, you can stay until morning," she said as a tentative invitation, while rubbing her hair dry.

"Hide? Who from?" He had a towel wrapped around his waist and a languid smile on his face. Anyone would think he'd recently had sex, whereas he'd recently had a wild old time almost making her beg.

"Trent. Do you want him to know we had sex tonight?"

"Apparently you don't." He tilted her face up to his with a forefinger and kissed her lips slowly and gently.

She breathed out, trying for a sensible expression on her face instead of a kiss-me-again one. "It wouldn't be a good look. Not when we live next door to each other."

"I see your point. Perhaps you could park your car behind mine. Then mine wouldn't be visible from the street."

So, half-dressed, they shifted cars in the dead of the night, Calli as guiltily nervous as a rebellious teenager hiding her naughtiness from her parents, something she had never done. She had been the quiet and obedient daughter. Antigone had been the rebel. Wondering what Tiggy had wanted to tell her, Calli raced back inside the cottage with Kell. She had barely crossed the bedroom threshold when he tossed her onto the bed and got her completely naked yet again.

In bed with him, she had nothing to prove. As a lover, the man was inexhaustible. When she finally slept, she slept like the dead. The ringing phone finally awoke her. Tiggy, again.

She sat up, this time too stupid with sleep to remember how to switch off the phone. Before she knew herself, she was listening to her sister's voice. "Calli, where are you?" Slats of morning light glimmered through the plantation blinds.

"In bed. Give me a minute. I'm not quite awake," she said in a grouchy voice, not immediately remembering what she had done with her clothes.

With a half grin on his face, Kell passed over the sheet that had somehow twisted into a rope on the bottom of the bed.

She draped herself, and trailing most of the sheet, she stumbled into the kitchen. "Okay, what's wrong?"

"Nothing. I haven't seen you for more than a month. Aren't I allowed to worry about you?"

"No need. I'm doing well, or I would be if people let me sleep."

"It's after nine," Tiggy said, indignation spiking her tone.

"It's also Sunday morning."

"Don't be a pill. How's the new garden coming along?"

Calli pulled out a kitchen chair with her foot, and sat on a lump of sheet. "As expected. I've done this before, you know."

"Not for a couple of years. You had your minions to do the dirty work for you. I don't think you've set a foot on a shovel for quite a while. Did you hear about Hagen?"

"What about Hagen?" Calli asked in a suspicious voice. Hagen, her older brother, the golden boy, had recently married a very beautiful woman. His lovely young bride had spent the past year modernizing his heritage house, apparently unable to see the beauty in his sparse but classy furnishing style. Every time Calli went to the house, a stark desolation filled her. The bright shiny objects that Mercia, his wife, had introduced made the whole area look as nondescript as a coat of paint on the *Mona Lisa*.

Tiggy snickered. "He told Mercia he wouldn't have the front garden redone. She wanted a lawn at the front, and the box hedges removed."

Calli gasped. "It took me months to get the box hedges shaped into those Georgian angles. Which was probably the problem. I designed the garden. I suppose most wives want to design their own." She made a rueful face to herself.

"Stop being fair. You know she is the most irritating woman in all creation. And that's exactly what she wants to be. It takes a lot to rile Ma, but she has even managed that. I heard Ma muttering to herself the other day, but she wouldn't say a word about whatever Mercia did or said. She wants to stay onside because, you know, grandchildren and all that."

"Yes. Mercia is now one of Ma's own and must be tolerated as such. So, how are you doing, Tiggy?" Calli watched the cat slink into the bedroom. Did she know Kell was there or was she simply trying to avoid Calli? Hobo had to be the most ungrateful creature in the whole wide world. At least she could smile at her rescuer once or twice, or even simply acknowledge Calli's existence other than at meal times.

"I'm still matching up the colors for the public areas in Aldinga. Far would like you back. He's not pleased with the garden design that has been presented to him for the complex."

"If I worked for him, it would have to be gratis, and you know he won't accept that."

"I think you need to get over yourself, Calli. Plenty of people owe money to their parents—you know, school fees, university fees, first home loans, et cetera. You don't have to pay it all back within months."

"I do. I lost the money. It wasn't Ma and Far's debt, but mine. I can't ever be independent if I'm leaching money from my parents. I don't want to be that sort of person."

Tiggy gave an audible resigned sigh. "So, what's he like?"

"Who?"

"The reason why you are whispering."

"I've had a bad throat, Tiggy," Calli said in a holier-than-thou voice, speaking nothing but the truth. She did have a bad throat a few days ago. "Anyway, thanks for catching me up." She ended the call and sat at the table, torn between two emotions. Like her sister and the rest of her family, she disliked Mercia, who tried to distance Hagen from everyone he knew, his friends, and his family. The woman was a troublemaker born and bred. Even so, Calli didn't want her design of Hagen's garden to cause a rift between the couple.

When she trailed back into the bedroom, Kell was lying on his back, the bed covers drawn to his waist, idly tickling Hobo who sat on his chest, interviewing him. "Bad news?" He glanced away from the cat.

"What makes you ask that?"

"The look on your face."

"That's my thinking face, not my bad news face."

"Glad to hear that. I don't feel in the mood for bad news. Come over here and snuggle with us."

She dropped the stupid sheet that had done nothing but try to trip her, and sat beside Kell, tentatively bringing her feet back onto the bed. He put his arm around her and she wriggled down until she lay beside him. Hobo frowned at her, apparently not willing to share her man.

Calli reached over to stroke the cat, who turned her back. "That's a statement, for sure. Look, Cat, I brought you in, I bathed you—"

"You bathed her?" Kell laughed. "Even I know that cats don't take well to water."

"She didn't mind. Until you came along, she thought I was okay." Calli continued to stroke the cat, whose fur quivered under the indignity. "I'm the one who feeds her."

Kell scooped one hand under the cat and held her straight up above his head at arm's length, her body supported by his palm, and her long skinny legs dangling helplessly. "Are you being ungrateful?"

The cat's head nodded.

"Are you sorry?"

The cat's head nodded again while the cat aimed her pretty golden eyes at Kell.

"Okay," he said, taking away the finger he had placed on top of her head to control her movements. "All is forgiven. We all snuggle together, right?"

The cat slitted her eyes, clearly disagreeing.

"She's not used to threesomes, and she doesn't quite approve. I think you'll need to tell her it's okay." Kell gave Calli a sideways smile.

"I don't approve of threesomes either." Calli smiled back at him. This might be the nicest Sunday morning she'd ever had, despite the early phone call.

"But a snuggle threesome is okay." He darted a glance at Calli. His arm moved under her shoulder, dragging her closer to his big warm body. Hobo frowned for a moment before deciding to settle between them.

"A man, a woman, and a cat are okay."

He nodded, his hand smoothing her shoulder, which he briefly kissed. His hand lazily massaged the back of her neck, and her hand toyed with the hair on his chest, while the cat purred. "What do you eat for breakfast?" he asked in a hinting voice.

"You don't want breakfast here. You wouldn't eat what I eat."

"Does it involve Brussels sprouts?"

"No." She glanced up at him.

"In that case, I would like it. I thought you would never ask."

"I eat cornflakes."

"So do I. What do *you* want?" he asked the cat, who appeared to have gone to sleep. He lifted his head so that his ear was closer to the cat's mouth. "Caviar? No. I'm afraid you'll have to have cornflakes like the rest of us."

Calli slid out of bed and into her robe. With the cat clasped to his chest, Kell swung his legs over the side of the bed. He put Hobo on the floor, where she stretched sinuously before strolling to the door.

"You'll need to put on your pants if you want breakfast," Calli said to Kell who appeared to either be losing an erection or growing one. The man was a gorgeous, sexy, wonderful lover. "I don't want any distractions."

He pulled on his jocks and his chinos, and found his cotton knit in the corner of the room. "What will we do after breakfast?"

"You will go home."

"It's Sunday. I might take a day off and do something lazy. Aside from that, Trent is home. I heard him drive in last night."

"What's wrong with Trent being there?"

"He might ask me where I've been. Could I tell a lie? No."

She placed her fists on her hips. "You're trying to blackmail me into doing something with you today?"

"Admit it. You want to."

She stalked into the kitchen and filled two bowls with cornflakes while she rattled around in her head for an answer. "I see you as a diversion," she said to him as he loomed beside her. "Good for sex—well, great for sex, but I don't know that I need anything else from you."

"You're getting way ahead of yourself. I'm offering you a visit to the library with me, and you're already seeing us in a relationship."

"The library?"

"That was an example." He firmed his perfect jaw.

"A better example might be going to the nursery to look at plants."

"If you insist."

"That was probably what I was going to do—go to the nursery." She hauled the milk out of the fridge, glancing at him over her shoulder, not quite knowing how she had agreed to spend a few more hours with him. Not that she really minded. The last few months of her life had been lonely. Now she had a cat and a date, a surfeit of company, though the cat preferred the man to her.

Right on cue, Hobo tapped her on the ankle.

"Yes?"

"I want to go outside," Kell said in yowly cat voice.

"Ask Kell to open the door for you," she said before she realized she was answering a cat who certainly didn't speak person.

Kell stood, walked to the door, and Hobo followed, showing that she must have channeled her thoughts to the only person in the room who was receptive. He closed the door behind her. "She'll knock when she returns." "I suppose she told you that." Calli slowly shook her head as she sat at the table, staring at Kell the Cat Whisperer. "That was good last night," she said in a friendly voice, not wanting to make too much of the mind-blowing sex she had participated in.

"I know."

"What do you mean, you *know*?"

"You might not have noticed but I was there, too."

"Oh. Yes. I thought you were big-noting yourself."

"I thought you were asking for a compliment." He stuffed a huge spoonful of milky cornflakes into his mouth.

She laughed. She didn't appear to be able to squash him. Well, of course not. The man was a demi-god and likely un-squashable. "Are you planning on shaving before we leave?"

"Nope. You only have a pink plastic razor, and I don't think that will suit my chin."

"The color?"

"The rust. I look okay, don't I?"

She pretended to consider. "Passable." Her heart flitter-fluttered. Best not to look at him too much or she would get a goofy expression on her face. "In the interest of keeping your car hidden, I think we ought to take the Jaguar out today."

"You have the keys?"

"I thought you might be able to hotwire it." She stood, leaned over, and took his bowl while he sat with his mouth half-open. After stacking the dishes in the dishwasher, she glanced back at him, hopefully.

He gave her a wide-eyed grin. Apparently he had taken a while thinking the matter over. "I'm surprised you can't."

"It's not a girl thing. I'll put on some lipstick, and we can leave."

"Do I hear a knock?"

She stopped and glanced at the door. "It's more of a scratch." Sure enough, when she opened the door, Hobo was standing there. She slipped between Calli's legs and bounded over to Kell.

He stood, and Hobo arose to her back legs, placing her front legs on his shins like a child asking to be picked up. Kell obliged and took her over to the couch, where she deigned to be dropped by him. "We'll be back later, puss. If you want a snack to tide you over, you'll have to be nice to Calli."

Calli waited, arms crossed. The cat considered for a moment and, after making her decision not to mess with the current situation, she curled herself into a ball and shut her eyes.

"I have half a mind not to leave out any food." With that, Calli opened the fridge, took out the remaining cat food, and scraped the lot into a saucer. "I won't bribe anyone to be nice to me." She left the food with Hobo's water bowl.

Ignoring her comment, Kell fingered his chin. "I wonder if I can sneak into my house to brush my teeth before we leave?"

"Are you going to try? Or do you want a toothbrush? I bought a four-pack."

"I'm rather keen on the idea of being a sneak."

"Suit yourself."

"Are you implying you'll miss me?"

"Sometimes I wonder if we speak the same language," she said, holding together the gaping sides of her dressing gown, which appeared to have distracted him.

"I'll get you to move your car so that I can back mine out. Then I'll cruise around the block and into my drive from the other direction. If Trent happens to be watching, he will see me coming from the city."

"So, you don't want to go to the nursery?"

"Sure I do. But first I want to clean my teeth, shave, and change. By that time, you'll be dressed and have the Jag hotwired."

"Do you care what we are going to do at the nursery?"

"Tell me."

"We're going to buy pots and potting soil, and then we'll come back here where you will help me dig up ten standard roses which we'll then pot."

"Okay." He moved to the doorway. "Not the way I would normally spend Sunday, but if that's what you want to do…"

"They will be the start of your new front garden. When you have chopped back the jungle and improved the soil, we'll be planting them along your front fence."

"Sounds good. Come out and shift your car."

* * * *

Kell strolled into his kitchen. Apparently Trent hadn't yet hauled himself out of bed, but Kell needed clean underwear and a change of clothes and so he continued on to the bedroom. The sound of the door must have woken Trent, who sat on the side of his camper bed rubbing his fair hair into a matted fluff. He yawned.

"Late night?" Kell asked, searching in his suitcase. He found clean jeans and a red sweatshirt Vix had bought him. She'd said he would look good in red but normally he preferred to look bad in blue. Today, good would do him.

"Not too late. Apparently *you* got into bed early." Trent sounded sour.

"Not too early." Kell grinned. "Did you get lucky?"

"I will not discuss my sex life with you."

Kell paused. "You're always wanting to discuss mine."

"That's different. Yours is casual. Mine is, well, nonexistent at this stage, but I have met the woman I intend to marry."

"Emily? Congrats, old chum. It's always good to have a goal, credible or not."

Trent rubbed his hair again. "I thought trying to talk her into bed after the first date wouldn't be the right thing to do. I want to show her I appreciate her first."

"Good move. That'll work."

"Says the king of one-night stands."

"C'mon. You've been my chaperone for the past two weeks. You know I haven't broken out once. Last night—after a day visiting wineries, I needed a little light relief. But I've got a date with Calli today so I had to rush home."

"A date with Calli?"

"She wants me to dig out her roses."

"Sucked in," Trent said morosely. "No wonder she's so successful at conning blokes. She doesn't ask you to do a thing and you find yourself offering."

"She asked me."

"She must have gotten to you in a weak moment. She's hard not to like, but that's her stock in trade. She wouldn't be any good at suckering people if they didn't like her first."

"What on earth are you on about?"

"Gossip. She conned some guy out of all his money. She broke him—sent him bankrupt, and he had to leave the state. It was in all the papers."

"When did you last read a paper?"

"I can't remember. Emily told me the story."

"I would guess it's complete rubbish. Calli makes sure of paying back any favors. In fact, that's how she is paying back yesterday's lunch, if I've got this right. I'm digging up the roses for the garden of this house. She will be potting them and keeping them alive until we're ready to plant, or so she said. Know how much a rose bush costs?"

"No."

"Neither do I, but she is giving us ten of them already grown. It's got to be at least a hundred dollars. So, she more than paid for her lunch." Kell grabbed his clothes and stalked off to the bathroom where he took a quick cold shower, needed because he was aggravated. Then he cleaned his teeth and shaved, surprised that Emily had gossiped about Calli.

So what if the guy, a boyfriend presumably, went bankrupt? More fool he. Anyone in charge of his money knew where every cent went. Kell sure did. He didn't spend wads on trying to impress women and he didn't spend much on himself. Instead, he worked hard and saved. As far as he could see, Calli did the same, though he knew something about her living next door was shady. She didn't act like a woman with a social circle, which was unusual. The part he didn't like about the story Trent had told him was the part about her boyfriend. He didn't want Calli to be thinking about another man, who had or had not lost his money and disappeared.

Dressed neatly, and more comfortably clean, he paced back to the house next door. "So, tell me about your last relationship," he said, spotting Calli in the kitchen as he walked inside her cottage.

"Relationship? So, Emily said something to Trent." She snatched up a big bag and pushed past him outside.

"Is that why you two weren't talking yesterday?"

"And I'm not talking about the same thing today."

"Fair enough, though I would happily tell you about my last girlfriend."

"I'm sure you would." She gave him cool glance. "But I don't want to hear about any of your girlfriends, because you and I don't have that sort of relationship. We are bed buddies, and that's all."

"Not quite," he said, heading for the Jaguar. "We're gardening buddies as well."

"I don't talk about my private life to my gardening buddies." She unlocked the driver's door with a click from a bunch of keys. Clearly she had the keys to everything on the judge's property. "Driving the judge's cars around at least once a week is in my contract. He doesn't want to come home to a dead battery," she said carefully. "So don't imagine we're going for a joyride."

"As you can see, I don't mind either way." He slipped into the passenger side, wishing he could drive the luxury vehicle. Owning an expensive car was his secret dream, but he was years away from owning anything but a tax-exempted work vehicle. "It's a shame the judge doesn't own a Ferrari. That'd be better for a trip to the nursery."

She reversed the car into the turning circle and drove out onto the street. "I don't think judges drive Ferraris. They need to own conservative cars.

The good thing about the Jag is that it's got a big trunk. We'll be able to put plenty in it."

And from there, she couldn't be drawn about a single personal thing. She told him the names of all the plants he ought to put in his garden, none of which meant a thing to him. He knew a tree, a bush, a flower, and a leaf, and that was about the full extent of his knowledge of gardens. They arrived at the nursery where she wandered around for a while until she spotted a tall guy in work clothes and an army-green hat marked with the nursery logo.

"Gary," she called in a pleased voice. "I was looking for you."

Gary, a fortyish redhead with a sunburnt nose, turned. "Calli. Nice to see you. You haven't been around for a while. Sorry to hear—"

"This is my friend Kell, Gary," she interrupted. "I'll be helping with his garden. What I want is ten recycled pots, plastic. And three big bags of potting soil. Can you do something for trade prices?"

Gary scanned her face. "Sure thing. Hi, Kell. You found a good designer. She bargains like her mother."

Calli laughed and turned to Kell. "My mother is Greek. She bargains for everything. I only bargain for items to do my job."

Kell nodded politely, as a client would, and followed her and Gary, grabbed the pots she wanted, loaded the bags of soil she wanted, paid twenty dollars and carried everything back to the car. "I presume that was a bargain."

"Twenty dollars for ten mature standard roses? That would be more than three hundred if you were paying normal prices."

"So, what are you going to charge me?"

"You've paid the twenty. And you'll be doing the work."

"Then I can charge you for the work."

"And pay yourself."

"But I'm getting rid of plants you don't want."

"Anyone would think your mother was Greek."

"You don't look Greek."

"Ma is Aussie Greek and Far, which is Danish for father, is Aussie Danish. So my blood flows with hot Mediterranean and icy Viking."

"The combination should make you lukewarm."

"What do you think?"

"Oh, you're pretty hot at times." He laughed. "I might check that out again after I've finished digging holes in your garden."

Chapter 9

"Dig down about this far from the roots." Calli glanced at Kell who watched, frowning, while she marked the dirt with the shovel. He took the implement out of her hands and edged her out of the way. Clearly, he knew the handle from the blade.

With a sharp thump of his foot, he jammed the blade deeply into the soil and she tried not to watch. A supervised man was one who would do nothing but show off, a trait she had noted during her previous experience of men helping her in the garden.

"In a circle or a square?" he asked with forced patience, the way men did when women gave instructions.

In a voice that made no attempt to bite back, she said, "Either. When you've cut the roots, put the shovel under and ease out the bush. Yes, that's exactly right. Now transfer the plant into here." She placed the pot near him and he neatly deposited the rose bush where she indicated. She gazed at the sky. Like yesterday, dark clouds loomed and the air smelled damp. The rain yesterday had loosened the soil.

Glad she had help in the perfect weather to move the roses, she slid the first filled pot onto the sack trolley, and pushed the two-wheeler around to the new bags of soil Kell had left near the judge's gardening shed. She intended to do the same with the following rose bushes and tend to the plants until Kell's garden was ready.

By the time she had patted the mix around the rose and bumped the trolley back, Kell had deposited two more bushes into pots and was well on the way to filling another. At this rate, she would lose him in ten minutes. Not that she'd ever had him. She had expanded her projected one-night stand a little, but she wouldn't be letting him into her bed again, not that he had made any sort of interesting suggestion about being there since he had asked about her last relationship, which he clearly presumed was sexual.

Half-offended and half-glad that him having the wrong idea gave her a good reason not to answer, she potted up the next bush, and when she arrived back, he had dug up the lot and dumped them all in their pots.

"It's a plot," he said, sounding disgruntled.

"A garden plot?"

"A gardener plot. You're dawdling back there. The only way to speed you up is to carry all these around to the shed for you." He put one pot on her trolley and grabbed up two, striding ahead of her to the shed, as if he might be carrying a bundle of feathers.

She wheeled along behind him slightly out of breath from handling one.

While she toiled at filling the three, he carried the rest to her and stayed watching. He stood, hip-shot, as sexy as a man ought *not* to be. She sweated under leather gloves and the weight of a guy's tool belt.

She hefted out her secateurs. "I'll leave the new growth," she said, glancing up at him, "but I'll trim them back a little to give them a good chance. I think they'll all survive. You haven't done much root damage and roses are hardy plants."

"They look good in a mass like that. Why don't you want them?"

"They're garden plants, flashy outdoors but not much use in vases. They're plants for the neighbors rather than for the householder. The others I'm planting will be lovely to pick for indoors as well as to brighten up the garden. Your house is edgy, not soft like this house. The icebergs are too regimented here with their upright stance, but they'd be very suitable for your garden." She thought he wouldn't understand what she meant but he nodded.

"You're right. My house is sharp-edged—the points of the roof, and the angles of the windows, and even the diamond patterns on the leadlight, which you will be interested to hear that I have decided to keep." Grabbing the nearest bag of soil, he upended it into the nearest pot, and then the next and the next until a job that could have taken her another ten minutes was finished in a couple. Clearly, he couldn't wait to leave.

Trying not to mind, she turned on the hose and wet the soil while he watched, his hands pushed casually into his pockets. He looked eye-catching in the red top, which brought out the bright blue of his eyes. If a scout for a modeling agency saw him, he would make a mint. Each time she glanced at him, she noticed more about him, like his hard firm lips and the way the autumn light caught on his cheekbones and shadowed the tiny cleft in his chin.

"What else do you have for me to do?"

"You've saved me half a day already with what you've done," she said reluctantly. The time had come for him to leave. She couldn't expect him to hang around forever because she had given him a bowl of cornflakes.

"So, this should be my time." He had a considering expression on his face and he stroked his chin like a villain in a melodrama.

She frowned. "What do you mean?"

"This should be time you spend with me instead."

"I am with you."

"I want to be with you the other way, you know, naked."

Her insides began to hum. Maybe he hadn't heard as much about her as she had presumed. Or maybe he had, and he didn't have a problem with dishonesty. Or perhaps he didn't believe the story he had heard about her *last relationship*. She almost held her breath while she decided not to worry either way.

"These plants are for you. It's my time we're using, not yours. So, you owe me half an hour." She crossed her arms, watching the interesting wheels of his mind turn.

His eyes hooded and he offered her an unreadable smile. "I could pay you back, naked in bed."

She breathed out. "I don't pay men to be naked in my bed."

"I'll have sex with you for nothing," he said, adopting an expression of mock offense. "You seem to think everything should be bought and paid for, but some things are free."

"Shh," she said, hearing the crunch of footsteps on the gravel path. She glanced toward the sound. "Hi, Trent."

"Calli," he answered with a nod. His gaze shifted between her and Kell. "I owe you a couple of hours' work. What can I do?" He plunged his hands into the front pockets of his jeans, his expression slightly sheepish.

She rose to her feet, hoping he hadn't heard Kell say he would have sex with her for nothing, and indicated the dumping ground behind the shed. "Rocks. All these need to edge the paths over there."

"Do you want to show me where?"

"I owe her half an hour, too," Kell said, casually eying Trent. "We could get these rocks out of the way today with the two of us working together."

"Right. Follow me. See the sprayed blue lines over here. This is where I want the rocks. Later on I'll lay down some wood chip paths. How was your date, Trent?" she asked him politely.

"Great." He gave her a wide smile, which he modified into a careful grin. "I have another next Thursday night. Emily works shifts and she waits until her days off for dates."

"Very wise. The wheelbarrow is in the shed."

Kell cricked open the shed door and Trent moved inside, grabbing the barrow. The two men crashed rocks into the tray until the tire on the wheel began to flatten, and then followed Calli down the paths she had marked, starting at the far end. She didn't need to supervise, and she was pleased to see her garden job cracking along so speedily, the roses shifted in time for the new paving, and her paths marked out with stone before the wood chips arrived. So far, her job was running to her planned schedule.

The least she could do was to make lunch for the guys who had been more than helpful—and on a Sunday morning, too—but she had almost no food to spare, as usual, except ham, lettuce, and tomato. Making a quick decision, she gave the Mercedes an outing to the large shopping complex a few blocks away. Being a set of boutique shops for the wealthy, the place was one where she could possibly be recognized, which had kept her away until now, but the tiny local shops stayed shut on the weekends, giving her no other choice.

She parked underground and dashed through the vine-covered arcade to the supermarket where she bought bread, butter, real milk, and another bag of self-raising flour. After she dumped the lot onto her kitchen counter, she went outside and found the guys still laboring away and doing a mighty fine job.

"Wow. There's nothing like having a cabinetmaker and a screen designer to make rock edgings for gardens. Very artistic." She narrowed her eyes critically, but the guys had gone to some trouble making sure that the various rock shapes worked together with unlike shapes and sizes mixed. "I'm making lunch. It will be ready in half an hour. Do you want to synchronize watches?"

"Midday," Kell said, concentrating on the rock he held in his hand.

"Right." He barely looked up at her. Clearly whatever job he did, he made sure he performed perfectly. Her sort of man, in fact. Slap-dash people puzzled her.

For a moment, she hesitated, shifting from foot to foot; then she decided now was the time to push her opinion, though she knew Kell was dead against enlarging his house. "If you built your extension out of your recycled bricks, you would have a classy feature wall."

Kell stopped moving. He shifted his gaze to her. "I'm not adding an extension. That would put the kitchen right in the center of the house."

"Yes, but you would have good light if you put in French doors or a wall of glass. I could design the perfect garden outside."

Trent glanced at Kell. "It's hard to see a garden growing there when now it's only dirt and trees and weeds. What do you think?"

Kell's expression remained inscrutable. "At this stage, I can't visualize making the biggest kitchen I have ever seen even bigger."

"When you've finished tidying up your garden, you'll see it. You ought to build a brick wall to hide the bins, too, while you still have all those good reclaimed bricks," Calli said as she went back to the cottage. There. She had said her piece. He could mull that over or ignore her at will. He owned the house, and so he could decide if he wanted to make real money or waste his time.

* * * *

"Did she try to get money from you?" Trent asked Kell in a stage whisper as he chipped off a corner of a rock to make a good fit. Although he disdained brickwork, he was a true expert. "I heard you say that she thinks everything should be paid for."

"Don't worry. I'm onto her little game. Lucky you warned me about what she did to her boyfriend, though," Kell said, thoroughly amused. He didn't want Trent to know that he was trying to romance Calli because so far, he wasn't doing too well.

Trent imagined Kell had a turbo-charged sex life, and Kell happily left him in ignorance about the true extent of his relationships with the various women he met. Women wanted permanency. The moment they began talking about the next weekend, or when he met their best friend, or any sort of future, he came out with a rash of excuses—he couldn't help himself.

He had no intention of being tied down. He didn't want to be slotted into a partnership. A woman would hold him back, would resent the hours he spent on his various work projects. If he settled down, he would get complacent, and his ambition would die. He saw that in his married friends, and a man who didn't learn by example would pay in the end. His plan to join up with a larger conglomeration wouldn't happen until he had managed to showcase his careful work in the Tudor house.

"This is looking good," he said about the job Calli had them doing. The paths meandered casually. He could imagine the wood chip base softening the appearance and he knew he would like this sort of garden for his house, not the one next door that he planned to sell, but the one that he would live in eventually...with a wife and children. He blinked, because he hadn't imagined a family before. A wife hadn't featured in his thoughts until he had met Calli, but he couldn't see her with children or with him.

She seemed to be marking time rather than looking for a relationship. Last night should be enough for both of them. That's what she had hinted before he had started acting out of character.

In fact, he rarely ate breakfast with a woman he had slept with the night before. Nor had he ever wasted a Sunday carrying bags of soil or carting rocks for anyone. Sunday was sacred, reserved for family or his down time, the time he worked on his accounts, payments in and payments out, quotes and estimates. Other than romancing the women who accepted him on a temporary basis, his life consisted of his work, because a man didn't get ahead without putting in the slog.

He considered Calli's idea of building an extension. Jay hadn't designed one because Kell decided the house was already large enough to show off his cabinetry skills which, combined with the money he would earn from the flip, was of prime concern to him. However, if he used the recycled bricks and the bricklayer he already had—Trent—the costs wouldn't be much more than for the roofing, which could also be made from recycled material such as the matching roof tiles from the garage.

A garden out the back, an entertainment area with a view through folding glass doors to the paved courtyard, and he had a plan for outdoor living. This could slot into the project quite well. Maybe. He didn't want to overprice the old house, but he could always run the idea by Jay.

In the meantime, he and Trent had finished the paths for Calli. By his calculations, they owed her no more time, either of them. When she started on his garden, he would owe her time then, but he didn't see much more he or Trent could do for her. She had a paving contractor and she could manage the planting herself. He almost regretted that she wouldn't need him because that would give him a good excuse to hang around.

"Lunch time," Trent said, interrupting Kell's musings. "I haven't had breakfast yet. I suppose you haven't either."

"I haven't even had morning coffee." Kell did his best to appear long-suffering.

The cat almost blew his cover by springing into his arms the second he walked into the cottage.

* * * *

Calli had arranged salad rolls on the table. She also had scones in the oven, which she slid out when the guys walked in and pulled up chairs. "I know you would prefer a meat pie and a carton of chocolate milk," she said with mock unconcern while she piled the scones into a breadbasket. "But you can't invite people to eat a pie with you unless you have made one. I don't make them because I'm not a very good cook. My one talent is scones, so I hope you like them."

Kell eyed her, clearly keeping his mouth shut about the rhubarb sponge she had presented last night. "I like scones. They're food, and I like all food."

And being just as discreet as he, she didn't say *except for Brussels sprouts*. She smiled. "I see you've seduced my cat again."

"This old thing?" Kell indicated the cat that sat perched on his forearm with the top of her head snuggled under his chin, her purring loud enough to rattle Calli's brain, or that might be her excuse for being so uncertain about Kell.

She thought she could remain casual about sex with him, but the idea of being naked with him one more time had grabbed hold and wouldn't let go. Never at any time had she honestly desired a man. Possibly, she should be glad of that, but as a twenty-six-year-old woman, she had remained cool about sex. She had dated a few men because, socially, she knew her family background was an appreciable asset. Mentally she had been involved, but physically she'd always been rather disappointed.

She had to admit that she appreciated a man who didn't pretend to be in love with her so that he could use her as an asset, too. The thought of stripping off a male's clothes had never occurred to her. Thinking back, she saw her previous relationships as asexual. No one would ever see a night with Kell as such. Sex oozed out his every pore.

"She's a hussy," Mr. Sexy said with an indulgent glance at the cat. "She throws herself at me, and I don't know what to do about it."

Trent chuckled. "You could do the same thing you do when any female throws herself at you."

"What's that?" Calli asked, her heart thumping nervously, knowing she had not only thrown herself at him but on top of him.

"Trent has no idea," Kell said, his expression wary. "You could find out if you threw yourself at me."

"I can't imagine anything less likely." She folded her arms, aghast that she had, and surprised that he didn't see her as needy and annoying as her last boyfriend had. Instead, he indulged her the same way he indulged the cat.

"Nor can I," Kell said in an impartial voice. "I'd like a woman gardener chasing me around. Then I would be sure of having a great garden."

"You can have me if you pay me. That's what usually happens." She raised her chin.

"Apparently, that doesn't work both ways."

She blushed, actually blushed, again recalling their former conversation about him being naked. "Are you going to try your lunch or do you need my cat's opinion first?"

Kell lowered his ear to the vicinity of the cat's mouth. "What? No tuna in the sandwiches. That's an outrage. But you have to remember, Cat, that this is people food. We don't eat tuna every day." The cat appeared to nod and then leaped down onto the floor, stalking to the couch where she settled, her unblinking gaze aimed at Kell. "She's trying to understand the strange diets of humans."

"He even gets cats on his side," Trent said to Calli. "I haven't seen that before, but there's a first time for everything. This salad roll is good. I'm getting used to not having a meat pie every day."

"You didn't *really*?" Calli asked, aghast.

"No, he didn't really. Some days he would simply have a hamburger. He won't know himself when he gets used to eating green food as well as brown and yellow food. What are you planning to do this afternoon?" Kell asked her.

"A spot of weeding."

"You can't do that on a weekend. How about if I take you to my brother's house to discuss this extension you think I should build?"

She took a bite of her roll and chewed while she thought. She would like to say *no*, but she was interested in his brother, the architect, not knowing why one brother would be an architect when the next two were tradesmen. Usually, most children in a family were university educated if the first was. Plus, she thought the extension was a good idea and couldn't imagine why his brother hadn't recommended building out. She considered for about three seconds. "Okay."

Kell smiled. "We'll leave as soon as you've finished eating."

"Are you going to check with him first to see if he's at home?"

"He is. He invited me to lunch, or his wife did. She does Sunday lunches for the family."

"Apparently you declined the invitation, or you wouldn't have eaten here," she answered, embarrassed that she had foisted lunch on him without asking if he had other arrangements.

"He hardly ever goes. I would if Vix was my sister-in-law." Trent took a huge bite of his roll, and used his fingers to cram in the part that didn't quite fit into his mouth.

Kell eyed him speculatively. "No, you wouldn't. You would feel as out of place there as I do. Both my brothers are married and week after week they expect me to haul along a date," he explained to Calli.

"The effort of deciding which woman to take exhausts him," Trent said, speaking and chewing at the same time. "So, he usually takes two."

Kell shot Trent a glance of annoyance. "Don't give Calli the wrong impression of me. I don't want to have to take a date. I don't want to ask someone to my brother's house because whoever I ask then has to pass the family inspection."

"But you can take me because I'm not a date," Calli said, rising to her feet and leaning over to collect the empty plates. "I'm the gardener who lives next door. You'll want to give them a chance to finish eating before we leave."

"They should be well underway in about an hour. That will give us time to eat scones—and drink coffee."

"That was a hint, I presume."

She turned on the coffee machine and put three cups on the hob to warm. Then she collected clean plates, butter, and jam.

"Often Kell doesn't know which date to take, though," said Trent, clearly not at all intimidated by Kell's reproof.

Kell leaned back and sighed. "He's about to enlighten you with a long running, fairly boring joke about me always having the choice of two."

"That's why he's called Killer. The Lady Killer."

"Killer." She shook her head, aiming a rueful smile at Kell. "That night you pounced on me and threw me to the ground…I thought Trent had called out 'kill her.' You can see why I was nervous about drugs and thugs. And then the blonde with the Ferrari. Only drug barons drive Ferraris."

Trent snickered. "That was Vix. It wasn't her car though, just a loaner until her car was serviced."

Calli glanced at him, surprised. "I'm missing out. The garage never gives me a Ferrari."

Kell shrugged. "She's a careful driver. Maybe all the other loaners were out and that was the only car she could get in a hurry. If I had a Ferrari, I would trust her with it."

Trent stared at him as if he had lost his mind.

She wondered what that was about while she waited for the coffee machine to squirt the first two cups through. "She must go to a pretty classy mechanic."

Both of the guys looked blank. She shrugged, mentally. Apparently cars and mechanics were a touchy subject, for reasons unknown to her. After her coffee had puttered into her mug, she sat at the table again, slightly entertained by watching the cat crawl her way back up Kell beneath his sweater. He scarcely winced, but he looked relieved when the cat finally settled under his chin again.

The guys had made a mess of the butter and jam, and she wished she had torn and spread the scones first. She had too many plates and knives and spoons on the table and had made the whole event too cluttered for them. Next time she would do better. That's what she always said to herself. Next time. She would do better.

* * * *

Kell removed the cat that sat between his T-shirt and his sweater where she had remained during coffee, and popped her onto the couch again. The little stray and Calli had the same characteristics, both waifs and both gentle with their clawing. "I'll wander home with Trent and bring back my car so that I can collect you," he said to Calli.

"I'll need to do something with my hair, so don't hurry."

He couldn't imagine what she would do with her short hair, but he strolled back home with Trent, heaving a sigh of relief. For various reasons, he didn't want Calli to know that his sister-in-law was the daughter of one of the richest men in the state. Not that he was embarrassed about Vix or her wealth. He simply didn't like talking about anyone's money. That sort of discussion brought out the envy in people and too often snide remarks, which Vix would never deserve.

"What was that rubbish about garages?" Trent asked.

"I don't think we need to share all our business with Calli."

Trent shrugged. "I told you what I heard about her. I didn't say I believed it."

"Nevertheless."

Trent shot him a mystified glance and disappeared into the shed. Kell slid into his car and drove next door, parking behind the Merc and the Jag. Before he could get out, Calli arrived, and she climbed in beside him. He reversed out and turned the car onto the street. She had done something fluffy to her hair, which looked good, and he wanted to taste the gloss of her lipstick. Too much gazing at her, and he would grow addicted to her high-boned, elegant face. He stared out at the road.

"Are you going to introduce me as a business associate?"

He laughed. "They would never believe that. It's Sunday. They know I wouldn't be driving around with a business associate. They'll assume you're my date."

"So, I'll have to pass the family inspection."

"It's subtle."

"I hope I don't notice."

"I hope you don't, too." He gave her a crooked smile. "But you have a smart mouth, and you'll manage."

She appeared to mull that before smiling. He might grow addicted to her smile, too, the way her mouth stretched into dimples, which gave the impression of impishness. Suddenly his jeans seemed too tight, and so he concentrated on the road, annoyed he still wanted her. She had gotten to him in the worst way, from his head to his zipper—*whoosh*.

He parked out the front of Jay's house and walked her to the code box on the gatepost, punched in the numbers, and led her down the side of the house, past the vehicles sitting in the carport to the gate behind. "Hey," he called to the group sitting in the pavilion beside the pool.

Luke's three sons spotted him first and ran over, the youngest, Oscar, grabbing his leg and trying to climb up him. "Hi, guys." With a finger on top of each shiny head, he named his nephews for Calli. "Max, Noah, and Oscar. This is my friend Calli." He swung up redheaded Oscar and carried the kid on his shoulders over to his brothers and their wives. "Calli," he said, in answer to the inquiring faces at the table while he dropped Oscar onto the bench seat Luke had just vacated to greet Calli.

Jay also rose to his feet to be introduced, which Kell did speedily, including Sherry, Luke's wife, and Vix, Jay's wife.

"There's plenty of food," Vix said with her lovely smile, indicating the remains on the table. "I'll get fresh plates."

"We've eaten. Calli's here to be inspected."

Calli stood, a bemused expression on her face. "I didn't think he would throw me at you quite so suddenly. I'm living next door to him for the next couple of months, and I'm going to help him with his garden. I'm a garden designer."

"That explains it," his younger brother Luke said with what might be termed an evil grin. "We're used to him bringing along his fan club. I can't remember the last time I saw him with one woman."

Kell tried frowning at Luke, but his brother gave him a light punch to the shoulder.

"You live next door?" Vix blinked. "I hope you inspected the place for her, Kell. There was a young lad, who Kell was worried about, hanging around."

Kell pushed his hands into his pockets. "Turned out to be Calli. She's doing the judge's garden and living in the place. She had an idea about my house, and I want to run it by Jay."

"What idea?" Jay asked, pulling up a seat for Calli, who sat, staring around at everyone.

"To use the old bricks to add on a room at the back."

"I thought you wanted to do as little as possible to the house?"

"She thinks I'll make a couple of hundred thousand more with the extra space."

"You're a garden designer," Jay said as a statement to Calli, drawing his eyebrows down and glancing at her. "How did you come up with a couple of hundred thousand for an extension? Kell has a four-bedroom house—at the top of the range already, I would have suspected."

She shrugged. "I worked for a property developer for a few years. You learn things when you're around the trade all the time. I also suggested another couple of bathrooms. He has the space. And the street, well, it's not so easy to buy into."

"I would say it's a good idea." Jay made a thinking face as he poured a glass of wine for Calli. "Do you want me to get it down on paper for you, Kell?"

Kell nodded, almost surprised. He had half expected Jay to reject the idea, but apparently he accepted Calli's calculations. She had the sort of casual plausibility that encouraged people not only to like her, but also to trust her—the perfect credentials for a confidence trickster. His mouth curved with amusement.

He thought she had the measure of his family. Even in the Garden of Eden, she would have the snake eating out of her hand. He settled in to watch his brothers and their wives check out his newest acquisition.

Chapter 10

Calli had to admit she'd been surprised when Kell drove her to the small expensive enclave where his brother lived. She had imagined he lived anywhere other than here, in this area of tall green trees and taller houses built of bluestone, sandstone, and untold wealth, but when she had spotted Vix Tremain in the back garden, she almost walked backward. His brother had clearly fallen on his feet by attracting one of the nicest, lowest-key rich girls in the state, most likely the reason why he lived in this gracious home in an exclusive area.

Vix had been two years ahead of Calli in school. She hoped, because of the age difference, Vix might not recognize her. In her private co-educational school, the older students had tended to ignore the younger ones, preferring to stick to their own groups. Calli tried to act unconcerned about being recognized, but she had the wild urge to grab Kell's big warm hand. Fortunately, she had managed to maintain her poise but only because he had been occupied with herding small boys at the time, which he found as difficult as mesmerizing cats. Consequently, she hadn't embarrassed herself by latching onto him.

Then, happily, she found she had no need to worry because Vix had waited for an introduction with a polite smile on her face. Well, Calli had never exactly been a star at school. Her only distinction was in having an identical twin sister who delighted in letting people guess which was which. Calli was the levelheaded twin. Tiggy was more open to wild ideas. And now barely eight years later, Calli was paying for organizing her life, but finally seeing the benefit of being open to anything, or rather, open to acting on her attraction to a man without first making sure that he was suitable marriage material.

A month ago, she thought she could only be happy with a man who had the same background as her, stable parents, a good steady income, and well-educated friends. These days she couldn't look past a man who had somehow brought himself up, and while bypassing a university education, had managed to start a thriving business of his own. Her father had done the same, though he had started with two very canny parents to help him. Kell was a rather marvelous self-starter.

After being seated, she scrutinized the rest of Kell's family of tall handsome brothers. Jay had a white scar on his cheek and Luke had red hair like two of his sons. Both of Kell's brothers were good looking. However, he had the edge, his coloring more dramatic with the contrast between the darkness of his hair and the lightness of his eyes. Sherry, Luke's wife, was pretty and pert, probably younger than Calli.

She took the glass of wine Jay handed her, noting only a single bottle sat on the table, out of which very little had been poured. This group didn't see drinking as a team sport, clearly. Nor did she.

Vix Tremaine, now Vix Dee, toyed with her drink, staring at Calli with a thoughtful expression on her face. She shook her head. "I can't believe Kell thought you were a boy."

"I can't either," Calli answered, now confident she hadn't been recognized and she wouldn't have to suffer the mortification of either being judged, or questioned about the truth of the story reported in the papers. "He tackled me and threw me to the ground. Very un-neighborly, I would say."

"He what?" Jay laughed. "I would have thought that by now he could tell the difference between males and females."

"Very funny," Kell muttered, folding his arms across his chest. "She took me by surprise."

"Are you house-sitting for the judge?" Vix asked, handing the middle-sized boy, Max, a halved apple.

"I'm living in the guest cottage, but I'm keeping an eye on the main house, too. The judge wanted his garden finished while he was away, and it's easier to get it done without having to worry that I might be inconveniencing a client while I was messing with the garden."

"How long have you been designing gardens?" Sherry passed the other half of the apple to Luke, who bit into the fruit while staring at Calli.

"Six years. For the first two I worked with David Bowden."

"David Bowden?" Vix gave a delighted smile. "He designed my grandmother's garden about five years ago. I was thinking that's where I might have seen you before."

"More than likely," Calli answered firmly, although she knew she hadn't seen Vix at her grandmother's home. She had been too confident too soon, and Vix was likely to remember where they had met before if Calli didn't keep cool. "Where is your grandmother's garden?"

"A couple of streets away, but she doesn't own it anymore. When my grandfather died, she moved to live with the rest of my family in my father's country house. David used a marble fountain reclaimed from an English garden as the centerpiece at the front—and he put in formal hedging, too. That was very much his style then."

"It still is, but I remember the garden with the marble fountain. It was one of the first I worked on. After being his apprentice, I took a job with AA & Company, and then I left to start designing gardens for my own business. I haven't yet had a request for a marble fountain. I mainly do less formal gardens now."

"You worked for Alexander Allbrook?" Kell squeezed his chin between his forefinger and his thumb, folding the skin into the cleft.

"For a few years. Then I branched out on my own."

"Brave," Kell said, his gaze intent on her. "I had a small catch-up job with them earlier in the year."

Jay leaned back in his chair. "If you were offered more contracts with them, you could set yourself up very nicely."

"Great minds." Kell shot a smile at his brother. "I'm angling for more, that's for sure."

"What about you, Vix? And Sherry? Do you have careers?" Calli smiled brightly at everyone, trying for a quick sidetrack. Although Trent had told Kell about Grayson, he clearly hadn't mentioned her surname. Her father, Alex Allbrook the owner of AA & Company, the leading property developer in the state, contracted his favorite companies and he rarely used others. She couldn't help Kell even if he asked her, not after the travesty of Grayson trying to worm his way in via Calli.

"I'm a set designer," Vix answered. "Sherry still has a boy at home. Are you going to design Kell's garden?"

"I'm going to give him advice."

"And she is *mighty good* at giving advice," Kell said in a mock dissatisfied tone before skimming a look at Calli. "She *advised* Trent and me to shift rocks for her this morning."

She noticed Vix and Sherry glance at each other while they laughed.

"Do you happen to have a best girlfriend?" Luke asked, drumming his fingers on the table, his expression mischievous.

She glanced at him, puzzled. "No. I have a sister."

"Leave it, Luke," Kell said in a threatening voice.

"A sister might do."

Kell rose to his feet, his expression dangerous. "You had your first and only warning."

Vix rose to her feet, too. "Sorry to interrupt a spot of family ragging, guys, but I'm needed in the kitchen, that is, if you want Pavlova. And, Jay, *leave it*." She aimed a steely glance at her husband.

He appeared taken aback for a moment. Then he nodded. "Sit down, Kell. We need to discuss your extension."

Kell sat, palms on his knees, his eyebrows lowered as he watched Vix cross the lawn to the house. Sherry, chewing on her bottom lip, arose and followed her. He finally said, "I'll want the roofline extended. We'll brick the side walls the same as the others and have a wall of glass at the back." He glanced at Calli for confirmation.

A tickle of pleasure warmed her chest. She leaned in to the conversation. "He needs sort of a family/eating room—big enough for the kids to do homework, et cetera. I wouldn't think a childless couple would buy a house with four huge bedrooms. Without the extension, Kell would only have formal rooms for the kids, like the dining and the sitting rooms."

"What sort of flooring would you use?" Jay asked his brother after considering Calli's words. He seemed to be the sort of person who would always consider before he spoke.

Kell lifted an ankle to his knee, blinking with thought. "I have flooring from the old laundry outside, and I could steal some from the upstairs bathrooms. It's all jarrah. I'd planned to use it in my business and tile the kitchen floor."

"Polished hardwood floors are on trend," Jay said, his gaze drifting to Calli for a moment. He blinked and concentrated again on Kell. "Using your wood and the reclaimed brick will give the old house an edge. Will Trent do the bricking for you?"

"I haven't asked, but he will. He doesn't plan to give up his free lodging, and he still has a couple of months before he leaves."

"I can do the plumbing next week," Luke said in a slightly chastened voice. He picked at his fingernails. "I'll start tomorrow, if you like."

Kell scrutinized his redheaded brother for a moment, as if examining the offer. Then he nodded curtly. "Trent would like that. Cold showers are getting to him."

Calli nudged Kell. "He knows he can have a hot shower in my place."

"You make him work it off." Kell eyed her sideways.

Calli glanced at his brothers, spreading her hands. "That's not as dubious as you might think. I used them both this morning to shift rocks around the judge's garden. They're probably owed a couple of free hot showers for that."

"You got Kell working for you on a Sunday morning?" Jay stared at Kell. "There's a first."

"I was working for me, as it happens," Kell said in a growly voice. "She offered to pot some plants for me that had to be dug up. So I dug them up."

"And another first, you working with plants," Luke contributed. "Being on the ladder to success is making a new man of you."

"Let's not get carried away. I felt no true connection to the plants." Kell leaned back in his seat, his fingers meshing behind his head.

The width of his shoulders and the hardness of his biceps showed far too blatantly, and Calli's lust for him almost stopped her breath. She glanced at his hard thighs and remembered him nudging himself between hers, and she groaned silently. In her whole life, she had never craved a man as much.

"Fortunately the plants didn't know," she said, clearing her throat. "Plants can be very sensitive. The rose bushes were very impressed by being handled so quickly and efficiently. I think that might be why Hobo, my cat, also is in love with him. I can't think of any other reason. He doesn't look after her or feed her."

"A cat is in love with him?" Luke let his jaw drop.

"She talks to him, and she answers when he speaks."

"A cat? What do you know about cats?" Jay asked Kell, appearing to be highly entertained.

Kell shrugged. "What's to know? Anyway, the cat decided on the relationship. I'm only going along with her."

"Sounds like you," Jay said, his mouth twisted. "Remember that old dog, Luke?"

"The stray?"

"This stray," Jay said, turning to Calli, "was the local beggar. He dragged himself along the street snatching up food where he could find it. The cat lady, who happened to live on our street, used to give him milk and table scraps. He took them without biting her, but he snarled at everyone else. Except Kell. Did you ever feed him, Kell?"

"Not initially. He smelled like the inside of a garbage bin," Kell said with clear reluctance. "He used to trail me and that annoyed me, but he turned out to be a good old dog in the end."

"He tamed Kell. Kell was a wild boy, but not when he was with the dog. We ended up adopting Scrappy, but he died within a couple of years. He was probably older than Kell at the time. What were you, ten?"

Kell shrugged and averted his glance. "Ha, Pavlova, at last," he said to Vix, who walked across the lawn with a tray holding plates and spoons.

Not following too far behind, Sherry carried the strawberry-topped meringue. "Make a space on the table," she said, and the guys moved glasses and dishes of nuts and dried fruit and little savory pastries out of the way. She slid the dessert onto the marble tabletop and Vix placed her tray alongside.

"Does everyone want a slice?" Vix glanced around, her eyebrows raised.

Five adults and three children nodded. She cut ten slices and handed the sweet around on plates. Calli slowly savored her treat. Kell ate his in about three bites, and when Calli finished, he stood. "We're off." He held out his hand to her.

One glance at him, and she took his grip, rising to her feet. "That was lovely, Vix, thank you. I hope I see you all again one day."

Everyone else rose, too, Sherry politely saying the very same thing about Calli. Jay and Vix walked Calli and Kell to the car. While Kell and Jay discussed the delivery date of the plans for the extension, Vix said in an undertone, "It will all go away before you know. You're strong. It took me a moment or two, but I remember you on the swimming team."

"You do?"

"And I had a terrible crush on your brother."

"Who didn't? Hagen the golden boy—not easy to live up to, that's for sure."

Vix nodded sympathetically, and Calli slipped into the car, rather impressed that Vix hadn't even hinted to the others that she recognized Calli. No doubt she would reveal that, if she hadn't already, and Kell would know within days. Despite being slightly apprehensive, Calli appreciated that the other woman hadn't started the old-school chat that never interested anyone who hadn't been there at the time.

Kell walked around to the driver's seat and started the engine while Calli absorbed the fact that Kell picked up strays, and she was also one. Like Hobo, she had decided to have a relationship with him, initially only physical, but now she wanted so much more.

Kell was not only handsome, but he was beautiful, too. She hadn't seen past his face, or his wonderful toned body, but this tiny glimpse of him with his family told her he wasn't her usual date, all show, no substance. He was a man. A real man, a man like her father—responsible, smart, and kind.

"I remember Vix from school," she said reluctantly, as he pulled into the traffic, struck by his profile, his straight manly nose, his chiseled lips, and his clean-cut jaw.

He didn't shift his gaze from the road. "And Vix went to a very expensive school."

"Yes."

"And you had parents who could afford that."

"Yes."

"I had an alcoholic father, and I barely matriculated." He clamped his lips.

She heightened her chin. "I have a tertiary degree, and I dig in gardens for a living. You asked about my last relationship. You heard something about me second-hand from Emily."

"I heard you bled the poor guy dry—bankrupted him."

She slumped down in the seat. "And what do you think of that?"

He drew a deep breath. "I think he should have watched where his money was going. I think he must have been a fool if he let you do that. And I think that if you did, you aren't the person I know. You are scrupulous about debts and money." He shifted one of his hands from the wheel to his thigh.

"I was, at the time, very stupid about debts and money. I had never had to worry about it, you see. I was given everything I would ever need by my parents, who have loved and supported me all my life."

"And so you didn't notice how much of his money you spent." For the first time he glanced at her, and her heart cracked. The expression on his face said that he was trying to make excuses for her. No one else had. The people who knew the truth of the story had told her she was an idiot to trust Grayson. This man who didn't know the story was willing to give her the benefit of the doubt.

"No. I didn't spend any of his money because he didn't have any. He convinced me to leave a good job and to go out on my own, with him. He assured me he could handle the business side, as my father had, and I would be in charge of the design side—which I hadn't quite been with my father. He had the ultimate decision about my gardens. I wanted to make my own decisions."

"So, the story about you is untrue?"

"The story about Grayson is untrue. He was impressed by my parent's money and he thought that when he had run through mine, my father would come to the rescue. And my father would have. I wouldn't let him."

"So, he tricked you, not the other way around?"

She nodded. "After he had spent all the money in my bank account, I had none left to pay the trades. And you said the person who had the money should have watched where it was going. I should have. I don't have any excuse for not doing so, other than I thought he and I were friends."

"He sounds like a man who needs a good throttling." His voice was matter-of-fact.

"I didn't have a magic people-meter in my head that sorted out the good people from the bad, after all."

"We all think we have one of those. Apparently, he fooled Emily, too."

"She would have read the newspaper story, which was a bit biased. And because my family refused to have me interviewed, the impressionable female journalist on the story took the view of a very handsome man. And what is written *can* be retracted, but it can't be unread."

"So, now you're bankrupt?"

She shook her head. "My father bailed me out. Grayson predicted that accurately. Far paid the tradespeople, but I don't have a house or a nice car now. I am as you see me, a garden designer who works in the gardens she designs and hopes for a cottage attached to the job. I don't suppose I will see that again, but it was certainly timely. At this stage I need to save every penny I get."

"And what about this Grayson. What did he do with your money?"

"While he was with me, he spent the trades' wages on impressing people, partying, drugs." She shrugged. "He cleaned out my bank account, and I didn't even notice because I left him to handle the money part of the business, though the only money was mine. My sister warned me, but would I listen? No."

He lifted his hand from his thigh and held hers. Tears drifted down her cheeks, but she didn't sniff or make a noise because she didn't want him to know how badly Grayson had hurt her. She had made poor choices in her personal relationships, and when she decided on a business relationship, she chose wrongly there as well. No doubt about it, she had no idea how to judge character.

Finally, she angled her head and wiped her tears on her shoulder, anything but let go of his hand and his incidental support.

"The worst of it is that he was such a stupid man," she said barely above a whisper. "All looks, no substance. And I was a stupid woman not to see him as he was." She cleared her throat, attempting to sit taller. "Anyway, with Far's help, the law will catch up to him, and he'll end up with nothing but a reprimand."

"Whereas you end up looking like a fool to have trusted him."

She swallowed. "How can I ever live that down?"

"By doing exactly as you are doing. By being yourself. I expect you are paying back your father?"

"I'll need to take quite a few more jobs before I can do that, but I'm well on the way. But the house and the car—well, the house was mortgaged, of course, but it was a start. If I want anything better now, I will have to marry a rich man, that's for sure," she said, trying to inject a lighter tone into her pity-party.

He squeezed her fingers and finally took back his hand. "I won't qualify for quite a few years," he said slowly.

She stared at him, surprised. "I'm not looking for a husband. I just didn't want you to think that I'm dishonest. I wanted to explain why I operate on a favor-for-a-favor system. That way I save on tax. Oh, hell. Now I'm outing myself as a tax-evader."

He made a wry movement of his mouth. "Have I done you a favor recently?"

"But for you, I wouldn't have had a slice of Pavlova. Why? What do you want me to do?"

"Tomorrow, I'm installing a kitchen in Richmond. The job will take all day and possibly extend to Tuesday. Meanwhile, Luke is going to start the plumbing in my house. He can start upstairs, but I'll need to find the space from somewhere for the third bathroom you advised. I'm thinking it ought be an en suite for the bedroom at the end of the hallway. I could possibly take off space from the hallway and the bedroom alongside. Or not. I would like you to go over the changes with me, if you would, because this is your idea."

"I'm no architect." She stared at his perfect profile. "Your brother could do it."

"He seems to think I should do the planning first. You women all say I ought to reinstate the butler's pantry. If I convert the bathroom there to a powder room, I'll want a laundry room somewhere else and all of those areas need plumbing." He waited.

"Okay, I'll do what I can. I have the graph paper and pencils I used for my garden designs. I'll want to be walked over the floor space, first. I haven't seen upstairs."

He turned and aimed a relieved smile at her.

Her heart leaped into her throat. A single smile from him, and she thudded with helpless pleasure. Giving him up would be very difficult when only a single night of sex with him had this effect on her.

She mentally talked herself down while he drove into his own place. Fortunately, Trent's car had gone. If he had told Kell her surname, Kell might not have mentioned his keenness to be employed by her father. So, at this stage, she had no need to be wary of Kell or suspect he might be interested in using her to get ahead. For reasons only known to a woman who had been chosen because of her surname to be fleeced of her money, she would prefer Kell not to know her Allbrook connection—not yet, not when she still hoped she could spend more time with him. She doubted Vix would call to tell him tonight.

In the meantime, remaining scrupulously business-like, she inspected Kell's upstairs' space and waited while he collected his house plans. He walked her back to the cottage and he settled with her at the kitchen table.

His plans absorbed her for the next few hours while together they plotted the position for each area, arguing over the space in the old butler's pantry before repositioning the sink. In accord, they re-designated the old downstairs bathroom as a modern powder room and found space for the laundry alongside, plotted for the new extension.

Finally finished, she stood, stretched her back, and raised her arms high. While she had been working over pages of graph paper, day had turned to night outside. She strolled over to the sitting area, turned on the table lamps, and closed the shutters. The cat awoke, stretched sinuously, and eyed Kell, who had begun rolling the paper sheets.

Hobo glanced at Calli as if asking a question. Calli shook her head, as disappointed as the cat to see the end of this over-full day.

For the past couple of hours, she had been Kell's helper, but now with night about to surround her, she wanted him to stay for selfish and possibly ignominious reasons. The longer she kept him away from Trent, the better.

"I would offer you a meal if I had anything interesting defrosted," she said to him in a tentative voice. Earlier, he had wanted to get naked with her and she had put him off. Now, she had changed her mind. Getting naked with him seemed about the best idea she had heard in a year.

He raised his gaze. "I can get us a pizza," he said, raking his fingers through his hair. "Do you have a preference?"

"Normally, but tonight I'm just plain hungry." And she hoped he took that two ways.

"I'll shoot off to the shop. Okay?"

She handed him his keys.

* * * *

The fact that Calli had given her trust to a lying loser tore at Kell. The fact that the guy had taken advantage of her because she had wealthy parents made him want to rip off Grayson's arms and stuff them down his throat. Anyone who hurt Calli would get the same reaction from him.

He had been looking all his life for her. Her smile had melted him from the start and her wobbly sense of humor killed him. She had never taken him seriously and for reasons unknown he loved that, too.

She never took a stance and crossed her arms. Her opinions were up for grabs and she didn't pass judgments on anyone. She didn't presume he was an uneducated lout. She treated him like someone whose opinion she would hear, although he *was* an uneducated lout with an uneducated opinion. He had a lot to learn about himself and about his business decisions. She accepted that, and she didn't push him in any particular direction.

Best of all, he loved the smell of her skin, he loved the gleam in her eyes before she laughed, and he loved that she fit in with his family. She hadn't acted possessive and she didn't try to find out what his brothers had been planning to rag him about. He suspected she would wait for him to tell her and he should—but the whole thing was too bloody stupid. He would sound bigheaded if he said he sometimes dragged two dates along in case one of his friends was interested.

He could only act laid-back and accept that what happened, happened, which was mainly nothing because as Calli had said, *what sort of woman would want to share a man?* But unfortunately, he'd spent years leaving his brothers to assume the worst. Trying to clear that up with them now would be far too late. He had needed to hold her in his arms since she had begun the story of Grayson. Now stuffed with pizza, and replenished with coffee, he looked into her eyes, accepting the sledgehammer hit to his heart.

He rose to his feet, folding up the pizza box, which he tossed from the table to the kitchen sink, still holding Calli's gaze. Then he began to remove his sweater. She stood, her expression watchful, and slipped out of her shoes. One bound, and he snatched her up, staring closely at her, noting the way she held his gaze, her mouth slack and her breath short. Slow and deliberate, he brushed his lips against hers, again, again, and again.

She tightened her fingers into his hair while he kissed her eyebrows, her eyes, the tip of her nose, and then her mouth. He slid his lips to her jaw, and she arched back, her palms flat against his chest. His heart reacted with a thump into his throat and he lost his breath. "I swear I'll get you naked any minute, but I have to finish kissing you first."

She laughed deep in the back of her throat. "I don't want to be greedy." Nuzzling into his neck, she licked him there, before kissing his jaw. She traded him kiss for kiss until he needed to explore inside her mouth and she needed explore inside his. Although he began to snatch at air, he could tell by the heat of her skin that she wanted him as desperately as he wanted her—but if he prolonged the inevitable for as long as possible, the build-up would intensify the climax.

When he thought the end of his tether had been reached, he walked her backward into the bedroom, trying to kick off his shoes. "Don't undress. I'm going to strip you."

"I don't think I can wait," she answered in a shaky voice. "But I want to undress you, too." She started by undoing his fly.

He pushed lightly at her hand, because if she had set that part of him free, he doubted he would be able to do more than toss her onto the bed. Now in far too much of a hurry, he pulled her shirt out of her jeans and sped each button out of each hole, his hands shaky. Finally he pushed her shirt off her shoulders. He would have undone her bra, but she moved back and crouched onto the floor to jerk off his shoes. She snatched off his socks. Then she waited, staring at his zipper.

"Your pants first," he said, undoing her zipper.

She wriggled her hips and he pulled the legs and with a kind of hop-step, she ended up in her bra and panties. Although slim of body and fit, she had beautiful breasts, a good handful each, but he assumed his jeans would have to go before he could fill his hands. She stared straight into his eyes. "I'm getting those jeans off you now and if you don't hang on to your interesting bits, I swear I'll grab you into my palm and play around for a while."

"Good God, you have a dirty mouth." He laughed as he let her drag down his jeans. Stepping out of them, he undid her bra. "I'm going to grab these and play around for a while," he said, staring at her lovely white breasts.

"Nope. You take your undies off, and I'll take mine off."

Because he couldn't wait, he did as instructed, and then he stood, erect and desperate to have her while she examined his body and then his dick, which had decided to preen.

She said nothing. She stared. "It's not fair," she eventually said, her eyes glossing slightly. "I've never thought the male body was more than mildly interesting, but yours is bloody perfect."

He cleared his throat. "How is that unfair?"

"Because your face is, too." Her lips quirked ruefully. "Just my luck."

"I'm not going to ask what you mean, and I'm not going to be coy because I can say the same of you. You are beautiful from the tip of your head to your tiny toes."

"Tiny toes?"

"Compared to mine."

She laughed. "May I touch now?"

He grabbed her by the hips and tossed her onto the bed, landing beside her with an *oof.* Then he lay back while she touched him all over, rolling on his condom slowly, stopping to kiss his belly while she did so, and exploring each of his reactions. Torture, but the best torture he had had in his life. And then he had his chance to reciprocate.

For him, sex had always been pleasurable, no matter with whom, but never so intimate, never so personal, never so real. He wanted to be with Calli for the rest of his life. But, of course, that would never happen. He wouldn't fool himself with the possibility now that he knew she had rich parents. When he finally entered her, each stroke was a groaning delight, each pass at her mouth with his lips was a last taste, and his final explosion no joy at all because he would have to give her up long before he wanted to.

He left her sleeping because he couldn't make plans for a future with her. Although he resembled Jay physically, he was nothing like his brother. He couldn't hook up with a rich girl, he shouldn't love one, and he wouldn't marry one.

During those few weeks at the beginning of the year with the biggest property development company in the state, he had worked with the best tradesmen in the business, people he would be proud to associate with for the rest of his working life. He saw how success bred success. Doing the odd flip once a year would help him buy a fancy house and a nice car, but expanding his company to accommodate the needs of Allbrooks would give him the professional standing he craved—but that was all.

If he was offered a commitment by AA & Company, he could possibly think about a life with a woman whose parents had the sort of healthy income he planned to make in the not-too-distant future. Long before that time, Calli would have moved on.

Chapter 11

Calli awoke to a cat sitting on her chest. "Good morning, Miss Hobo." The bright sunlight streaming in through side cracks of the blind showed rumpled sheets but no Kell. He must have slipped away in the middle of the night. Calli frowned. "What happened to our pet man?"

Hobo offered a blink before leaping to the floor, where she waited to show Calli the way to her food dish.

"It's no use trying to pretend you don't know because you must have seen him leave. Since you only speak person in his presence, I'm guessing he wanted to get to work early. You cats have it easy. He has to earn a living like the rest of us humans."

Hobo stalked off to the kitchen. After swinging out of bed, Calli grabbed her bathroom robe and followed, barefooted. No man before Kell had considered kissing her all over. He had even resorted to licking at times. Last night had been Super-Callistic-Extra-Stylosis, or something like that.

"Don't be huffy." She filled Hobo's bowl while the cat frowned with annoyance. "He wouldn't have left early to avoid the morning after. He's not that type. He has a lot of confidence, you know. I suppose because he doesn't expect to be rejected." She made an uncertain face.

But apparently Hobo had no doubt about Kell's confidence, and she munched her breakfast while Calli spooned cornflakes into her own mouth, showered, and dressed, hugging herself with the knowledge that for the first time in her life she had been cherished. She had finally met a man expert enough and generous enough to make sure of her satisfaction. She had never imagined making love would be so leisurely, so wonderful. A tickle of heat warmed her lower belly.

If she hadn't heard the rumble of a truck in the driveway, she might have wandered around for quite some time with a dreamy smile on her face. Instead, she had to dash outside before five pallets of paving blocked the driveway. The orders on the delivery sheet should have directed the driver to the other side of the house where he could leave the pavers without impeding her access. After a short discussion, he backed up into the street and forklifted the pallets over the front fence. As he finished, the paving team arrived and stood discussing their weekend activities until the sand was poured into a pyramid near the pavers.

Then the work began, the old pavers lifted, and the new boundaries of the paths correctly marked with string lines. As soon as she had a moment, she dashed next door where Trent appeared to be stacking the old roof tiles into a neat pile by the back of the house. "We're building an extension as soon as Jay has drawn up the specs," he said, shading his eyes against the early morning sun as she walked toward him.

"Have you spoken to Kell?"

"This morning? Sure. That's why I'm getting the tiles over here. I had them in the dumpster."

"I hope you haven't already, but please don't tell him my surname."

"I don't know your surname."

"Didn't Emily tell you?"

"No. She said your family is rich. No point in me knowing your surname. I wouldn't know it anyway."

She grabbed his shoulders and kissed him on the cheek. "Allbrook," she said. "That's why I don't want him to know."

"Oh," he said, glancing down while he spread the dirt in front of him with the toe of his work boot. "If he knew, he would drop you like a sack of potatoes."

"Really? I was more afraid he would ask me to help him get a job with my father. I can't. My father would instantly mistrust anyone I recommended. He thinks I'm a poor choice of character." She moistened her lips. "And I don't want to be dropped."

Trent sighed. "He thinks I don't know he's been seeing you. I'm happy to keep out of this, but I have to tell you that Kell has never asked for a favor from anyone in his life. He's a proud bastard." He carefully neatened up the edges of two tiles. "Normally, I don't get a chance to give advice to women, but I think you need to keep your secret a little longer."

"I probably can't. I went to school with Vix Dee. She knows who I am."

Trent considered. "I might give her a phone call and see if I can get her to keep quiet, though I don't know. Kell has been bitten before. More than that I won't say. But," he said with a shrug and a sigh, "good luck."

She ran back into the judge's garden, absolutely certain she could trust Trent not to betray her, knowing that if she hadn't told him, she would be a double rat. She hoped Vix would entertain keeping a secret from her brother-in-law, and she decided Vix would, or else she would have outed Calli as soon as she recognized her. Gaining confidence, she directed traffic on her site.

During the rest of the morning, she had few moments to think about Kell and the next time she saw him. He had his normal job to do, and so did she. She had barely seen him last week, and she would barely see him this week. Then again, he hadn't mentioned seeing her. Well, he would have to because he lived next door. He might want to ask her something. She might want to ask him something. He might want a cup of coffee. She might want...him. She sighed. And of course she did. Any woman would.

Emotionally, she shouldn't be able to come out of a string of dysfunctional relationships and throw herself straight into another. Anyone with a gram of sense would see Kell as he was, a delightful interlude in an otherwise dull existence. As long as she continued to treat him casually, and as long as he didn't know that she was Alex Allbrook's daughter, she would be safe from being wanted for the wrong reason. She wouldn't call him or drop by. He could set the pace—if he wanted any sort of pace, if he wanted her.

In the meantime, her own pace grew frenetic. While the paving plodded along, she had a call from the bricklayer who had been hired to build her planter boxes. He'd had a cancellation and could start today as well. A delivery of gray slate arrived and then the bricklayer's sand. She ordered fresh new soil for the planters, the best quality, and a load of compost, realizing that she may as well mound up everything now while the place was a mess.

She thought she could dig holes awaiting the arrival of her new plants, but whenever she settled in to do a task, she was wanted for a decision. She thrived on this. Organizing gardens and coordinating her designs kept her mind alert and brought her plans to life. The morning hurried into the evening, and she barely had the energy to make herself a meal. However, her only dependent needed clean water, an amenities break, and food. Hobo took her time outside before she came back through the door that had been left open for her.

"I think we ought to come to an agreement," Calli said, bending down to look the cat in the eye. "I can hardly see your hip bones now, and I think

I can trust you with the key to the door, relatively speaking. I'll leave the window open and you can come and go as you please. Just promise me to keep away from the trucks. Nobody likes the look of a squashed cat."

Hobo considered and showed great interest in the open-window policy. She sat on the sill and breathed in the cooler night air. Apparently cats didn't like cooler night air, because after filling her lungs, she settled back in her own warm spot on the best part of the couch. She even conceded snuggling closer to Calli and that night, for the first time, she shared her bed.

By midday Thursday, Calli and the cat were bed buddies. As well, the paths delineated the garden beds and the planter boxes stood awaiting the fresh soil. Calli trudged back to the cottage, deciding on a salami sandwich and a cup of tea before loading the dirt into the planters. Hobo bounded along behind her. Freedom to come and go meant she followed Calli around the garden, supervising.

"Who's this?" Calli muttered to her only advisor. A dark-haired woman dressed in jeans and a green sweater strode down the driveway. A welcoming smile plastered Calli's face as she recognized her visitor.

"Sherry," she called in delight to Kell's sister-in-law. "I'm just about to have a cup of tea and a sandwich. I hope you have time to join me?"

"Tea would nice, but I'll be taking Oscar home for lunch any minute. At the moment, he's helping Luke. We've been next door to see the renovations while the other boys are at school. Luke's almost finished the plumbing in the upstairs bathrooms. Kell decided on two en suites and a main, and he's also having a half bathroom downstairs. I wouldn't mind a house with three and a half bathrooms if I didn't have to clean them."

"There's that," Calli said with a laugh, plugging in the electric kettle and taking two mugs from the cupboard. "But each bathroom adds value. Take a seat. I need to wash my hands."

Sherry settled herself at the kitchen table while Calli hurried off.

In the bathroom, she glanced at herself in the mirror, making a rueful face. Without a doubt, Sherry had come to talk about Kell. Calli didn't want to talk about Kell. She wanted to see him, grab him, hold him close, kiss his wonderful face, nibble his ear, and love him. Love him?

Shaking her head, she moved back out to the sitting room. "I hope you don't mind me eating in front of you," she said to Sherry while she turned and inspected the contents of the fridge.

"You eat, and I'll talk," Sherry said, settling her elbows on the table. "Luke's guys will be finishing up tomorrow. They won't be back until the tiling's done. The master en suite bathroom is roomy—a double shower and a double vanity. I can just see Luke and me having a shower at the same time. Not. We would have three kids in with us, splashing water everywhere, either that or find out they had destroyed the house while no one was watching them. All this stuff, and most of it's useless."

Calli laughed, now certain that Sherry had not been told Calli was the daughter of a rich man. If she had, this talk of wasted money would never have happened. "I would be surprised if anyone with small children bought the house. Double basins *are* useful, though. It's a pain having to wait to clean your teeth while someone else is cleaning theirs."

"The other en suite is quite small, really just closet space, but it's still bigger than my only bathroom. You would think if you married a plumber, you would have the very best bathroom, wouldn't you?"

Calli shook her head, watching the water boil while she put teabags in the mugs. "If you marry an electrician, you're stuck with faulty wiring. A doctor, and you can have the flu with no sympathy whatsoever. I hear that sort of thing all the time. People don't take their work home with them."

"Kell takes his home. He always has, his paperwork, that is. He's a workaholic. As for the kitchen he's putting in, and I can only judge by the plumbing prep, wow. The butler's pantry is bigger than my whole kitchen, too. I think I'm going to have to talk Luke into upsizing as soon as we can afford it." With a grin, Sherry rose to her feet as the kettle turned off. "You finish making your sandwich. I'll pour the water. I drink mine black."

"Me, too." Calli slapped tomato on top of her salami and sat with her sandwich while Sherry brought around the tea mugs.

"I heard an earful from Trent about Emily," Sherry continued, sliding back onto her seat. "I met her at Kell's barbeque last. Trent has a date with her tonight."

"So I heard."

"I've known him for years." Sherry squeezed out her teabag and left it on a spoon. "I hope it works out for him, but he's planning on leaving for Sydney in a month or two. That will complicate their relationship." She made a wry mouth. "He's started to brick the new extension, and it's going to look good. At the moment, he's showing Oscar how to lay a line of bricks. I expect I'll be brushing cement out of the little pest's clothes when I get home." With a mock doleful expression, Sherry dropped her face into her hands.

Calli grinned. "I love renovations. Some of them can take forever, but Kell's seems to be racing along." Not that Calli knew, though she could see the various trades' vans parked outside the house.

"Your garden is speeding along, too. When do you think you'll finish?"

"Most of it this week, hopefully."

Sherry's face dropped. "Oh," she said blankly, and then she straightened. "I thought you would be here longer."

"I will be. I'm here until Christmas, house-sitting. I'm hoping Kell's work will be finished by then so that I can help with his garden."

Sherry fiddled with her wedding ring. "We couldn't help noticing, Vix and I, that he likes you. He doesn't look at you like you're a new toy he hasn't quite decided to try out. He listens to you. Vix told me not to interfere, but I've known Kell since I was in primary school. I love him. He's my family, but he's not like Jay and Luke. Jay is totally confident of himself and what he is doing. He always was. Luke is a family man and a good father. Kell is a loner. He thinks he has to be self-sufficient."

"Is that a bad thing to be?"

"No. Vix was right. I shouldn't have said anything. It's just that Kell is determined to be everything his father wasn't—you know, responsible, successful, and in control. That doesn't leave him much time to laugh, is all."

Calli reached out and squeezed Sherry's hand. "Like the rest of us, he'll laugh when he finds time. That's an enormous job he's doing next door while he's also working at his nine-to-five job. I don't know how he finds time to blink."

"Could you ask him to go to a movie or something? He never relaxes."

Calli shrugged. "We don't have that sort of relationship." And she sat staring at Sherry because she didn't know what sort of relationship she had with Kell. He helped her, she helped him, but no money changed hands. She used him for sex. He didn't mind. In fact, he seemed quite happy with that, but he hadn't made another date to see her, which meant that he would either drop by when he could or that he didn't want a date with her. Then again, if he was a loner, he wouldn't make dates. He would let dates find him, which seemed to happen. Emily had turned up without a qualm for a lunch, not knowing if he had other plans. "I'll think about it. Now, do you want to see my garden?"

After she had taken Sherry for a quick tour, she thought about Sherry's proposition and decided against asking Kell to go to a movie. If he wanted her, he would have to make the effort. She was no maiden waiting to be rescued. She had almost turned her life around and would, once she had consolidated her finances and found another couple of jobs. A man was the last thing she needed at this time. She had proved herself able to manage her sparse finances. She had proved she could keep on track. She had proved herself capable of independence.

She didn't need to prove herself worthy of love. Been there, done that, and all she had proved was that some other woman was always more worthy than she.

* * * *

Kell arrived back at the house that night after spending the day inspecting a couple of old kitchens for women who wanted a new ones, and one for a family who had begun to build an addition to their house. He planned to draw up his measurements tonight and work out the pricing for his quotes.

First, he bounded up the stairs to see the progress Luke had made on the bathrooms. Trent had built the walls that allowed for the two new en suites, making five good-sized rooms into one large bedroom and three smaller. The upstairs plumbing had been finished and the waterproofing applied to dry out overnight. Sometime next week, the bathroom tiling would begin.

Luke had chosen the tiles and the fixtures. That was his specialty. Kell opened the boxes to check his brother's choices. Each bathroom would feature white gloss subway tiles and stone-colored floors, a good neutral, suits-everyone plan. The more people the house suited, the higher the bargaining. Jay had raced through the plans for the extension. After the approval of the building inspector, the downstairs plumbing would begin.

Kell paced back to the kitchen where Trent stood chugging down a beer. "Don't look at me like that. I'm having one for courage."

Kell planted his hands on his hips. "Emily's not all *that* scary."

"Maybe not for you because you're not interested in a relationship with her. When you find the woman of your dreams, you might understand nerves, buddy. Rejection is hard to swallow and this might be my last chance."

Kell leaned against the doorway and adopted a smile smug enough to irritate Trent. Old habits died hard.

With a puff of disgust, Trent turned away to put his empty bottle in the bin. "You don't ask women for dates. You let them ask you, and Calli is never gonna. And there she is day after day alone in that cottage. Why don't you take her out tonight? Do the lady a favor." He faced Kell.

Kell lowered his chin and stared at Trent for a few seconds before he indicated absolutely nothing, he hoped. He strolled into the bedroom and sat on the side of his camper bed, legs apart, elbows on knees, and his chin in his palms. Without a doubt, if he went to Calli and said, *let's get naked* he would be in with a good chance.

He had no illusions about himself. He could please a woman in bed. He could also pass as a relatively silent handbag for the women who invited him to various functions from work dinners to weddings. He passed because of his looks, and he didn't hang around because he had nothing to say to these women who preferred him not to mention he was a cabinetmaker with his own small business.

"It sounds as if you're trying to get more work, Kell," one woman told him as an excuse, because he knew that wasn't true. She was simply ashamed to be with a man who wouldn't impress her friends with his money or his glib tongue.

In truth, he was little more than a gigolo. He wasn't very interesting. He wasn't educated or the life of the party. He was introspective and boring. Women didn't see past his looks. His policy had always been not to get too close or he would feel insignificant. Calli was bright and beautiful. She wouldn't be interested in him if she knew him out of bed.

He, in fact, knew more about rejection than Trent, starting with his father and continuing throughout his life. One day he would be successful enough to impress the sort of woman he would want to impress. If Calli could wait for five years, he would have enough money to support her in the style she would expect, though of course by then, she would have happily married someone suitable from her social circle of private schools and wealthy successful parents. He sat staring into space, afraid to ask her for a date, afraid to start a relationship that had no future.

Finally Trent left after a moody, "Hope I don't see you until tomorrow morning."

"Good luck," Kell called after him, rising to his feet.

He needed a meal before he started on his pricing. His books and pencils in hand, he walked to the stark uninteresting kitchen that would soon be the focal point of the house, and opened the fridge, seeing nothing but Calli opening her fridge in her lonely kitchen. With a "what the heck?" moment of resignation, he tossed his books onto the old tiled countertop, and pulled his phone from his back pocket. He would have her any way he could for as long as he could.

Finding her number, he texted, *Want to go to the pub for dinner?*

Who's paying?

He laughed. *The cabinetmaker.* And then he smacked his head with his palm. He should have said something light-hearted rather stating his lowly trade.

The gardener is ravenous. I'll be ready in 5.

"This is a lovely surprise," she said five minutes later, standing in the doorway of the cottage. She looked beautiful in her form-fitting black slacks, a loose rusty colored shirt, and black-and-white high-heeled shoes. Very feminine and very smart.

He wanted to grab her into his arms and walk her backwards into her bedroom. "The one thing we have in common is a need to eat a few times per day."

"Idiot." She pulled the door closed behind her as she stepped out the doorway, tucked her bag under her arm, and tilted her head to kiss him, a light kiss, a friendly kiss, and the kiss of a woman who liked him. "We have far more in common than that."

He could have grabbed her and given her a real kiss, but tonight would be a test of whether she liked him or whether she merely wanted him for his body.

Naturally he couldn't take a woman like her to a greasy suburban hotel, so he drove into the city. His luck was in, and he found a park a few paces away from a new boutique pub Vix had mentioned a few weeks ago. The building had been renovated a few years ago, the old wood floors sanded and polished. A marble-topped bar in front of shelves of glasses stood parallel to the front door. The trendily dressed patrons either sat on stools at the bar or at the scrubbed wooden tables in front.

Farther inside, where he led Calli, the place opened out to a dining room with the same wooden tables and comfortable black upholstered chairs. Apparently, local artists decorated the walls. The paintings looked interesting, one depicting Napoleon with a bow and arrow and his foot on a supine giraffe.

"Choose where you want to sit," he said to Calli who led the way past various patrons to the back.

A waiter followed them with a carafe of water, glasses, and a menu. A woman at a nearby table called *hi* to Calli, who smiled and wiggled her fingers back. "If this is one of your usual spots, it's amazing we haven't met before," she said to Kell. "I used to come here a lot."

"It's my first time," he answered, half-pleased she already liked the place and half-disgruntled if that meant she might keep seeing people she knew. "So, tell me what you recommend on the menu."

"Anything. I'll have a Thai salad."

"What about wine?"

"I'll have a glass if you do. If not, water is fine."

He ordered a steak and wine. Another woman came over and kissed Calli on the cheek. She said, "Glad you're back," and gave him a very significant glance.

After a few pleasantries, she left. Calli's smile at him was full of mischief. "I think you're about to fill my social calendar for me. She only came over to find out who you are." Her phone started to ring. Frowning, she began a search of her bag. "Sorry. I didn't mean to bring it with me." She glanced at the number and turned off the phone. "My sister again. She seems to know when I'm with someone. I'll call her back later. Now, I hear from Sherry that your bathrooms are almost ready to be tiled."

"The guys will start on the main bathroom next week."

"What sort of tiles have you chosen?"

"Luke brought along the usual. White subway for the walls and stone for the floors." He frowned. "Why?"

"Although I haven't worked as an interior designer, I have a few design contacts. Your house is Tudor on the outside, but you have art deco ceiling roses and cornices. I think it would be a shame not to build on the theme you already have."

"I was going with the vintage look."

"That's certainly trending for new builds." She gave him a dubious glance.

"You're saying vintage wouldn't suit Tudor?" He leaned back, staring at her with a crease between his eyebrows.

She shrugged. "Your house was built in the early twenties. The bathrooms would look wonderful in a modern art deco style. You can see that in the cornices you have in your downstairs rooms. You could show that upstairs with glossy white and black, and with the tiling. Modern, but themed."

"And you think I should use black or white cabinetry in the bathrooms?"

"Not necessarily. I'll find you some pictures on my phone."

After a few minutes of thumbing, she passed him her phone. "In these bathrooms, they've used black and white, but look at the tiling. Most of the tiles are tiny and intricate. The gray coin marble on the floor of the top picture looks pretty classy. Also that basket cut marble. This bathroom is gray and white. And see this one with blue walls? A pure color looks pretty fantastic with the black and white, or gray and white, and paint color is easy to change. You might want green, or red, or pink."

"And a similar design in the kitchen? I was going to tile the floors in the kitchen for easy cleaning and use the recycled jarrah for the extension. And match this with reused wood cabinetry. What do you think?"

She made a wry face. "I would keep a hardwood floor throughout the house. That with black and white would be appropriate."

He tapped his fingers on the table. The bathrooms she had shown him were spectacular, and his business brain told him the edgy tiling would cost very little more while having a far greater impact. "You're not just a pretty face, are you?"

"I'd settle for that, though." She gave him a hopeful smile.

"I wouldn't want you to settle for anything. I would want you to have exactly what you want." He held her gaze, knowing he really meant that.

She drew a deep breath. "In the case of your kitchen and bathroom, you must make the choice. I'm only suggesting you emphasize the integrity of your house's past."

"Integrity. That's a word I rarely consider when talking about making a profit." He drummed his fingers on the table, knowing he gave customers the kitchens they wanted rather than making suggestions that might cost them less.

She looked incredulous, which pleased him. "You're a perfectionist. Integrity is your middle name."

"Calli! Why didn't you tell me you were back?" A well-presented fair-headed woman about Calli's age leaned down and gave Calli a smothering hug. Then, grabbing Calli's hands in hers, she crouched beside Calli's seat to talk to her on the same level. "I keep calling your parents, but they won't say a word, other than you would let them know when you return. And your mother promised to tell me." Then she glanced at Kell. "I don't want to break into your date. Give me your new phone number."

Calli considered the request for some seconds. She locked her gaze with Kell's for a moment. "I've only been back for an hour or two. I have your number on my phone. I'll call you, and then you'll have my number. Maggie Masterson, meet Kell Dee."

Maggie straightened, smiled at Kell, and said, "She's been a bad girl. A very good friend, who happens to be me, has some stupendous news she wants to share and she hasn't been able to talk to her for *two months*. Where on earth have you been? Croatia?"

"Not quite as far as that. What's the news?"

Maggie held up her left hand, her fingers splayed. "Engaged. Yes, to Drew. And I'm having the official party next Saturday night. You have to be there, Calli. I can't celebrate without you. Bring a date, or not, but come. It's too late to send an invitation, but I'll send the details via the phone. You have to come."

"I will."

"I want you to be one of my bridesmaids as well, but we'll talk about that. I have to go. We just stopped in for a quick drink."

"I'm glad you found me in time." Calli stood and hugged and kissed her friend, who left in a tangle of scarves and goodbyes. When Calli glanced at Kell, she had glossy eyes. "I didn't think about anyone but me and my problems for a very long time. I think she brought me back to reality. Do you want to be my date for the engagement party or should I find someone else?"

"Don't even consider that," he said in a growly voice. "If you're sleeping with me, you're dating me. Those two things go together."

"You mean if I don't date you, I don't get sex?"

He had a moment of taking her seriously and his heart thumped. "Isn't that the way a relationship normally goes?" he asked, his face stiff.

"I don't know that I've ever had a healthy relationship with a man. I have dated men that I rarely had sex with, and I have supported men that have sex with other women. If I date you as well as have sex with you, I'm liable to take our relationship a little seriously. Is that what you want? I had the impression that you don't want to get too close to me."

"I couldn't get closer than naked."

Her phone chimed and she shook her head. "That's what happens when a conversation starts getting interesting. I'll turn it off. One moment." She scrabbled around in her bag and pulled out the lit-up phone. "My sister again. Oh, no. Now she's sent a text. She says to pick up the call because it's urgent. Do you mind?"

"Go ahead."

She pressed reply. "This had better be urgent, Tiggy. I'm at the Toz waiting for a meal." She listened and then her face froze. "Is he okay?"

She sat very still, her forehead propped on her closed fist. "Yes...yes...yes...he would be devastated. I'm with someone. We'll eat, and then I'll come over. Maybe an hour." She ended the call.

She lifted her head and stared at him. "My sister-in-law was killed in a car accident this afternoon. The family is rallying around my brother. He is with my sister and our parents at their house. My brother will be heartbroken. He was madly in love with Mercia. She was his whole life. I need to be there for him, too." Her expression looked pleading.

"Do you want to leave right now?" he asked. For sure, he would lose his appetite if either of his sisters-in-law had been killed.

She thought for a moment before she shook her head. "We've ordered. If you don't mind, though, I would like you to drop me off right after we've eaten. It won't be out of your way. In fact, my parents' house is on our way home. St. Peters." She picked up her wine and drank the rest in her glass. "Dutch courage. I haven't seen my family since before I took the judge's job. I swore I wouldn't until I had earned enough money to salve my pride, and I haven't until I have paid back my father. That won't be for at least another few months, and only if I get a design job after this one. So, I won't be running home a success after all."

"I'm betting they couldn't care less."

"You're right. They don't. I do. I think you're the same, trying to prove yourself to yourself. It's a human failing."

He thought about that after he dropped her off at the front of a gracious two-story Georgian home built on one side of a double block.

Yes, he had spent a lifetime trying to prove to himself that a man with his background could have a work ethic second to none.

Chapter 12

A purring furry head snuggled under Kell's chin. He automatically made accommodation for the soft little feline in his camper bed, a vague thought wandering through his half-awake mind that his window was open, and he fell asleep again. Sometime later, he heard a car crunching down Calli's driveway, and he knew she was safely back.

In the morning, the cat was nothing but a memory, and Kell left early for work. The earlier he started, the earlier he could return to begin on the extra tasks in the house. Trent could have the new extension walls built in a week, as soon as Kell had the go-ahead. In the meantime, Kell could prepare the floorboards he had salvaged and measure out the rafters. His days would be full, with scant time to be with the woman who occupied his constant thoughts.

He dropped by to see Calli when he arrived home a little after four. The cat bounded up the path to greet him with a yowl, and walked her front paws up his shin. He lifted her to face height so that she could inspect him and then he tucked her under his arm while staring at beautiful Calli who strode toward him, her eyes big and sad. Apparently the funeral arrangements would need to be delayed because of the coroner. "Next Wednesday," she told him, holding his upper arm lightly, and placing her forehead on his shoulder.

"Do you want me to go with you?" he said, his hand slowly rubbing the back of her neck.

She shook her head. "But thanks for offering. Do you want to stay tonight?"

He nodded and wrapped his arms around her. She needed him, and that was a warming thought. The cat struggled out of the embrace, bounding onto the ground, but Kell kept Calli in his arms, resting his face against her soft hair. "But I can't. I'll be plastering in the upstairs rooms until midnight." He kissed the tip of her nose. She smelled of lavender and sunshine. "I don't want to wake you."

"If you need help, say so. I'm not bad with a broom, and I can paint."

"But can I afford you?"

She laughed and reached up her face to kiss him on the mouth. "Some things are free. I won't be here most of Wednesday. I have to go home early to change for the funeral. All my proper clothes are in storage at my parent's house. And then Ma is catering after the funeral. If you want to make a date with me for Wednesday night, I'll be able to offer you leftovers. My mother is a habitual over-caterer."

She spoke the truth. Her haul after the funeral included Greek pastries, a large bowl of salad, keftedes, an untouched dish of moussaka, and a basket of shortbreads. He stayed the night and he wished he could be with her every single night for the rest of his misbegotten life. He loved the softness of her skin, he loved the fragrance of her hair, and he adored the sensual expression on her face while he made love to her. Each time he left her bed seemed harder than the time before.

He couldn't be in love after knowing her for not much more than a month, but somehow his heart had made a space that expanded each time he saw her.

The next day, while buying new folders for his files in his lunch break, he grabbed up a newspaper, too. Normally he only read the football pages but while he idly bit into a Greek pastry back at the works, he flicked past the politics and a story about a young family with a sick child. Then a half page photo of mourners outside a city church stopped him. With funerals on his mind, he began to skim through the narrative.

Mercia Allbrook, wife of Hagen Allbrook, died on impact when her car hit a tree on Strathalbyn Road. Allbrook. Frowning, he quickly scanned the photo and saw an almost unrecognizable Calli—Calliope Allbrook dressed in black and wearing one of those big hats that women wore to the races, with a pair of sunglasses hiding her face. Nothing hid her graceful posture, the clean line of her haircut, or the curve of her cheek that he knew so well. He put the paper on his knee, his head spinning. Calli Opey. Calliope. *Allbrook.*

He sat perfectly still, filled with dread and with a kind of sadness, a loss of hope.

He could aspire to marry the daughter of wealthy parents, but the Allbrooks were more than wealthy. They numbered on the rich list, not at the top, but there, nonetheless. He was a tradesman and always would be, not an architect like his brother.

At Jay's house, Kell had mentioned her family's company and she had not said a word. She could have spoken then, although he would have looked like a fool if she had done so at that time. Knowing his aspirations, she should have told him who she was later. Had she tried? He rubbed his forehead. Not that he recalled. She said she'd been used before for her money. Clearly she didn't intend the same thing to happen again. Apparently she didn't trust the man she had been sleeping with not to take advantage of his relationship with her.

He couldn't remember having ever met the families of his dates. That would imply a relationship and he couldn't say he had ever had one until this past month with Calli, but he knew and she knew that a cabinetmaker didn't fit into an Allbrook's social calendar any more than his trade had suited most of his other dates. Had he known she was an Allbrook, he wouldn't have touched her, but he had and now he had to pay for wanting a woman so badly that he had taken her, losing his sense of self-preservation in the process.

Within the next couple of months, he and she would finish up in this area. Until then, he would take as much of her as he could get. He hadn't had that same chance before he had lost his mother to breast cancer and his father to drink.

Now older and harder, he knew that no matter how little a person could have of someone he loved, that would have to suffice him forevermore.

* * * *

Kell was the perfect escort for Maggie's engagement party. Not only did he look jaw droppingly fabulous in dark trousers and a tan striped shirt, but he took the time to learn the names of her friends and their friends, and he stuck to her side. He didn't ogle other women, and he didn't get loud with drink. She had never been so proud to be with a man in her whole life.

Not knowing whether to introduce him as a cabinetmaker or as a neighbor, she chose the former, which might boost his business. All her friends were either married now or about to be, and would need referrals to a good tradesman some time or other.

She couldn't count on the fingers of both hands how many times she was asked if he was *the one,* and she could only say she needed to wait and see, but of course she already knew she was hopelessly stuck on him. Unlike his predecessors, he was smart and hard working. Her parents would be proud of her if they knew, after the poor choices she had made previously, but she couldn't build up their hopes of her finally settling down. Although she thought Kell was the one, she had assumed the others were, too. But none of them happened to love her. Kell also hadn't mentioned the L word.

"You have a fan," he said to her in the car as he drove home through the swishing rain. "While you were doing your girl-hugs, an older woman sidled up to me and told me she has known you since you were very young and you're one of her favorite people."

"Was that Maggie's mother?"

"No, you introduced me to her mother. This woman was a bit shorter than you with gray hair. Nice looking. She said you were a good catch."

She tilted up nose. "I hope you told her that I have other attributes."

"I told her that you are perfect, and in fact the woman of my dreams, the sort of friend who'll help sand down a wall so that she can help paint it." He gave a casual laugh, a throwaway laugh that said the opposite.

She ran her tongue across her lips. "Couldn't you have said something more romantic?"

"More romantic than you being the woman of my dreams?"

"You have a point."

"She mumbled something about working toward a common goal and then she disappeared."

"You should have pointed her out. I would love to know *whose* favorite person I might be." And then she shut her mouth.

She couldn't expect Kell to return her feelings. She knew he liked her, but love was a whole different bunch of roses. Most people didn't fall in love over incidentals like good sex, laughing at the same jokes, and liking the way the other person kissed. Or because their cat had fallen in love with that person. More than likely, she and the cat simply had a crush.

She couldn't imagine who might have said Calli was one of her favorite people and she rubbed the back of her neck, thinking. Far and Ma could easily have been invited to *pop in* on Maggie's casual engagement celebration if they had the time. Forewarned was forearmed in the case of her mother. She liked thinking Ma had heard she was Kell's dream girl, though she would be more thrilled if Kell meant what he had said. But if her parents had dropped in to see Maggie, why hadn't Calli seen them?

To find out, she drove over to visit her parents on Monday night. After a hug and a kiss, she mentioned Maggie's party.

"We did drop by." Her mother evaded her gaze. "But just for a quick moment to give Maggie our best wishes before we had to dash off to another function."

"Do you have anything to confess, like trying to find out from Maggie where I live?" Calli used a severe voice. "Because it's not a secret any longer. I've been working in Adrian Ferguson's garden, but I've finished the job, and I'm still living in his guesthouse. I only have to earn another three thousand dollars, and I will have paid back all I owe to Far. For sure, he will see the money in the next month or two."

Her mother laughed. "That's good to know, darling, but if you didn't want us to know where you were, you should have turned off the location thing in your phone."

Calli placed her fists on her hips. "You've known all along?" She frowned.

"We knew you wanted privacy. I hope you have been spending your time productively." Demi, her mother, spoke in dulcet tones.

Calli drew a deep breath. "I think I'm in love."

"In love?" Her mother grabbed her and examined her face.

Calli shrugged. "I'm sure it won't be fatal."

"Does this man love you, too?"

"I've wondered, but he hasn't said so."

"I've never heard you say 'in love' before." Her mother frowned. "Is he suitable?"

"Not at all. He's the son of an alcoholic from the wrong side of the tracks. And even worse, he wants a job with you." She aimed her words at her silent father. "But if he gets one and he finds out I'm your daughter, he'll think I used my influence. He's a very proud self-made man. He would then refuse the job and dump me."

"You can't know that." Her mother lifted her eyebrows.

"Oh, yes I can. I can tell by every favor he refuses, how he makes sure he gives more than he receives. He never wants to be beholden to anyone."

Her father frowned. "So, he doesn't know who you are? Is that a way to start a relationship?"

"I didn't know I was going to fall for him," Calli said indignantly. "He thought I was a boy. That wasn't a very promising start."

"You'd best tell him the truth."

"Then he'll never apply for a job with you."

"Stalemate, Calli, but I still think you ought to tell him the truth. Are you going to tell us who he is?"

"I don't doubt you could find out if you want to." She kissed her father on the cheek and gathered up her bag, ready to leave.

She gave her father's advice some consideration in the car on the way home before deciding that if Kell didn't love her, he didn't ever need to know she was an Allbrook. Then he could apply for whatever job he chose without worrying about his pride. She would be nothing but the gardener next door with whom he'd had a pleasant fling until *surprise, surprise, who would have guessed*?

During the week, having finished the judge's garden, she had time to find casual employment without worrying about her surname, which she did with comparative ease. On Tuesday she began her first gardening job.

"Two hundred dollars a day," she said to Kell, waving a wad of cash under his nose when she popped in to see his progress on his house after she had finished work for the day. "Not bad. I can take you out for dinner."

He grabbed her and hugged her tight. She knew he liked her a lot, but that would never be enough for her. Of course, she would be shattered if he didn't return her love, but she was willing to give him until the judge returned to see how perfect they were for each other. Her cat wanted him as much as she did.

By the end of the week, the electrician had rewired Kell's house, minus the final details, and the tiler finished his three upstairs bathrooms, the main with gray marble coin flooring and gray subway tiles. He used the same flooring in the guest en suite with white tiles on the walls. The pièce de résistance was the master bathroom featuring gray and black basket-weave mosaic marble flooring and black railway tiles on the walls. With all the baths and basins white and all the fixtures bronze, the effect was dramatically art deco and elegant.

Downstairs, the new extension had been approved and Trent hammered in the joists for the floor. Over the weekend, Kell and Trent built the rafters. During the week, Trent added the flooring and the roof tiles. Calli watched the installation of the bank of glass doors at the back, plotting the plants she would want in view. Kell finished polishing the upstairs floors. The end was now in clear sight.

After the walls for the downstairs laundry were erected, only waterproofing remained until Kell had his new half bathroom and laundry. He worked into the night during that next week and she desperately wanted to help him, if only to see him, but he had nothing for her to do but sweep, which of course she did.

However, he deconstructed his old kitchen the next week, which worked in her favor, because Trent finally decided to move in with Emily. Although he could have a hot shower now, he couldn't manage without somewhere to prepare meals, or so he said. Emily, apparently, had fallen as hard for him as he had for her. Calli couldn't have been more delighted. Trent had been caught from the start, and he deserved an A for persistence.

"You couldn't say a P," Kell said. "Since that would be a bathroom reference and after he went without for so long…" He grinned.

"I'm sure you can't cope without a kitchen either, so you could move in with me," Calli said to Kell, clinging onto his arm and kissing his stubbly cheek.

"That'd mean I would be living off the judge. Not cool, Calli."

She sighed, having heard clear confirmation of the pride she had described to her parents. Not for a moment had she expected him to agree. She turned on the coffee machine. Today she had done a full day's casual laboring in a nearby garden. "I was offered a design job today, too, off the street. Kerin Haslam, a woman who walks past daily, asked me to do some planting in her garden, too. How about that?"

"I'm not surprised. The judge's place is a great advertisement for you. I hope you make mine look half as good."

"Half? I don't do anything by halves."

"I know. We'll soon be ready to start my garden. The construction is finished and as soon as the inside is done, we can do the outside."

"I'm starting on Mrs. Haslam's garden as soon as she approves my plans. I only need to finish the drawings, and I can do that tonight while you're sanding your upstairs floors."

"I'll be prepping for a few more days before I'm ready to sand, but as soon as we've eaten tonight, I'll make a start. Then I'll move into the small bedroom upstairs while I polish the downstairs floors."

"Takeaway pizza?"

"You order, and I'll get it." He left after they had eaten. Rather than watch television with Hobo, she helped Kell pull the old carpet nails out of the floors until her knees refused to click one more time. He kissed her goodnight and went on with the work. Trent now only worked during the daytime.

In the morning, she dropped her design plans into her prospective client's letterbox. The next day she started ordering pavers, sand, laborers, and plants. During the previous week of sunny summer days, and with Christmas looming, the judge's garden had hardened off the new growth. The roses had their first showing during spring and had already developed the next the plump buds. The salvias, geraniums, dog's bane, lavenders, Mexican sage, and Felicia still bloomed in a swathe of blues and purples among the silver foliage of the Artemesia. The pinks hovered, waiting for their big moment.

The judge's pool glimmered sparkling blue, his fountain twinkled in the sunshine, and the spent plants had been removed from the vegetable garden. Spinach glistened in the sun. Tiny peaches and apricots had already formed on the fruit trees. Bees hummed through the air, and butterflies flittered erratically from leaf to flower. She needed to plant Kell's garden before the summer heat turned scorching.

"Could you cut down all the shrubby rubbish in your front garden this weekend? I'll need to get a start on the soil and the plotting," she said to Kell, after he had crawled into bed with her that night. The light from the moon slitted through the blinds. Hobo, her creamy pale coat rippling with health, sprang onto Calli's pillow and snuggled between her chin and shoulder while purring into Calli's ear. Neither she nor the cat could have been happier, sleeping with Kell most nights.

"I don't expect you to do the garden." He rolled to face her and with a single finger he pushed her hair back behind her ears as if to see her better. "You have more than enough to do. Our deal was for a plan."

"And then you would pay someone to work on my plan?"

He kissed her chin. "I suppose."

"Pay me then. I'll give you mate's rates. I'll work on your garden during weekends once you have cleared the area. Hobo will be thrilled. She'll be able to see you more often."

"Are you planning on keeping her?"

"What else could I do? She must have adopted me for some reason."

He considered. "I wonder where she came from?"

"She'll never tell, but the vet said that judging by the condition of her paws, she had travelled a long way."

"To find you." His breath whispered on her cheek. "Where will you go when the judge comes back?"

Her heart dropped. She had to face the fact that soon she would have to leave Kell—but not quite yet, not for a couple of weeks. By then, she could be bored with his conversation, tired of wonderful sex, and anxious to be alone. "I don't know. I might move in with my sister for a while. Where will you go?"

"I'll stay in the house until it sells, and then I'll move back into my caravan. I have a spot at the warehouse reserved. When I have the money, I'll buy another renovator's delight, but for me."

Three weeks was all she had left with him, three weeks until Christmas day. She longed to ask if he planned to continue their relationship, but she couldn't face a question whose answer she might not be able to bear. Best not to know, and enjoy the relationship while she could. She didn't intend to be one of those women who waited and waited for a proposal. Her own mind was made up, and she would marry him on the spot, but if he loved her as much as she loved him, he would *want to* marry her instantly.

Her friend Maggie waited four years for a proposal. That was right for her, but not for Calli. By now she knew she had never been in love before. The men who hadn't loved her had never given her these feelings of desperation, the longing to see them, the great warmth inside when she did, or the smile she wore when she was expecting Kell to arrive home from work.

Whatever money or property woes she and Kell had could be solved together. If he didn't see this, if he didn't love her so deeply that he wanted her no matter what, he didn't love her enough. And perhaps he didn't.

She might be another Hobo to him, for all she knew, simply a stray to be nurtured.

* * * *

Kell straightened and leaned back, his palms pressing on the small of his back as he watched Calli crawl around on her hands and knees joining the rolls of sod they had almost finished laying. Trent brought another barrow-load from the front where the grass had been dumped early this morning. "That's the last. I'm ready for a nice cold bottle of beer."

"I'm looking forward to sitting for a while." Emily had also come along today with Trent to help finish the garden. She had wanted to look at the inside of the house, but Kell didn't have time for a tour, not yet.

Laying the green lawn front and back was the final task. He kicked, and the new section slowly unrolled to the red brick garden border. Calli scooted along on her knees to join the edges while Trent dumped another roll and Emily walked the sod flat.

Calli and Emily had evaded each other's gazes for a while after Emily had turned up, but either something had been said that Kell hadn't heard or they had conceded to working instead of letting a tense atmosphere ruin the day. Now after three hours of working together, they were as pleased with each other as two women could be. "Emily, if you want to sit, you could get into your car and drive down to Mama's on Portrush Road," Calli said, her face serious. "I ordered lunch and it will be ready to pick up."

"Where do we plan to eat? On Kell's beautiful new shiny floor?" Emily sounded reluctant.

"Next door, in my place. I've got the table set up there."

"Okay," Emily said, rising to her feet. "I'm feeling a bit old after all this physical work. The rest of you are used to it, but I normally work inside an air conditioned building."

She left and Calli began watering in the new lawn at the front of the house while Kell and Trent barrowed and spread the spare soil over the joins at the back. Grassing the front garden had taught them the routine Calli clearly knew so well.

This final touch of green made Kell want to stand back and enjoy the view. He and Trent had paved the patio with herringbone reclaimed red brick, old fashioned, but in keeping with the design of the house. The new wide front path had also been herringboned and with the lawn on either side and the iceberg roses along the red brick fence, the garden looked plain, neat, and strangely right. Trent had also added some fancy brickwork to the low front fence, copying a pattern of herringbone twist Calli had shown him on a picture of Hampton Palace, an old Tudor house in England. Between the pillars sat plain iron railing in dark gray. Calli knew her design.

The back garden was another matter, lushly planted with a rainbow of colors along the new gray fence. A big old elm had been kept in the middle of the lawn but the rest of the trees had gone with the chainsaw. Kell had painted the window frames to match the fence iron. The front door was pale aqua blue, and the diamond-patterned leadlight sparkling in the top of the windows looked perfect.

Other than the last painting of the walls downstairs, only the kitchen inside remained waiting to be installed. Strange, that. The cabinets had been ready for a couple of weeks, but Kell had a childhood hangover he had never been able to shake. *Leave the best for last.*

By the time Emily returned with lunch, a sprinkler had been set on the back lawn and everyone was ready for a break. Calli led the way to her cottage next door where they could comfortably eat the chicken and prawn salad she had ordered last night.

When Trent and Emily clicked together the small bottles of ice-cold beer Calli had taken from her fridge, Kell sat up straighter. The couple had been strangely jubilant this morning.

"Are you going to tell, or am I?" Emily glanced at Trent.

"You."

"I've quit my job, and I've found another one in Sydney." Emily gave a little hitch to her shoulders and a bolstering smile at the persistent, hard-working, easygoing bricklayer who had made sure Kell reached his goal. "I'm leaving with Trent when he goes after Christmas."

Without Trent and his patience, Kell would be renovating his house until the middle of next year. He reached over and ruffled Trent's hair, delighted for his friend. "Good news, buddy."

"We're getting engaged," Emily said, staring at her bare ring finger. "Probably not until June or July, though."

"If you don't mind." Calli rose to her feet. "I must kiss the happy couple." Trent being the nearest, she kissed him first, and without any hesitation she kissed Emily. "He's the best. You are a lucky girl." She collected the used plates and stacked them in the kitchen, her smile somewhat wan.

Kell covered her unusual behavior by talking about places he would like to live in Sydney, and listening to speculation about how busy the set design business would keep Trent. Trent decided that he would show Emily over the renovated house before the couple left to spend the afternoon with Emily's parents, who apparently knew and approved of goofy Trent.

"You need a dripper system for the garden now." Calli sat at the table again after watching Trent and Emily walk down the driveway.

"I'm pretty well on budget, so I'll buy the makings and put the system together during the week. Why the lack of enthusiasm about Trent's good news?"

"I wanted her to love him as much as he ought to be loved," she said, her voice fierce.

"How do you know she doesn't?"

"She's made plans to make a plan to marry him. Engaged in six months? Why not married in six months? If I thought someone wanted to put off marrying me for years, I wouldn't consider him as a partner. I would go on my merry way. I want much more than a tepid relationship."

And so did he. With her, his relationship had been anything but tepid. Flaming hot, would describe their interactions. He rubbed the back of his neck while he considered the passion in her tone. This woman didn't want half of anything. She worked in her gardens with the same passion that she showed when she made love to him. She plotted, certainly, but if her design didn't quite work how she saw it in her head, she had no hesitation in moving plants again and again until her mind picture satisfied her. Nothing but the best was good enough for her, and he wasn't that by any means.

"You deserve nothing less," he said, keeping his voice tight to cover his hopelessness. And then the damned cat leaped onto his lap and started purring. His neck stiff and his emotions deliberately blocked, he put her onto the floor, stood, and walked to the door. "I'll move the sprinkler. You can have the rest of the afternoon off. I'll measure out the positions for the kitchen units."

"Don't you want me to hold the end of the tape?"

"I'll be okay alone." Alone. Without her.

As soon as he sold the Tudor, he would need to settle the huge mortgage he had taken out on the place. He stood to make one hundred thousand plus his own stake of one hundred thousand if he sold for a million. Two hundred thousand would never be enough to buy a house he would want to renovate for himself.

If he sold for 1.2 million, he had another two hundred thousand in his pocket, less taxes. He also had the quarter acre next door to the Tudor, which he could possibly sell for three or four hundred thousand, most of which he would have to plough into growing his business, or at least in mortgaging his own premises. The rest would get him the mortgage for an ordinary sort of house in a newer suburb, not a home he could bet Calli had been brought up to expect, and certainly not in an area commensurate with her family's position.

What he wanted more than another house to renovate, was to build his company into the biggest and the best. If he had an assured future, he would have the right to ask Calli to marry him. Maybe. He couldn't offer her less than a husband with assured potential, not an Allbrook.

At this stage, he had nothing to promise but a caravan on a concrete pad and the use of a bathroom in his workshop—unless AA & Company took over the empty plot and offered his team a place in their company, taking the bribe of him paying half the costs, which meant the land.

The rest of his life hinged on the impression he made on AA's representative.

Chapter 13

Kell's team installed his kitchen. He was his own customer, also his own designer, his own craftsman, and his own worst enemy. Glancing at patient and lately very solemn Calli, he shrugged. "What do you think?"

"The workmanship is perfect." She ran her hand over the white marble countertop, a considering expression on her face.

"Is that all?" he asked, disappointed. Normally she couldn't hold back her enthusiasm, which was another trait that endeared her to him.

"It's beautiful. I love the black cabinetry on the bottom and the white on the top. I love the cool marble countertops. I love the basket-weave splash backs. I am insanely crazy about the butler's pantry, and I think the powder room is glamorous and just right where it is."

"You talked me into putting it where it is and all the rest was your design, too." He pushed his hands deep into his pockets, disgruntled for reasons unknown.

"Which is why I couldn't praise it. I commented on your effort without which the magnificent art deco look couldn't have been accomplished half as well. All you need now is a bright color on one of the entertaining area's walls, some expert staging, and you can put the place on the market for 1.2 or 1.3 million." She shot a quick glance at him, as if expecting an argument.

He nodded. "I thought I would match the carpet color upstairs and in the formal rooms to the hardwood floors in the entertaining area."

"Good move. When's that happening?"

"As soon as I've finished painting the downstairs walls." He heaved a breath.

He had two weeks with Calli, minimum, and she wouldn't wait if he didn't love her enough to marry her instantly. She'd said those words about her dream husband and for the past few weeks, he had mulled the repeating echo. He certainly loved her enough, and right now, faced with losing her, he almost didn't give a damn about what her family might think of him aspiring to marry her. Almost, but not quite.

A small home in a working class suburb would not be enough for a woman who had been brought up with wealth, who had a university degree, and a successful and respected family. She had probably never seen an alcoholic stumbling around and kicking his children out of the way so that he could reach his next drink. She didn't know what it was like to arrive at school in dirty clothes without a lunch and to sit and watch the other kids eat.

She would want her children to have the same advantages as she'd had—clean clothes, warmth in winter, and a good education. Her children shouldn't only have the choice of a state school and a trade. Kell might never have more, and he might never make more than a living from his business. If he married Calli, he didn't want his trade causing people to wonder why she married him. And he was getting too far ahead of himself.

She had never said she loved him. Hell, she had never even mentioned she liked him, but every kiss of hers told him she did, and he knew she respected him. She had introduced him to her friends without a hint of embarrassment that he wasn't a doctor, or a lawyer, or a property developer. If she loved him…but he couldn't ask her that or to marry him, not when he couldn't offer her anything but hope.

He could only have the woman if he had the means to keep her. Drawing a deep breath, he stared at the scuffed toes of his work boots. "Would you like to live here?"

"Who wouldn't? But I couldn't afford this house on my salary."

"I can't afford it on mine, either. Its only use to me is the profit it will make. But this is the sort of house I will have one day."

"In the not-too-distant future, I would guess so, based on your work ethic."

"Work ethic?" He managed a twisted smile.

"My father brought up his kids with those two words firmly planted in their brains. We've all got one: a work ethic. We know we can't spend money we don't have and we know if we want it, we have to earn it. We had to earn our pocket money, and that drove my sister wild. She calculated to the minutest degree what she was owed, and she was never handed all she thought she deserved." She laughed. "We're twins. We look alike, but we're not at all alike. I'm the good twin, by the way."

"I wouldn't be surprised if she says that, too." Somehow, he smiled.

"She doesn't want to be good, whereas I do. Or I did. I'm not sure that's my goal now."

"Too bad. I think you're bloody perfect," he said, his tone unfortunately sincere.

She stood there, staring at him, her eyes big and glossy. "And..."

He breathed out, trying to shake off the urge to grab her into his arms and tell her he loved her. Instead, he stared through the bank of folding glass doors to the new garden beyond—Calli's garden, the garden made for him by the woman he wanted by his side for the rest of his life. "You said something about staging."

"My sister could help you with that, but she charges a fortune."

"What sort of fortune?"

"Somewhere between two and three thousand."

"Hell."

"Maybe I could wangle friend's rates for you."

"Not on your life. I pay in full or not at all."

She pursed her mouth. "I thought you might say that, but she owes me big-time."

"Then, she would be doing it for you? I would owe *you*."

"Remember that. I might want to call in the favor sometime. Shall I call her to come and take a look?"

He considered, perhaps a little too long. "At the end of the week," he said reluctantly. She gave too much, and he took too much. At this rate, he would rack up far too many lost opportunities to give more than he took when she left him. "By then I should have the kitchen finished."

"What color are you thinking of for the walls?"

"Aqua blue?"

"That would look great. Having a bit of color there will help Tiggy with her design scheme." She glanced at him as if waiting for a comment.

He nodded and busied himself. She walked off without another word.

Perhaps letting her think he was moody and impatient was all for the best. He had to have a reason for keeping out of her bed.

* * * *

At nine the next morning, a full hour after Kell should have been at work, Calli's sister stood in the doorway of the Tudor. Her eyes widened with the same surprise that his did on seeing *her*. She looked like Calli would with long blond hair in varying shades. She had the same sparse figure and the same come-and-go dimples. Her expression quickly changed into one of snooty superiority. "Nice garden. Calli's work?"

"Yes. You'll find more of her work inside." He held open the door so that she could stride past him down the hallway, past the newly carpeted stairs to the wide-open kitchen and entertaining area. She wore a pink shirt and yellow tight-fitting pants.

"I'm Kell, by the way."

"Tiggy," she said tersely. "Do you want to give me a brief?"

"Do you want to give me a price?"

She shook her head. "Calli called in a freebie."

He drew a deep breath. "Do you want me to show you around?"

"I think better alone."

And so did Kell. While Calli's terse, unfriendly sister did a tour with her notebook, he waited in the kitchen, leaning against the countertop of the kitchen island. Clearly Tiggy knew nothing about him other than he was a charity case. Since she hadn't used her surname, she had been briefed not to, which was fortunate because now was not the time for him to reveal he knew who Calli was.

Tiggy arrived back in under fifteen minutes, tucking her notebook into her bag. "Art deco. Nice. I have a few pieces I have never used before that would look great here. Calli did a good job, as usual. I hope you're not doing a job on her. If you are, I'll personally rip off your balls."

He laughed without mirth. "It runs in the family, I see."

"What does?" she said with a frown that was almost, but not quite like Calli's.

"The need to threaten me. I'm beholden to Calli, and I know that."

She faced him squarely and appeared to read the stark expression that he wished he didn't have on his face. Her eyes blinked a couple of times and she turned away, ostensibly to haul out a scrap of paper. "Next Friday," she said in a husky voice. "Your furniture will arrive at nine in the morning. You'll be doing the unloading. I'll be here at about midday to start arranging things. I'll want a couple of men to help with the heavy stuff. See you then."

As she turned to leave, Calli arrived through the back door, trailed by a bouncy Hobo. "Hey, Tiggy."

"Hey, Calli. I'm off—got a thousand things to do today. The house looks fab. Bye, Kell."

"And that was Tornado Tiggy," Calli said as her sister sped to the front door and left.

"I don't think she liked me. She threatened to rip off my balls."

Calli shook her head and angled her mouth into a half smile. "That's weird. She doesn't usually start her conversations with clients that way. What did you say to her?"

"That I am beholden to you."

She ran her tongue over her lips and gazed around the room, leaving his words to dissolve into the silence. Finally her gaze settled back onto his face. "I can't believe this is almost over," she said, as if she had papered over his ridiculously husky tone. "The judge will be back in two weeks, and I'll be gone."

"I'll be moving out next Monday for a couple of weeks when the sale sign goes up."

"It's been fun. We've both accomplished our goals. I've finished the judge's garden, and I'm almost back on my feet money-wise. You've finished this house, and you're set up for life. You'll make a mint, and you'll sell that land and…" Her evasive gaze eventually met his.

He breathed in. "And I couldn't have done this without you." The cat sat in front of him, staring and frowning.

"Not exactly this, no, but you would have done something wonderful." She traced a vein in the marble countertop with one finger.

"So, wish me luck. On Monday I'm hoping to make the greatest deal of my life. I have someone coming to look over the house, and if he likes my work—"

"Whoever it is will love your work. Those long banks of closets you made for the bedrooms are perfectly done, modern, but in keeping with the art deco theme."

"…if he likes my work, I will be recommended to a company who will take over the block next door for me. I can't run a successful business and build a house at the same time. When I sell this, I'll want to put the profits into growing my business." He jammed his hands into his pockets.

She nodded. "You'll succeed, Kell."

"It's almost over."

"We're both about to start new lives, me without a business, and you with a better one."

"I would offer you a job, but I don't have another house to renovate."

"You know who to call to do the garden when you do." She smiled lightly. "I'm off to work now. Will I see you tonight?"

His heart lurched. He could hear goodbye in her voice. "I'll be working late again," he said to her back.

* * * *

Calli wiped the sweat from her forehead. Today she only had a light gardening job, but the summer had begun with a burst and her client wanted white petunias bordering all her paths for her pre-Christmas party.

While breathing in the scent of the flowers, Calli thought over Tiggy's words to Kell, trying to make sense of them. Apparently her sister had interfered in Calli's life in some way, inferring that Kell owed her for the staging, which was ridiculous. The family had a warehouse full of furniture that Tiggy brought out to stage every project AA & Company completed. Yes, Tiggy would have to spend quite a few hours organizing that furniture, but Calli had never known her sister to be ungenerous. If asked, Calli would give gardening time to one of Tiggy's friends.

And Calli sniffled, miserable as she could be. She didn't know if another man was about to love and leave her, but she still had a week to find out. At least Kell had showed how much he enjoyed her, unlike the others. She had never had a relationship like this one, where she knew she was head over heels, but too darned defensive to say so.

That night, he popped in to have coffee with her, but the conversation ended with him rising to his feet after one last pat of Hobo's head. Apparently, Kell preferred to sleep alone in his camper bed in the smallest bedroom of the house next door than with Calli. At least their conversations never trailed off and at least he didn't stare into the distance when she spoke. Mentally, she still interested him. He still continued to smile as if he liked her and didn't find her the world's greatest bore. He had lovely manners if nothing else.

During the week, she saw him, and he waved, but he seemed not to have a whole lot of time to spare, which certainly rang true. On Monday morning, he expected an early morning visit from the land agent who would give him an estimate of the price he might expect for the house, which he had prepared for sale.

Calli gave the house one last inspection, too—twitching a few cushions and lifting a speck of dirt from the carpet near the front door. And now she expected him to move out. She had experienced men walking out on her before and the other times she had been impatient and had insisted on saying the goodbye words. This time, she let the situation drift. If she had to end things with him, she would waft off with her best smile.

Kell would never know she had hoped for more. Her pride insisted on that.

Chapter 14

Kell packed his bags into his car on Monday morning. He didn't plan to move back in the Tudor until after the inspection from the man he had let Calli presume was a land agent.

The man was not a land agent and not Andrew Simmons, the project manager at AA & Company with whom he had worked a few times, but her brother, Hagen Allbrook, the business manager of the company. Kell had been told on Friday to expect him at around eight in the morning rather than Andrew.

Kell made a determined effort not to let his nerves get the better of him. He had no idea why the plan had been changed, the change made him twice as determined to remain cool and calm. If Calli knew about this, she was a better actress than he could possibly have imagined. He stood in his new kitchen, leaning against the marble countertop, hearing a car pull up outside. The car door slammed shut. Footsteps paced up the path—leather-soled shoes. The doorknocker was used abruptly for the first time. He strode to the door to let in the man who held all Kell's hopes in his decision. If Hagen offered Kell's company a position with AA & Company, Kell would be able to offer Calli his heart.

"Kell Dee." He gave a firm smile and shook Hagen's hand.

"Hagen Allbrook. I know you were expecting Andrew, but he snapped up the offer of a job in his hometown, Brisbane—leaving us without a project manager for the time being." Hagen paused. "The front garden is excellent. Your design?"

Kell shook his head. "The neighbor's work."

Hagen gave a terse nod. Tall and fair, he had eyes as blue and cold as a glacier, dead eyes. Barely widowed a month, he clearly hadn't taken time to mourn.

Kell led him to the kitchen, indicating the cabinetry. "This is my work." He stood, his back stiff while Hagen opened a drawer and watched the steady slide and the silent closing. He checked a door, inside and out, and the fittings inside the cupboards, the pantry shelves, the precision of the banks of drawers.

"Very nice," he said in a voice that sounded remote. "Show me a bathroom."

Kell led the man upstairs into the master bedroom that Tiggy had styled in black and white, with a high black-padded headboard against the burgundy accent wall. Three cushions sat in a squared off group, one burgundy, one orange, and one patterned black and white, on a bed covered with a white bedspread dressed with a black turned back quilt.

Hagen stopped at the bank of closets and ran his hand over the polished wood. "Your work, too?"

Kell nodded. "I reused and built up the original wardrobe doors from the house because of the inlaid art deco design. For the other bedrooms, I modified the design, but it complements these. Inside this room, I built his and hers sections totally separate."

Hagen said nothing as he opened each door, checking out the jeweler lock-up and the slide of the shoe racks, and then he entered the en suite bathroom where Kell had installed a makeup drawer and plenty more shelves and cupboards. The man checked the work in the other three bedrooms in total silence. Finally, Hagen's gaze met his. "Shall we take a seat downstairs?"

Kell hid his apprehension behind a confident smile, leading the way to the now furnished sitting room at the front of the house. With Calli's help, and his muscle, Tiggy had surpassed all expectations using a fan-shaped sofa in black and two matching white armchairs. Where she would have found art deco seating, he couldn't imagine. With his latte carpets and a few framed black-and-white posters of old movies on the gray walls, the room was the epitome of sophistication.

For a moment Hagen frowned at the furnishings, but he sat in one armchair while Kell sat in the other, leaning forward.

Hagen crossed his legs in an elegant movement rather like Calli's. "You did all this while operating your workshop full-time?"

Kell nodded. "I worked at night and on weekends with the help of a bricklayer—and a friend."

Hagen held his gaze too long. "There is no doubt you are competent," he finally said. "But…" The last word hung heavily in the air.

Kell let out all his breath in one aching *whoosh*, his lungs deflating with his hope. He had aimed too high. Being with Calli and her enthusiasm for his project had given him grandiose ideas of himself. Wanting to be good enough for her, and being good enough for her, were two entirely different things.

"…but our usual contractors will be finishing the Aldinga job. We can certainly offer you work there. We have tenants for five shops at this time awaiting fittings. Also a restaurant and a coffee bar that need a few ideas before we lease them."

"You want me to work with your usual contractors?" Kell tried to relax his shoulders. He had set his sights on becoming one of the usual contractors, taking a full-time permanent place for his business with AA & Company. Not another piddling one-off job.

"For the time being." Hagen leaned back.

With his dream dead, all Kell had to do now was leave. His bags were already packed. He glanced down at his clenched hands, massaging his white knuckles. "I have a few small jobs to finish first, but I don't doubt I can manage extra." Since he couldn't assure his future, he wouldn't have a chance to leap over the barrier that separated him from Calli, the money and the class barrier. If he couldn't claim her as her equal, he would have to walk away from her.

Hagen's mouth relaxed. "As for your offer of a partnership on your subdivision, you'll want a lawyer to renegotiate the conditions, and we'll work something out there, but we no longer have a project manager."

Kell let a cynical smile curl his lips. "If you assume I can fit out shops and restaurants as well as houses, you are assuming I can manage without a project manager."

Hagen nodded. "Normally we call for written applications. But since Andrew recommended *you* for the job…what do you say?"

Kell gripped the arms of the chair, his breath suspended. "To the offer of the job as your project manager?"

For a moment, Hagen sat silent. "The starting salary is one hundred and fifty thousand a year. After that, if all works well, you can renegotiate. My father is trusting me on this one, but if you agree, he wants to see you in his office at nine tomorrow."

"I have the job?" The pulse in his neck thudded.

Hagen nodded. "It's yours if you want it. As my father said, we can always redeploy you if you don't work out."

"I want it."

Hagen stood. "Welcome to AA & Company." He moved across to Kell, hand outstretched.

Kell rose to his feet and shook Hagen's hand. "I'll walk you out."

Dazed, Kell stood watching the least outgoing man he had met, but the fastest to make a decision, drive off in his red Porsche. As reality hit him, he punched the air. His first thought was to leap the fence and tell Calli his dream had come true. His second was to slow down. Now almost nine in the morning, she was expecting a sometime bed partner, full-time tradesman to drop by and tell her the land agent's estimate of the value of his house. He had half expected to be saying his final goodbye to her this morning. The last thing she would want would be to have him swing her off her feet and ask her to marry him.

He had the job of his dreams, not one that he had ever imagined on his résumé. If he could do that, perhaps he could have the woman, too.

* * * *

Calli dressed for gardening in old jeans and the khaki work shirt that had been washed often enough to form soft creases. The judge would be back at the end of the week, and she would be moving out. She would only have a week of not seeing Kell in the doorway, idly stroking the cat, instead of grabbing Calli into his arms. Even she knew that a quick break was the best.

The small hand on the kitchen clock moved to nine. She hadn't promised to wait to hear what the land agent said, but she had heard his car leave five minutes ago. At least she had only known Kell for three months, which should not be long enough to cause her any lasting distress when he moved on. She might sob into her pillow for a month or two, but that would serve her right for thinking she could have a purely physical relationship with a man.

Of course she would have to like him a whole lot to virtually cohabit with him for months, and she liked him more than anyone she could think of at this moment. She would be hard put not to assume she loved him so much that when he left, her heart would be well and truly broken for the very first time.

Neither had expected any more than a sexual relationship and initially she would have settled for that, but the ache in her heart said Kell was different. He had been there for her when she needed him, unlike her sensible choices. He had helped her whenever she needed help. She would need to accept the fact that she had met him on a working holiday, and that was all.

Easing the tension in her back, she practiced the light-hearted smile she would offer him as he left. The hurt of not being *the one* for a man who was definitely her *one* was too much to handle. This time, she would square her shoulders, smile blandly, and walk off into a perfect sunshine.

Hobo rubbed against Calli's shins. She bent down and collected the cat in her arms for comfort. Hobo struggled herself into a position where she could lie on her back and pat Calli's face with a soft paw, like *there, there.*

"I hope you won't miss him too much," Calli whispered onto Hobo's belly fur.

Hobo purred, apparently quite confident that her life could be complete without seeing Kell again. She put a paw on either side of Calli's head and rubbed faces.

Accepting the gentle caress, Calli said, "I'm going to have to leave for work any minute, but I'm just waiting to see him one last time. You don't begrudge me that, do you?"

Hobo gave her a sympathetic glance, her purring vibrating through her soft little body as light footsteps disturbed the crushed granite path outside.

"Shoulders straight," Calli whispered to the cat as she placed her on her own four paws. She opened the door. "How did it go?" she asked Kell.

He stood there, glancing warily at her. "Pretty good."

"Are you going to talk to other land agents, or was that it?"

"I'm going to talk to a couple of land agents, yes." He touched his tongue to his bottom lip. "First, I—"

"I'm off to work now, Kell. Let's not worry about any parting speeches. I'm glad the house pleased the agent, but I knew it would. Tiggy always does a fantastic job, but you had the bones there. I know you will send the furniture back to the warehouse when the time comes because I know you are utterly reliable."

He drew in a breath. "Thank you for your faith in me, but I don't have a parting speech prepared. I've been offered more than the opportunity I wanted, Calli."

"And you're moving on. I know. I've always known. I'm moving on, too. It's been wonderful, these last few months, the sex, I mean. You're the best lover I've ever had but I have places to go and jobs to do."

A crease formed between his eyebrows. "I'm sure you do."

She waited for him to turn and leave. "I'm not in debt any longer, and I can get out of here and start enjoying life."

"You haven't enjoyed life here?" He folded his arms across his chest.

"I'm a garden designer. I don't mind weeding and planting, but I don't want to make a career out of laboring for someone else. It does no favors to my skin." As her voice grew snootier and snootier like every mean girl she had ever met in her life, her heart was breaking. She glanced at her rough hands, which trembled.

"I understand. I don't want to cut lengths of wood forever, either. I have the opportunity to—"

"I know. We both need to move on."

He raked his fingers through his hair. "I love you, Calli."

"Loveable Calli, everyone's best friend, everyone's best bet not to make a scene. Yep, that's me," she said with bitterness in her tone. "And now I'm going to have to hear that this morning, or even last week you met *the one.*"

"I met *the one* a few months ago."

"Isn't that par for the course?" Her eyes prickled. "How would she feel if she knew you'd been bonking me with so much enthusiasm all that time?"

"Are you planning on telling her?" His lips formed a thin line.

"Unlikely. What's that saying? What happens on holiday, stays on holiday." Hobo tapped her leg. She glanced down. "No, not you. You're a keeper," she said in a voice husky with suppressed tears.

Kell swooped up the cat. "Are you taking sides?" he asked Hobo, frowning.

The cat shook her head. Kell leaned lower to hear the cat's whisper. "But she won't let me," he said in answer to Hobo's silent comment. "I told her I love her, and she seems to think I said something else."

"Put my bloody cat down."

He faced her. His mouth curled into a reluctant smile. "She loves me. She has from the start. Strays tend to fall for me."

"No, we don't."

"You're hardly a stray." He reached out, gently cupping the side of her face, as Hobo had done, his smile tentative.

"That's all you know. I've had a very hard life. My parents love me, my siblings are kind to me. I've had the education I wanted, and all the men running after me who wanted my father's influence used in their favor. I had monetary help in buying my first house, which I lost because I'm prone to judging people on their looks. For example, I thought you were tall, dark, and handsome."

He raised his eyebrows. "I am. Everyone says so."

"See?" She sniffed back a tear.

"I do see. I'm insane about you, Calli. You must know that." He wiped his thumb across her cheek.

"But you're moving on."

"I have to take the opportunities as they present. I have worked hard for the chance to have this one and even harder because I know you are Alexander Allbrook's daughter. I didn't know if he knew about you and me, or not."

"You know? You know?" She blinked hard, trying to absorb any sign of tears. "He didn't. Know." Her throat ached, but she managed to woman up. "And I made darned sure he didn't by not accepting your offer to support me at the funeral."

"So, I got this job on my own merit?"

"What job?"

"Your brother Hagen has offered me a job at AA & Company."

"When did you talk to Hagen?" She placed her fists on her hips.

"A few minutes ago. He inspected the house and said the company would come in with me on the next build, and then he offered me the full-time job of project manager for the company."

"That's quite a deal." She glanced at him, wishing he would leave. "And now you have what you want. I had no hand in it. I needed to make sure we were together because you liked me for myself."

"I know." His hand shifted to her shoulder.

"You couldn't possibly know," she said crossly. "Being Alexander Allbrook's daughter quite often makes me attractive."

With the cat still resting on his arm, he moved closer to Calli, a breath away, staring down at her. "Exactly how attractive do you need to be?"

Her mouth curved into a cynical smile. "When did you find out who I am?"

"When I saw your photo in the paper attending the funeral of your brother's wife." He sighed. "The same brother I met this morning, next door, who offered me a contract based on my work in the house, my work and yours." His gaze met hers. "That's what we've been doing for the past three months—working toward a common goal. I didn't realize that until the woman who spoke to me at Maggie's party said so."

"That was my mother."

"Tell me you're joking." He examined her expression.

She shrugged. "She thinks that's what makes marriages successful. Hers and Far's is blissful sometimes, noisy sometimes, but no one would ever doubt they are crazy about each other, and they've worked together since day one."

"Whereas, I'm crazy about you and you are not so crazy about me. You want me to rack off." He dropped his hand from her shoulder, tilting his mouth wryly. "You used me and now you're moving on. I'm not good enough to be with the daughter of Alexander Allbrook, despite being good enough to share her bed."

She glanced up at him, slightly shocked. "You mean 'used' as in connection to sex? Well, isn't that just like a man? I was in that relationship, too, you know."

"If you're attractive because of your family's influence, I'm unattractive when a woman finds out I'm a tradesman."

"You're accusing me of being a snob."

"And you're accusing me of only being interested in your family's influence. I made as sure as possible that I kept our relationship quiet."

"So did I. Tiggy might have suspected something, but I said *don't ask* and she didn't." Her voice quavered.

He drew in a long deep breath, offering her a half smile. "I fell for you the moment you accused me of running a meth lab. You knew you were wrong, but you wouldn't give in. And you don't. That's a quality to love, and I'm in love with you, Calli. I'm crazy enough about you to want to marry you." He stared right into her eyes.

"Is that a proposal?"

"Darned right, it's a proposal. I love you, and I want to spend the rest of my life loving you."

"*Please*, put the cat down."

"Not quite the answer I was hoping for." With a wary smile he let the cat bound onto the floor where she sat glancing up as if also waiting for an answer, too.

"The answer is..." she flung her arms around his neck, "... yes. Yes, yes, yes."

He held her close. "We could get married as soon as we can get a license," he murmured into her ear.

"Did I tell you I love you, too?"

"I was hoping that's why you decided to marry me." He kissed her lips, once, twice.

"Hobo will be pleased. She was asking this morning where I intended to go."

"You can move into the Tudor with me." He cleared his throat. "Let's hope it doesn't sell too fast. If it does, I'll find somewhere, don't worry."

"She was quite happy when I suggested asking my father for one of the houses he has sitting around waiting for renovation." She glanced at the cat. "Right, Hobo?"

He remained silent for a moment. "He rents them?"

"Yes, but I'll be working for him again, and we could take one that needs the garden redone."

"No handouts, Calli."

"Of course not. But it makes perfect sense to help him out."

"I'm guessing this is my first lesson in how to compromise," he said into her hair. "Do you have to leave for work?"

She backed into the cottage, dragging him with her. "It's not every day a girl gets a marriage proposal. I'm sure my client will see reason." When she started kissing him, she couldn't stop, but he wouldn't let her, because he showed her with his soft kisses and his hard kisses and his passionate kisses how much he loved her.

Finally, he leaned back and stared into her eyes. "I'm meeting your father tomorrow," he said, straightening her shirt collar. "What's the protocol? Should I tell him I'm going to marry his daughter before or after he makes me a formal offer for the job."

She brushed his cheek with her fingers. "Don't say a word to him. I'll call Ma in the morning and make a time for us all to meet."

If her father had found out who the tradesman next door was, and if he had offered Kell the job because his daughter loved him, she hoped Kell would never find out. She hoped she would never find out either, but even so, her father now had the perfect son-in-law. He needed a man like Kell in the company.

* * * *

At nine the next morning, she called her mother and told her she was about to have a son-in-law. "He's being inducted into the company by Far this morning. I thought it would be a nice idea if you met him, too. You'll be the only member of the family who hasn't."

"He's being interviewed for what job?" her mother asked in a suspicious voice.

"Project manager. Does Far know?"

"That he's about to employ the man who is his prospective son-in-law? No. We both decided not to check up on you. This is very good news, darling, and I did like him when I talked to him at Maggie's engagement. We'll have to have a very makeshift celebration in the staff room."

"Let's meet there at ten o'clock." Calli knew her mother would come armed with food, but the employees would be pleased to have an excuse to eat more of her offerings.

Calli took the day off work, promising herself to finish Mrs. Haslam's garden during the week. By the time she arrived at AA & Company, the tables in the staffroom groaned with sweet pastries and pink roses. Kell looked bemused as he walked in with Far. Hagen came behind, and Tiggy followed.

She smiled at him. "Hi. I couldn't be nice to you when I was staging your house because I didn't exactly know what you meant to Calli. She refused to say, which is often a bad sign. If you were going to be a rat, I wasn't about to be friendly. But I can now that we're going to be related."

Hagen looked at him, blinking, and he slowly nodded. "Your garden was Calli's work. I should have realized." He touched his earlobe, a habit that he adopted when he was thinking. "I knew I had seen that art deco lounge suite before."

Tiggy laughed. "It used to be in your office, but it was burgundy then. I had it reupholstered."

"Lovely to see you again," Ma said, presenting her cheek to be kissed by Kell. "Have you settled on a wedding date?"

Kell laughed. "We only settled on a wedding yesterday. Calli doesn't want to wait. Nor do I. I'll apply for a license as soon as I get a spare moment."

"A Greek wedding would be too big, and a Nordic wedding too sparse," Ma said, passing him a glass of champagne. "You'll want something in between," she told Kell.

"The registry office would do me."

"Now, now," Ma said, patting him on the hand. "Calli is my first daughter to marry. I've always known I will have to restrain myself because both my girls have too much Nordic caution in them to tolerate the enormous wedding I had. But like Christmas, weddings are just as much for the family as for the happy couple. We could keep the guest list to a hundred or two if we tried."

"Try, Ma," Tiggy said earnestly. "Because we don't want to scare Kell off before we've quite got him. I say fifty or sixty. Have you made a list, Calli?"

Calli shook her head. "We have thirteen close relatives between us, and three grandparents. That's sixteen before we start counting. I have a few friends who must be invited, and so does Kell. Sixty would work."

Kell looked horrified. "Whatever Calli says."

"Right. What theme are you planning?" Tiggy glanced at Calli. "You don't want Greek—are you going to grow your hair?"

"Nope."

"Then we can't have a Viking wedding."

"Don't worry, Kell." Ma patted him again. "She's teasing you. Where do you want the wedding, Calli?"

She glanced at Kell. "We want an Australian wedding, Tiggy. Some thing cool and simple, and in a garden. Then you could deck out that restaurant on the river for the reception. Does that suit everyone?"

"It seems too easy." Ma relaxed. "Who wants another custard tart?"

* * * *

Kell barely remembered the wedding ceremony. The bride stole his breath, standing in her parents' beautiful garden smiling up at him. Calli wore shades of autumn in a drifting fairy-like gown that suited her long-limbed elegance. He had been coerced into a light suit, and he wore a tie in the autumn tones that matched the bride's dress and the setting and the day.

He had sold his house days after the first viewing for one and a quarter million. The settlement had been banked, and as his workshop would now be an adjunct to A A & Company, he didn't need to buy a larger truck for deliveries. He had employed another three cabinetmakers, he had almost finished his first office fit-out for the company, and Calli was proud of him.

The wedding presents almost overwhelmed him, but after the wedding, he had moved into the best-established house he could afford on the best street he could afford, not too far from Calli's parents. He would renovate this house, too, and move on and up. Although he had nothing left to prove, he didn't intend to grow fat and complacent.

He now had a beautiful and successful wife, and he would never stop trying to earn her.

"When do you want to start having children?" she asked him in the honeymoon suite that night.

"You might want to wait until Vix and Jay have produced two," he answered with a grin.

And then he explained the alphabetic naming in his family.

She mulled over Max, Noah, and Oscar. "I understand your qualms," she said laughing. "But if I have to, I can always skew this by changing Hobo's name to Quasimodo."

After the weekend honeymoon, Calli collected her cat from Tiggy. She put the question of a name change to Hobo, who violently objected. She squirmed out of Calli's hold and stalked over to Kell, whom she beseeched to pick her up.

"There, there," he said, using his smoochy face to calm the cat. "You might have to take one for the team, but don't worry because the name has only been used once before by a human who saved a beautiful young maiden. Since you also did, the name makes sense."

Hobo managed to do one of her Kell-nods.

Kell laughed. "She says 'purr-fect sense.' Get it?"

Calli did. Somehow meeting the cat and Kell at the same place made perfect sense.

Don't miss other books by Virginia Taylor

Sets Appeal

In the cosmopolitan coastal city of Adelaide in South Australia, two theater lovers create a little drama of their own . . .

Twenty-seven-year-old divorcée Vix Tremain nally has her rst job—as a theater-set painter—and is ready to leave the past behind. What better way to get her con dence back than a ing with a handsome stranger? She isn't looking for anything emotional, she's had enough heartbreak. Rugged Jay Dee, the set construction manager, ts the bill for no strings fun perfectly.
What Vix doesn't realize is that Jay is not exactly a stranger . . .

Jay would recognize wealthy, spoiled Vix anywhere. After all, she's the ex-wife of the man who destroyed his career. Naturally, Jay wants a little sweet revenge—at rst. To his surprise, Vix is far from the ice princess he expected, and spending time with her changes everything. Soon he realizes he's actually falling for the vulnerable beauty. But becoming entangled with her will mean revealing who he is—and opening them both up to more pain. With their dreams at stake, is their connection strong enough to weather the truth—and take center stage?

Chapter 1

Her shoulders almost creaking with tension, Victoria Tremain turned off her car engine. Tonight, as one of the crew, she had attended the first party she had been to in a year, a pre-production getting-to-know-you function held for the cast and crew of the stage version of *High Society*. Experiencing a deadly case of stage fright, she aimed the huge smile she had plastered on her face in the direction of her wildly attractive passenger. He had told her he would make her a cup of coffee if she drove him home.

Behind him, the blaring streetlight reflected on the outside of a suburban redbrick bungalow with no fence and a front garden that had been dug over but not planted—a work in progress, but not out of place in this narrow street of tidy post-war houses. Shadowy stacks of planks lay in his concrete driveway.

"So, this is where you build your theater sets?" Her voice sounded suitably low and husky, not because she was at all sophisticated, but because she was terrified.

Picking up men wasn't as easy as... Actually, she hadn't imagined picking up men would be easy, not for someone as naturally awkward as she. She had almost fallen over her feet in her hurry to get the hunky set-builder into her car. Or maybe she almost fell over her big yellow heels, which took some getting used to—for she was now flashy, single, champagne-drinking Vix Tremain, trying to find the life she had missed during the past seven years. Married at the age of twenty, she had divorced eleven months ago.

He shook his head. "The wood belongs in the garage, but I haven't had time yet to shift it." Muffled *doof-doof* music rocked the air as he opened the car door on his side.

She opened her side, stepped out, and caught her bag on the handbrake. Muttering under her breath, she untangled the strap and closed the door, hoping he hadn't noticed. His coordination was as notable as his big, honed body.

She cleared her throat. "When did you finish your last set?" Scooping her hair back, she followed him along an overgrown path to the low front porch.

"A couple of weeks ago. My team does four a year." He fumbled for his keys. A sudden gust of wind blew a sheet of newspaper across the road and an orphaned takeaway coffee cup rattled against the fence. As she took a step back to give him space, her spiked heel caught between two slats and she stumbled.

He grabbed her, steadying her against his chest, his shaggy brown hair idly teasing across her cheek. "My woman trap." He set her back on her own feet. Suppressed laughter deepened his voice.

She gave a careful smile, scoring herself a ten for not apologizing. The man smelled like pine chips and the fresh sea breeze blowing in from the port. He opened the door, a forest green blistered over white undercoat and slivers of ashen wood. For a moment, his arm blocked her as he reached around his doorframe for the light. The pulse in her neck thudding, she waited until he stepped back. This could be her first one-night stand if she didn't mess up or say something dorky. Tonight, she had great expectations of herself. She had scrubbed-up quite well and now she only had to follow through.

He placed his hand on the center of her back and guided her through a bare hallway to an open space containing a sitting room at one end and a dining–slash–kitchen area at the other. Tossing his leather jacket over a chair, he stepped behind the kitchen countertop and began to pour coffee beans into a grinder sitting beside a basic espresso machine. For a moment, she experienced stark disappointment. Perhaps when he had said "coffee," he had meant "coffee."

"Take a seat." Using his eyes, he indicated the sitting area, painted in faded magnolia and furnished with a floral two-seater couch and a couple of stiff-backed chairs upholstered in gray.

Keeping him in view, she sat on the edge of the couch, clutching her handbag to her chest. Her mouth was as dry as the recent winter. "What's your real name?"

"JD." Resting his work-roughened hands on the countertop, he flitted his gaze over her legs.

Her skirt had hitched up too high. She thought about using her handbag as a cover but she had worn the bad-girl, tight red skirt to change her image.

Breathing out, she put the bag on the floor, giving him a sideways glance. "I'm guessing. An abbreviation of Juvenile Delinquent?" She held her breath. He smiled, forming creases that were almost dimples. "From *West Side Story*?" He scooped the ground beans into the measure. She half-relaxed. He recognized the musical, and most men didn't. "Just Deciding might suit you better." She laughed at her blatant hint but when his gaze connected with hers, her face warmed. He could take all the time he needed and if he didn't plan on having sex with her, the world wouldn't end. He might simply have wanted a comfortable ride home. Men invariably preferred using her cars.

Fortunately, he gave her an amused look. Reaching for the mugs, he showed her an impressive back view, wide at the top and angling to lean hips and a tight, hard rear. Although stacked, he couldn't be called handsome. The left side of his face had been puckered by a scar that wove up his cheek and toward his eye. He looked like the tradesman he was, an appearance he emphasized with his faded jeans and cotton shirt.

"How do you like your coffee?" He stared at her over his shoulder.

"Plain black, please."

At the party for *High Society*, she'd used champagne to segue into the new sophisticated Vix Tremain. Awkward, tactless Victoria Nolan had barely spoken to a man in this past year, let alone stumbled into his house. Married young, she'd never ventured into the dating scene. Instead, she had accepted the first man who had shown an interest in her, impressionable fool that she had been. "How complicated was your last set?"

"A single room." He shrugged. "Three entrances and a flight of stairs." He brought over a brimming coffee, placing the mug on the blue-painted table adjacent to her seat.

"Sit here," she said, amazing herself by patting the cushion beside her. She even considered adding a casual touch by kicking off her heels, but couldn't with any semblance of grace. Her legs were long and her skirt was a size tighter than she usually bought. She should have worn fitted pants. Then she could have crossed her legs or casually hooked one up onto the couch. Dressing to pick up a man needed more planning than she had imagined. She dragged in a breath. "I see we have ten scene changes. That's enough to keep me painting solidly for the next three months."

He lowered himself beside her. For a few heartbeats, he sat silently. "Are you being paid for your time or the job?"

"For the job. My specialty is set design, but I've never worked. I have to start. So, I thought taking on the painting first would ease my way in, which makes the money immaterial."

He gave an almost imperceptible nod. "When did it happen?"

"Getting the job?"

"I'm asking about your divorce." He lifted her third finger, left hand, which still held an indented reminder of the wedding ring she no longer wore.

She no longer owned the platinum band, either. Although she should have flushed the meaningless thing into the sewer, she couldn't stand waste. Instead, she had gone out to buy herself a box of celebration chocolates, the last she had eaten since then, and sold the ring, dropping the money into the hat of the first street musician she saw on the way back to her car.

"You're observant. I've been free for a year."

"Good."

She tilted her head to the side, trying an unconcerned smile. "Because?"

His eyebrows lifted.

Her insides began to quiver with hope.

He settled his arm along the back of the couch. His hand touched her hair, and he tugged a lock. "What am I going to do with you?" He used a deep, soft tone.

"Did you have anything else in mind when you offered to make me coffee?" Her tentative gaze met his.

"Not my thinking mind, no."

"Your thinking mind as compared to…?"

He drew air through his teeth. "As compared to the mind I don't often use when I'm with a beautiful woman. So…" He rested one large hand on the side of her neck and his thumb under her jaw. Leaning over, he touched his lips to hers.

A delicious shiver ran though her. His eyelashes were thick and brown at the tips and blond near his lids.

When she could breathe evenly, she said, "You have nice, soft lips."

"That's my line." His steady gaze held hers.

"I thought you might need encouragement."

His mouth tilted at the corners and his eyes gleamed. "More likely discouragement."

She gave an off-hand shrug, smiling inside. "I'm just not in the mood to do that," she said, trying for a mock snooty tone.

"To discourage me?" He glanced sideways at her. "Let me get this straight. You want to encourage me?"

"I drove you home. What would you expect if you had driven me home?" She lifted her eyebrows.

He nodded. "I would hope for much more than a cup of coffee."

She couldn't look away from him, and she certainly couldn't breathe.

He meshed his fingers with hers. "And, fair's fair." Staring at her face, he put his other arm along the back of the couch behind her. His hand shifted to the nape of her neck and she found herself tucked into his frame. She glanced up, hoping to be kissed again.

He obliged, dropping his mouth lightly over hers and testing her upper lip with his tongue.

She drew back. "The bedroom?"

"Right now?"

Experimentally, she brushed his upper thigh with her knuckles, noting an exciting shape expanding his jeans. "I can't possibly give you time to change your mind."

He picked up her hand and gently took the pad of her forefinger between his lips. "Why hurry? We're going to be working together," he said in a relaxed voice.

"Not often. When your job ends, mine begins. I can't paint a set before it's built."

He toyed with her fingers.

She wriggled uncomfortably. "If you're afraid of awkwardness when we meet again, I'm sure we will hardly ever meet again. I mean…"

"So, you want to get into bed with someone that you expect to hardly ever meet again?"

Her insides began to shake. "If you don't want to, you can say no. I thought… Well, it's kind of normal, isn't it, to have an instant physical attraction to someone? Well, it's not normal for me, but…"

He leaned back, staring into her eyes. "I didn't plan on saying no."

"Are we arguing about what happens next, or are we agreeing?" She started to chew on her lip and, mindful of looking insecure, stopped.

He glanced away. "What color are my eyes?"

"You have light brown hair, so you probably have light eyes."

"Your eyes are blue."

"You're looking straight at them now," she said indignantly.

"How does that follow? You're not naturally blond."

"I almost am."

He laughed.

Embarrassed, for she had been born blond and had remained that way until about the age of ten, when her hair had turned a pure shade of natural mouse, she said, "Hardly anyone is at my age. If you are only interested in natural blondes, you're doomed to disappointment."

"I didn't say I was disappointed. My mind was simply trying to connect eye color and hair color."

"I can only judge your reaction to me by your, um..." She stopped, knowing she shouldn't tell a man that from the moment they'd met, his smile had lured her on, way past her normal comfort zone. Most men preferred assured women who knew how to tease.

"My *um*?" His expression blanked, and he stood.

Her stomach dropped to her toes. Being knocked back on her first try at propositioning a man would probably put her off ever trying again. Any other unnatural blonde in a tight red skirt would get the man she wanted... or leave with her dignity intact. She rose to her feet, avoiding his eyes. "So, I'll say goodnight and thank you for the coffee."

He stood. "You read my *um* right. That's one of the disadvantages of being male."

She nodded, reaching for her handbag. A tall, confident man like him was possibly propositioned twice a day, at least. He could afford to pick and choose. Her breath stopped as she realized what he had implied and, her mouth not quite shut, she lifted her gaze to his.

"And thank me in the morning," he murmured as his mouth slowly connected with hers.

At first stunned, she didn't respond. Then he settled a palm on the small of her back, drawing her close. Her insides began to hum, and she leaned away to struggle out of her jacket. He helped, tossing the distraction onto the chair with his. She started to work on the button of his jeans, her brain a maze of unfinished thoughts. Unfortunately, in her confusion, she tangled her fingers against his flat belly.

"I'll do that," he said, his eyes glinting with humor. "I think I ought to head for the bathroom for a condom. The bedroom is through there." He indicated the room in the hallway closest to the front door.

She glanced at his chin, traced her gaze over his scar, and straightened her shoulders. Then, picking up her jacket and her bag, she went into his bedroom, where after undressing quickly, she arranged herself in his bed. With her arms at her sides, she lay staring at the flaky ceiling, forcing in long, deep breaths. He gave her time enough to ease the nervous flutter in her chest and time enough to justify acting out of character.

She had never before let anyone think they owed her a favor. A good girl all her life, she had been called prissy and conventional. She'd watched the bad girls grab whatever they wanted while she'd stood back and hoped to be valued for being honest. No more.

She'd been cheated on, taken advantage of, and left humiliated. If she had any sort of courage, she would stop living for tomorrow and start living for today—tonight. What sort of person had no regrets? Wincing, she glanced at her clothes on the floor. If need be she could make a quick getaway.

In half an hour, with luck, she would find out if sex with a wildly attractive bad boy would change her attitude. She didn't care about competing with other more attractive, more confident women, and she didn't hope for love. One single bout of satisfying sex would do her. Then, she would know she was not as frigid, repressed, and sexless as she had been told.

Staring at the door, she waited for the big, inscrutable hunk.

* * * *

Jay shut the bathroom door behind him. Last year, he had built the set for *South Pacific*. Although he hadn't attended any rehearsals of the show, while he had been bumping-in the set, he had heard an actor going over a schmaltzy song about spotting a woman across a crowded room and falling instantly in love.

Jay hadn't fallen instantly in love with Vix Tremain, but lust had featured strongly. Spotting the blonde, he had pushed through the usual crowd to introduce himself to a sleek beauty who seemed genuinely glad to talk him. Normally a woman with skin as smooth as rich cream and a long-legged, toned body would act like a show pony, but she had a rare natural charm. She also showed a clear interest in him, demonstrated by the odd self-conscious gesture, like touching her hair and moistening her lips. Every move of hers reflected his purely animal attraction. He'd thought the last theater set he ever meant to construct would easily be his most interesting.

Set painters could be anyone—male or female, old or young, ultra-serious, control freaks, or dreadlocked posers. Not often did he get assigned to a beautiful woman who looked as interested in messing around as he was. He didn't have the time for a relationship, but he could fit in a casual affair that lasted the length of the production, and he could certainly handle one with a golden man-toy. He'd been blatant about his attraction to her, and he'd intimated that a sweaty night would be had by all if she accompanied him home.

The dazzling smile she gave him in response hit him like a punch to the head. He'd seen that smile before. Only last year, when skimming the newspaper, he'd noted a photograph of the Nolans, plain, plump Victoria with her incredible smile and her older husband, Timothy, architect and millionaire entrepreneur.

Jay ran his fingers over the scar on his cheek, a memento from her husband.

For at least a year, he'd thought about revenge on Timmy-boy. Although Jay was visibly scarred, he'd never been handsome. Nor did he make his living out of his looks. Bygones had been bygones, but knowing she was

Meet the Author

From art student to stylist, to nurse and midwife, **Virginia Taylor's** life has been one illogical step to the next, each one leading to the final goal of being an author. When she can tear herself away from the computer and the waiting blank page, she immerses herself in arts and crafts, gardening, or, of course, cooking. You can visit her website at www.virginia-taylor. com, and tweet her @authorvtaylor.

Tim's ex added to her appeal. In fact, he'd seen screwing her as some sort of compensation for having his future screwed by Tim. His dick had largely guided these self-serving thoughts.

Now, although still influenced by a keen body part, he found he couldn't use Vix in an act of silent revenge. Perhaps if she had been the woman he'd always assumed she was, a rich bitch with haughty opinions, he wouldn't have changed sides, but a sophisticated man-toy she was not. Instead, she was bright and wryly funny, both of which he found more sexually stimulating than a bored divorcée looking for a night on the wild side.

Crap! He couldn't knock back a woman with so little confidence in herself. If he had her, he would be all kinds of a heel. If he didn't, he would be all kinds of a fool.

He massaged the back of his neck, undecided.

Finally, he eked out a breath, opened the cabinet door, and glumly reached for a condom. This had to be his unluckiest night in his whole misbegotten life.

Printed in the United States
by Baker & Taylor Publisher Services